FRIEND OR FOE?

"One more thing," Davies said. "Be very, very careful. If the deaths of Rolly and Susan Eastfield were not incidental, someone knows you as well as me. And is watching you. I can take care of myself, Alex. But I may not be able to help you, as well."

She shrugged, indifferent. No one had ever promised her safety. Once she'd hung from a rope over the edge of a building with Rob Rangel, shouting questions at a demented would-be jumper who'd taken his daughter out on the ledge with him. Rob had taken the pictures.

Alex remembered that sensation of swinging in the wind, helpless.

"Tell me one thing," she said, and that same feeling welled up in her stomach again, of arrested falling. "Can you swear to me, absolutely swear, that you've never killed anyone?"

His smile vanished. There was nothing in his face, nothing. His eyes were flat as glass, and his muscles were neither tight nor loose, just there. *Dead,* she thought again. He looked dead.

"Of course," he said.

She knew he was lying.

S0-AAE-157

ROXANNE LONGSTREET

RED ANGEL

ZEBRA BOOKS
KENSINGTON PUBLISHING CORP.

ZEBRA BOOKS are published by

Kensington Publishing Corp.
475 Park Avenue South
New York, NY 10016

Zebra and the Z logo Reg. U.S. Pat & TM Off.

First Printing: April, 1994
Printed in the United States of America

DEDICATION

To the Wednesday Weirdos—
Pat, Rebecca, Steve, Julie, Bob,
Margaret, and Dale—for going with me
into the dark.

ACKNOWLEDGMENTS

Thanks to Cat, for his continuing, unfailing confidence—and for putting up with my psychotic episodes; to Jim, for lending me lots of research material; to M&M, for technical and emotional support; to Alice Cooper, Melissa Etheridge, and Fish, for musical support; to my editor, Jennifer Sawyer; to my agent, Donald Maass; and last, but never least, to P.N. and Mark Elrod, my buddies, who *still* don't really think I'm too crazy to be around. Yet.

Chapter One
Davies

The following is an excerpt from *The Casebooks of Gabriel Davies*, published by Omega Press in 1992. The edition is unauthorized by Gabriel Davies.

May 26, 1986

I wonder, sometimes, if I'm insane.

They say that if you wonder, you can't be. But don't the insane wonder? Don't they fear?

Don't they fear more than other people, actually?

I've spent a lot of time thinking about the symptoms of psychopathic and sociopathic behavior. It's disturbing to examine yourself this way, to look at all of your private thoughts and hold them up to the light. I wonder if anyone else does this. I'm terribly afraid they don't.

My family history seems to point toward typical sociopathic tendencies: emotional dysfunction, heavy psychological abuse. I can recall clearly how surprised I was when one of my teachers hugged me in first grade. No one had ever hugged me before. I didn't like it.

I hate being touched. By anyone. Another traditional sociopathic trait, as demonstrated by Barnes Broward. I still have a ridged scar on my arm, a souvenir of grabbing for his as he fell from the roof of the Montroy Hotel.

I almost lost the use of my left hand. He fell anyway.

I seem largely unable to initiate violence, even against animals. That is somewhat comforting, since torturing pets or strays is a traditional sociopathic indicator. I dismembered dolls quite regularly as a child, but never (so far as I remember) a living thing. I boiled my turtles in the tub, but I believe that was entirely accidental.

Still, you'd think I was sociopathic, wouldn't you? Given the evidence?

Chapter Two

"Wow. Jeez, that's a mess. What do you figure, a forty-five, something like that?"

"Shit, she wouldn't have a head. Thirty-eight, maybe. Wonder where the hell the slug went."

"Ask her. Must've been the last thing on her mind," one of the junior-grade detectives said, and grinned. "Hey, Alex, wanna call it?"

"Killed somewhere else, dumped here—see the splash marks?—and whoever it was just sort of pitched her out here pretty hard. Otherwise half her brain wouldn't be on her face," said Alexandra Hobbs, who stood with her arms crossed and her stomach held tightly under them. Her voice was steady. Somehow. The junior-grade detective, who probably felt as nauseated as she did, grinned again.

"It's what we call the mushroom effect." He looked around at the two other cops, both older, but neither of them seemed to appreciate his humor. "Get it? Mushroom?"

"The slug's back where he killed her. What're these marks on her wrists? Rope, or tape?" she asked.

The senior detective, Markovsky, just shrugged. It was the first sign of life he'd shown since she'd arrived. She continued, encouraged. "Maybe a sex crime, a bondage thing?"

"Maybe." Markovsky was stunningly uncooperative. Nothing new. Alex snuck a glance at her watch.

"Witnesses?" she persisted.

"We got shit," he said indifferently. With meticulous care, he unwrapped a thin stick of Dentyne and folded the paper into a tiny square before putting it back in his pocket.

He never looked at the dead woman, though she was hard to miss. She lay in the middle of the broad sidewalk, a round pattern of blood around her head like a red Chinese fan. Her hair was blond where it wasn't matted and clotting. Her skin had taken on a bluish color, but her lips had stayed unnaturally scarlet. Fresh lipstick.

"The left eye's probably wherever the slug is," Markovsky said. He continued to stare off toward the sunset, chewing his gum.

Oh, yeah, the eyes. She'd been trying to avoid that sweet detail. One of them was a gelatinous sludge smeared over her cheek and nose. The other one was gone, too, but it hadn't been knocked out by a bullet. Somebody'd had to dig hard to remove it, by the gouges.

The right side of the corpse's head was smashed open by the exit wound. Her brain squeezed out of the hole like sprouting gray fungus.

Think of something else, Alex told herself. The body's hands were a little wrinkled, dry, probably the hands of somebody in her late thirties. She had medium-long fingernails. Several of them were broken.

Alex pointed toward them, stooping down, careful not to touch anything.

"You gonna bag her hands?" she asked mildly. Markovsky shot her a wearily hostile look.

"Christ, Hobbs, of course we're gonna bag her hands, you think we're all blind? I'll bag your *ass* if you're not careful." He glanced around and checked his watch. "It's almost TV time. Better hit the road."

His voice was flat, uncompromising. Alex nodded her thanks and walked away, back toward the yellow crime scene tape. She checked her watch. Ten 'til four. She'd give it to four, and then she'd split. She didn't want to be late, not considering what she had waiting for her.

She got close enough to the tape to draw attention from the clot of reporters on the other side. Three or four of the quicker ones started pacing her at a trot.

"Hey! Hey, Hobbs! What's it like?" a reporter from the *American Sentinel* asked. Somebody elbowed him aside. "Hobbs! Give a pal a chance!"

He wasn't her pal. She stuck her hands in her jacket pockets and strolled serenely along at a safe distance inside the crime scene, heading for the corner of Meadow and Arcadia. They followed for a while, howling, but as she'd figured, they were loath to get too far from the action and dropped back. Even her pal.

There were a few more guys hanging around the corner, but she knew most of them. Didn't like many of them, but they were either too discouraged or too indifferent to hassle her. Most days.

As Alex ducked under the tape, Rob Rangel shaded his eyes against the afternoon sun and looked her carefully up and down. His eyes came up again and stopped somewhere around her breasts.

"Don't you ever get tired of showing Markovsky your tits?" he asked, as she sat down next to him. She just shot him a look and held out her hand for the Coke he was holding, a cold one, sweat beaded on its sides. He handed it over. She took in a big, greedy drink. The can tasted bitter and salty, but the liquid was sweet and cool and carbonated. She handed it back to him and watched him wipe the rim before drinking.

"Thought you feminists hated that shit," Rob said. She rested her elbows on her thighs and shrugged. She wasn't watching him. She was watching Markovsky, the two junior detectives, the distant blot of the body.

Jesus, she thought suddenly. Her arms broke out in hard, cold goosebumps. *Jesus, her eyes. Why would he do that to her eyes?*

Rob, after waiting unsuccessfully for a fight, put the Coke down and popped his Nikon open to load more film. In the afternoon sun he looked innocent and priestly, a young man already showing a ring of bald pink flesh on top and wearing his hair excessively long, as if one balanced the other. He stored his exposed film in a gray plastic case and tossed it into his open camera bag beside him.

"Didn't get one single decent shot," Rob groused. She signaled him for the Coke again, and he handed it over. "Hey, the forensic assholes finally showed. If they think they're going to get fiber samples or some such shit on a dirty city sidewalk, they're nuts."

She pulled out her notepad and doodled on it a little, thinking about the gouges and the bloody red hole where an eye had been. Her doodles looked ugly and thick.

Rob shifted and pointed to the other side of the street. "Hey, is that Channel Twelve, Live at Five?"

Beyond the black-painted police evidence van the first of the TV parasites had arrived. The truck bristled with intimidating microwave technology, and as the van door slid aside, the Live at Five team bailed out like SWAT commandos, walkie-talkies to their mouths, cables slithering like jungle pythons. Rob stood up and took a look through the Nikon. His smile was blissful and pure.

"Oh, yeah," he murmured. "Here she comes, oh, baby, this way, come this way, I'll get you a story. Man! Look at that."

Her name was Therese Villarreal, and she was, if you believed the TV promos, the hottest investigative reporter in the business. Therese Villarreal had about as much depth as her pancake makeup.

But a great ass. World-class.

Alex sucked down another mouthful of Rob's Coke and got a faraway, dreamy look in her eyes.

"Oh, man, you gotta see this to believe it. One of those wrap-skirt things, all we need is a good breeze—think she's wearing anything under there? It's pretty tight—" Rob adjusted the focus. "Turn around, sweetheart, show me something—"

Therese Villarreal, umbilicaled to her cameraman by a microphone cord, strode up to the crime scene tape. The detectives turned their backs.

"Cold shoulder time for the star—hey! Panty line alert! Woop! Woop! Yep, she's got 'em. Too bad."

Villarreal was having no luck. The detectives continued to ignore her. The uniformed cops manning the line continued to stonewall her. She turned to one of the print reporters hanging around nearby, and he shook his head.

He pointed down the block, toward where Alex and Rob sat.

"Holy shit," Rob said. His voice had jumped up an octave. "Christ, she's—she's coming over—"

He had enough sense to take the Nikon away from his eye. Alex refused to look, just listened to the approaching sharp tap of heels.

A shadow spilled over half her lap. It had big hair.

"How'd you get inside, Hobbs?" the shadow asked bluntly. Alex shaded her eyes and looked up. Villarreal's makeup, seen up close, looked like she'd had it mixed in a cement truck.

Alex just looked at her. Villarreal's eyes narrowed.

"Tits," Rob said suddenly. They both looked at him.

Villarreal straightened her back, the better to display her advantages. She gave him a slow, confident smile.

"Tits," she repeated. Rob nodded solemnly. "No problem."

With one more scornful look at Alex, she tapped briskly away. She stopped to give her cameraman a one-word command, like *Stay*. She went on without him.

Alex took the last drink of Coke from the can and handed the empty back to Rob. He dropped it and fumbled the Nikon back up to his eye.

"What an ass," he breathed. "Oh, Christ, look at it, just look at it. Hey, Hobbs?"

"What?" she asked, as she checked her watch. Four o'clock, straight up. She didn't want to be late. She got up and took one last look back down the block, to where Villarreal was pressed against the tape.

"You're not pissed I told her, are you?"

"You," she answered, "have got to be kidding."

He never looked back at her. He was adjusting the Nikon in tiny, sure, professional flicks of his finger.

"We're talking major crisis here—whoops, she's going for it—one button—two—oh my God, three! Bra line! We've got a bra line! She's breathing deep—nice, nice—uh-oh."

Alex dusted off her butt. Rob's body froze, leaning forward as if he'd like to crawl through the camera.

"Jesus Christ," he breathed. "Penetration! We've got penetration!"

Villarreal's in, she thought. She just shrugged and walked on. Behind her, Rob's autowinder powered up with a sound like a jet engine starting.

Villarreal's vomit hit the sidewalk like a cloudburst.

"Je-*sus!*" one of the cops screamed, as the heaves

15

continued in prolonged wet gasps. "Christ, not here, that's evidence, lady!"

"All right, who let the bitch in?" Markovsky's voice echoed.

Alex felt a genuine smile break over her lips as she heard the *whirr* of Rob's Nikon, capturing every moment in perfect detail, suitable for framing.

The Arcadia Street side was deserted except for a forlorn-looking flower seller at the far end. The crowd had all gravitated to the crime scene. Two or three blocks away, people were shopping, unaware of the mayhem. Cars detoured around the police barricades in frustrated clusters. Here, though, it was eerily silent. Alex felt a definite chill as she walked down toward the bar.

It was not a fern bar. It was a neighborhood bar, the kind with uneven yellowing linoleum flooring and smoke swirling like thick milk around the lightbulbs. The smell was a mix of old grease, spilled beer, workday sweat. The air felt thick and hot, like sweat condensing on her skin. Alex blinked rapidly and looked around. There wasn't much to see. The tables were just tables, if a little dingier and more rickety than usual. The chairs looked weatherbeaten. Only the bar looked freshly stocked, unlike the bartender.

She checked her watch. Five after four. Not too late. Markovsky had no witnesses, he'd said so.

That made hers an exclusive.

He was sitting nervously in a booth at the back. She wasn't a moment too soon; the bottle on the table was perilously drained. He looked up at her approach and she was surprised by the pallor of his face, the

16

tremor in his hands. She'd thought the booze would have steadied him a little.

"Hey, take it easy. You want something to eat?" she asked him, and slid onto the bench seat. He was an older man, over fifty, and wore a bright red running suit. The only thing he ran to, in Alex's opinion, was fat. His eyes, small and brown, were squinted, although the lights were low. He had a thick fan of wrinkles from his eyes back to his temples.

"No, no, I can't eat," he mumbled, and grabbed a broken piece of pretzel out of the bowl on the table. His teeth were yellowish and strong, like a mule's. "They take her away yet?"

"Not yet. Listen, I'm sorry you had to wait so long, but I couldn't be too careful. Somebody would have tipped to it if I'd taken off, and you don't want a media circus, do you?" There were certain buzzwords that were sure to panic witnesses. *Media circus* was an exacta every time. Alex mentally hummed a few bars of "Send in the Clowns". "Hey, you don't mind if I take notes, do you? So I get everything right?"

"Nah," he said, and took another drink. Not a sip—a drink. "Look, I'll tell you what I saw, but I gotta stay out of it, right? No cops, right? I can't be placed down here."

Alex made a show of searching for a pen in her pocket. While her fingers were in there, they turned on her tape recorder. She slapped the pen down on the table and dug her notepad out, too.

"Why can't you be placed down here?" Alex asked neutrally. He looked up. His florid, uneven face took on a few more splotches of color. She didn't really

17

need his answer; he was a successful man (the running suit was designer), long married (gold band sunk deep into his sausagy finger), and philandering. Probably with a firm-fleshed young woman just out of college, looking for a steady income without a steady job. Alex wasn't making a moral judgment. Hell, she worked for the *National Light.*

"Well, uh, there's—a—" The man coughed and drank again. He finally got his nose out of the whisky and met her eyes directly. "Another man."

She blinked. Again. He seemed to expect some answer, and she tried to think of one. It took a minute.

"It won't go in the story, and I don't reveal my sources. Now, you say you ducked the cops? Didn't make a report?" Alex said, and took a note. It looked like she was taking a note, anyway. Actually, she doodled a fat little man with a gold ring through his nose.

"No, no, I saw the body and I threw up and I ran. That's all. I just ran." His shoulders drooped miserably, and he breathed noisily through his mouth. From the stuffy sound of his voice, his nose was running. "I'm a fucking coward, I know that. Listen, what about the money you promised?"

"In a minute. But you saw the body," Alex repeated. He nodded convulsively. His neck looked so tight she was afraid a muscle would rip. "Did you see who dumped her?"

For just a minute she thought he wouldn't answer, but he'd gone this far, drunk this much. He nodded.

"Yeah. Yeah. Sort of. It was a red van; the side door slid open and there was this white plastic sheet, like a dropcloth or a real big garbage bag, and she pulled up one end. And the—the body, it sort of rolled out. Hard. Onto the sidewalk."

Alex felt her heart lurch and speed forward, taking her stomach with it. *She.* She looked at him, memorizing the moment.

"You're sure it was a woman?" she asked, and kept most of her excitement out of her voice. "Did you see her?"

"She didn't get out. I just saw her hands, you know, and this shiny red glitter nail polish on her fingers, and when she leaned forward I saw she had breasts." He sounded faintly ashamed for noticing. "She had big boobs."

"Hair?"

"Yeah," he agreed wisely. Alex's smile tightened on her lips, and she forced it back to something more agreeable.

"What color?"

"I don't know, brown, maybe blond. I couldn't see much, I told you. She had on blue jeans and some kind of sweatshirt. It was a red van, late '70s, I didn't see the plates," he apologized, and gulped another mouthful of whisky. It must have burned, from his grimace. "I was busy, you know, looking at—the stuff on the sidewalk. The blood."

If he'd been close enough to see all that, he'd been close enough to see the brain mushrooming through the skull, and the eyes. Correction, lack thereof. Alex looked down at her pad and sketched something amorphous and ugly. He looked down into his glass.

"You think I ought to talk to the cops?" he suddenly asked her. Alex shrugged. She colored in the sketch and made it a thick, uneven pool of blood.

"Buddy, it's your life. But anybody who would kill that woman and dump her cool as ice on a busy street is gonna do it again. That's all I'm gonna say." Let him, she thought, decide whether the killer would go after another woman or after him if he talked. She wasn't going to give him instructions.

"Yeah," he said, and looked away again. "Look, I told you everything I know. I'm not giving you my name, understand? I don't know you. I wasn't here. I didn't see it."

"So you didn't see a dark-haired woman in a red '70s van dump the body."

"That's right."

Alex reached in her pocket and clicked STOP. He looked more than a little green around the gills. She reached in her pocket and found a bent, sweat-damp card that read ALEXANDRA HOBBS, INVESTIGATIVE REPORTER. The logo of the *National Light* loomed over her name. The eagle looked like a vulture, which was more than appropriate.

Food chains.

"You think of anything else, you call me, okay? I'm going to feed this stuff to the cops anonymously. You don't have to worry about it. Here." Alex slid his agreed-upon fee, five hundred dollars, across the table toward him. She also slid over a ten-dollar bill. "Have another drink."

It wasn't a wise suggestion. He turned even greener. As she drew back, he lunged out of the booth and staggered for the restrooms in the back. He got as far as the hallway.

His vomiting was as noisy and indelicate as Therese Villarreal's.

Alex scanned the bar automatically to take her mind off the smell filtering back from the hall, filing away in her mind the chipped tables and uneven floor and sparse selection of bottles over the counter. She filed away the faces of the customers, who were mostly looking toward the hallway where her witness was depositing her expense budget.

One of the faces hit her like an electric shock. She blinked, studied him, and felt her heart kick into overdrive. Her muscles tightened convulsively, her skin burned, and her breath rasped in and out of her lungs faster than she could absorb the oxygen.

She was having a religious experience. An *orgasm.* She knew this guy.

Gabriel Davies was at the bar. Gabriel Davies, sitting there as casual as anything, watching a Celtics game on TV, ignoring the world.

Alex flicked her pocket recorder on again. Her knees felt weak and trembly when she stood up, but she made it all the way across the room to where he sat. He didn't look like much, a wiry guy in a loose cotton shirt and pants, only a few years older than her own thirty years. He'd started to lose his thinning brown hair to male-pattern baldness, and his scalp looked pink and newborn in a circle at the crown of his head. Like Rob Rangel's.

He'd been five years younger and a little beefier when she'd snapped his picture in front of his office. Gabriel Davies, boy wonder detective. How many serial killers had he caught by then? Three?

Yeah, three at least. And then there was Barnes

Broward, and then there were the illegally published *Casebooks,* and then he wasn't quite such a hero anymore.

And nobody had seen him since.

He was drinking something dark and carbonated, rum and something. He didn't look at her directly, but she saw him watching her in the mirror over the bar. His eyes, as she remembered, were a light brown, almost gold.

"Buy you a drink?" she asked, and waved the ten at the bartender. Davies didn't look at her.

"No, thank you." The amazing thing about his voice was that it didn't sound like anything, really. Just a voice, not too deep, not too high, not too interested. The voice of the clerk at the grocery store.

Yeah, she thought. *In the meat department.*

"Okay, buy me one. Mr. *Davies.*" A long muscle in her back tensed as she said it, reminding her how stupid she was, how totally reckless. In spite of that, Alex smiled, but the smile was hard to hold. His eyes, when he turned, were so unnerving. So direct.

"You have me confused with someone else," he said. She swallowed and kept looking. The muscle in her back twitched painfully.

"Not a chance, friend, and you remember me, too. Alex Hobbs. I write for the *National Light* now."

"Oh, too bad," he said politely, and sipped at his drink. "Goodbye."

He stared at her, waiting. His expression was as cold as the ice he rattled in his glass, and his eyes looked supernaturally brilliant buried in the middle of all that blandness. She had a visceral flash of memory, of his face stark-white in the strobe flash of cameras, his eyes wild and catlike. Before or after the *Casebooks* went on the bestseller lists? Before, she thought. In her memory, Gabriel stood over the bloody sheeted lump of Broward's body, and trembled. Nearly every reporter had put it down to shock.

But Alex had interpreted it—correctly—as triumph. As ecstasy.

"I'm not leaving," she said. Davies had an absolutely terrifying stare, a predator's stare, never varying. She held it even though her stomach clenched and quivered with the strain. "Mr. Davies, I'm not going to blow your cover, if that's what this is. All I want is a comment, I won't give your location."

"It's not a cover, it's my life. What's left of it." With the same sudden disinterest as the cat he resembled, he swiveled away from her and set his empty glass on the bar. "What people like you left of it."

"Hey, I didn't write the book," she shrugged, and started to touch his shoulder. Something in his body language told her she'd better not try it. "Look, really, what do I have to promise? I swear, you've got complete confidentiality."

He laughed. It sent chills through her and made her glad she'd gone with the nontouching decision. His laughter was quiet and composed and not at all amused. She remembered the look on his face five years ago, caught in the flash of her camera.

"Why, thank you, Miss Hobbs. I recall getting a similar promise from Mr. Landrum when I lent him my casebooks. Background, he said. And within six weeks, five hundred thousand people were devouring

23

my thoughts, just like little maggots." He rattled the ice in his glass. His fingers were white where he gripped it, the only real sign of his tension. They were big, square fingers, neatly manicured. He didn't work with his hands. "I'll decline your offer."

"So you have no comment about the body found around the corner on Meadow?"

"None." A quiet, composed answer.

"Well, okay, if it doesn't interest you, I don't suppose you'll be particularly interested that she nearly had her head blown off. Brains everywhere. Blood." Alex realized that she was babbling, and knew she'd misstepped. Badly. But she'd figured the blood would attract him, like a sharp-toothed piranha.

"No," he said more slowly. She slid off of the barstool with a guilty feeling of relief and felt her shirt cling unpleasantly to her back. He swiveled slowly to look at her again, nailing her in place with those large-pupiled eyes. "Robbery?"

"Probably not. Probably killed somewhere else and dumped on the sidewalk." Alex swallowed hard. She was gripped by an eerie feeling of triumph and terror.

He leaned forward, eyes widening, face going even more expressionless than before. His hands dangled limply between his knees, but there was, if possible, even more tension in him than before.

"Shot, you said?" he asked. She nodded. "Shot from the front?"

"No, the back."

He rubbed his thumbs together, stared at her.

"Do you have an identification?"

"Her ID said Dianne Gardner."

He came up off his barstool, an explosion of muscle that made her take a couple of quick steps backward. His expression wasn't blank anymore. It was full of sudden, complete concentration.

"Show me," Gabriel Davies commanded.

Chapter Three

He didn't want to approach the scene while the cops were still looking around, and Alex didn't have any intention of leaving him. They sat together, tensely, on a shaded bus stop bench as the reporters packed up their gear and the TV trucks rolled away. Alex fiddled with her pad and paper, nervously scratching down ideas and marking them off before Davies might look over and see them. He just sat, waiting.

Markovsky was the last of the cops to leave, walking from one end of the block to the other, pacing, thinking. Alex felt a surge of relief when he let his pacing carry him over to a parked white Ford; he scanned the street as he got in his car, and she looked away. When she turned back, he was in the car and driving toward them. She dropped her notebook and bent over to get it, but a quick glance assured her that Markovsky hadn't looked her way.

"Let's go," Gabriel Davies said, and was already walking by the time she understood what he'd said.

He took long, quick, eager steps. She had to trot to keep up with him.

"What are we doing?" she asked. She wished she'd had time to reload tape; her recorder had long ago clicked off. "What are you looking for?"

He ignored her, crossed the street. A car zoomed by, headlights painting him in harsh light, but he didn't notice it. Alex darted across after him and felt an instant's panic as a car roared over the hill toward her. She jumped for the curb and felt the tug of wind as the station wagon flickered past.

Gabriel Davies was at the crime scene.

He stood there for a long moment, looked up and down the street. He crouched down and bent close to look at the bloodstain. She thought for an eerie instant he was smelling the blood, tasting it in some bizarre way. He leaned back on his heels and looked down the block. His eyes began flickering rapidly, focusing, unfocusing. He tracked something she couldn't see to the bloody spot, then tracked it away. Into her. Past her.

Past is right, she realized. He was watching the past. Reconstructing it, with a sense of reality that she couldn't hope to understand.

"Well?" she demanded. His face drained of expression again as he focused on her.

"She was dumped here out of something like a van. If they'd tried to dump her from a car the splash pattern would have been different, there would have been a door in the way. She died on something nonabsorbent, like plastic or a dropcloth. I see she left smears of brain. I presume the bullet took quite a bit of it out."

27

Alex nodded, unable to speak. He stood up and began walking again, casually now, and she followed.

"I presume the police have nothing much to go on."

"Well—probably not," she admitted. He nodded and walked on to the alleyway a few feet away, stopped there and squatted. He stared at a puddle of something she could barely see in the dim light.

"I presume that the man in the red running suit was your witness. The one who stood here," Davies said. She felt her skin tighten over her arms and back. Was he seeing him now? Or had he seen him—then?

"You remember him," she said, and he twisted to look over his shoulder at her, smiling slightly.

"It's hard to forget a man who vomits so loudly. For the second time in one day." He indicated the pool in front of him. "The police haven't talked to him."

"No."

Davies nodded and stood up. He took one last look down the alley and spun around to view the street. Alex turned, too, and it flashed in front of her. A corona of blood. The eyes—

"She didn't have any eyes," Alex murmured. Davies didn't answer.

He made the trip from the bloodstain to the alleyway three more times, slowly, deliberately. It was already dark. Streetlights flicked on in unsteady spurts, one after another, marching up Meadow Avenue toward them. A light buzzed and hummed and caught fire over Davies' head as he stood looking at the stain.

It looked black in the halogen glow.

28

"Thank you, Miss Hobbs. I've seen everything I need to see here," he said, and her heart lurched suddenly at the dismissal in his voice. *Hang on to him,* her mind screamed. *Hang on, no matter what.*

"Mr. Davies, how about that interview now?" she asked quickly, as he began to leave. He didn't even hesitate, didn't seem to hear her at all. She felt anger spread under her skin in a thick flush; unwilling to be ignored, she followed him. She reached out for his shoulder. "Hey!"

She never touched him. Never saw him spin around. The only clear thing she saw was his fist, held trembling and suspended an inch or so from her face. The fear took a second to register in her, but when it did it hit with a vengeance, like an electric shock down her spine. She didn't dare move, not even to back up. His face was blank, strange, impenetrable. And his eyes were savage.

And then they were afraid. He lowered his fist and uncurled it, took a step back.

"Don't follow me," he said. "Don't ever do that again."

She couldn't have followed him, not then. He walked away, passing in and out of the streetlights until he reached the corner. After he'd turned it, she heard his footsteps continue on into the distance.

You fucking coward, she thought shakily. *Why did you let him get away with that?*

Chapter Four
Davies

An excerpt from *The Casebooks of Gabriel Davies*. Published.

August 16, 1986

I wasn't sure the man responsible for the child murders was Barnes Broward. They think I made some magical leap of logic to figure it out; I've heard that I deduced his guilt from the wear pattern on the bottom of his shoes, like Sherlock Holmes. Truth is, I never saw the bottom of his shoe until he kicked me in the face. But they'd never believe me if I said that I just saw him, saw the way he touched the little girl. I still wasn't certain, even after the Cassetti child disappeared, that I was really on the right track. I wasn't certain right up until the last one.

At least, I hope I wasn't sure. The alternative is that I followed him around knowing he was killing them, and didn't do anything to stop him.

As I watched him that day in the park, I began to see why the bodies were divided into so many pieces.

It was a terrible, familiar feeling, like looking at some horrible mask in the mirror and recognizing yourself. Barnes Broward did love them. Every part of them. We found semen traces consistently in the wounds.

The worst thing, the very worst, is that sometimes I lie awake at night and dream about it. The knife feels cool in my hand, as hard as the lump of my erection. I see the child. I feel along the cool, fragile flesh to the bumpy joinings of her bones, hear her scream, feel her blood washing over me. And I cut, in my half-dreams, like Barnes Broward cut, meticulously, carefully.

He learned how to joint them, like chickens. The Pitney girl, Caroline, showed trial cuts on all of her long bones. He had trouble locating the joints at first, but he learned quickly. The second and third children must have taken remarkably little time, given the circumstances. There were no trial cuts on the bones, just perfect precision.

They called him a butcher. He wasn't. It was important to him to do it right, to have the flesh divided just so, the bone intact and pearly-pink. He didn't hack. He carved.

All of this frightens me sometimes. I know I shouldn't allow myself this, shouldn't get aroused when I think of those children.

But I do.

Chapter Five

He'd saved Shalanna North from Barnes Broward, at the end. But nobody cared.

The Broward chapter was deceptively matter-of-fact, but Alex could almost feel the anguish seeping through the pages, could nearly see the look in his eyes as he stared at himself in the mirror. What was frightening was the possibility that someday he'd look in the mirror and wouldn't find anything strange there at all.

Alex put the book aside and wandered toward the kitchen. On the way she found herself putting a hand on the apartment door, making sure the deadbolt was turned. She was angry at herself for letting it spook her, but she hooked the chain, too.

In the kitchen, two days' worth of dishes lingered in the sink, beginning to smell like old socks. Alex ran hot water over them and dumped in a spray of blue detergent. The feel of soap suds on her hands was soothing, a perfect distraction. She rinsed old lasagna from a blue-flowered plate her sister had given her and tried to imagine what Gabriel Davies must be thinking.

The water was warm. Warm as skin. As blood. A chunk of lasagna came loose from the plate and floated away; it bumped gently against her fingers, soft and pulpy.

I should have followed him, Alex thought, as she had a hundred times since coming home. But she knew it wouldn't have done any good. If Gabriel Davies wanted to talk to her, he would. If he didn't, the best she could hope for from him was indifference. Her neck prickled with the thought of what might interest him.

The telephone rang as she set the last dish on the drainboard. She put her hand on the cool plastic, felt the vibration of the rings through her damp skin, and finally picked it up. She held it to her ear and silently waited.

"Your witness," Gabriel Davies said tinnily through the receiver. "I want to talk to him."

Oddly enough, she felt no surprise.

"Nope." Alex hoped she sounded cool enough; her fingers were aching, little pinpricks, and she held the phone between her shoulder and ear while she rubbed them. "No can do. I promised him confidentiality."

"I'm hardly likely to run his name in the paper."

That might have actually been a joke. Alex heard a distant echo of thin applause behind him. Was he watching TV?

"Miss Hobbs?" he asked. She pulled her thoughts back together again and shoved her hands in the pockets of her robe. It was pink, fuzzy, soft as a child's skin. Her fingers felt frostbitten.

"Alex."

"I hardly think we're on a first-name basis, Miss Hobbs. I need to talk to your witness. It's important."

"No, I can't allow that, not you, not the cops, not anybody, unless he comes forward on his own. You may think I don't have any ethics, but I've still got this one. No deal."

Davies was quiet again. Behind him, the clapping changed to a familiar theme song. *Jeopardy!*

"Then play me the tape of the interview," he suddenly said. She flinched in surprise. "I know you've got one. That's no breach of ethics, is it? You can edit out the name, if you even have it. But I need to know the rest."

"Why?" she asked. There was a click on the other end of the phone, and for a second she thought he'd hung up. *Jeopardy!*'s theme song stopped. "Mr. Davies, why?"

"Because this isn't the first time a body has appeared near where I'm staying," he answered.

Alex breathed in again, held it, breathed cautiously out. She reached for a pen.

"Tell me where to meet you," she said.

Weirdly enough, it felt like a first date. Alex swallowed hard as she opened the door of DelVecchio's and stepped inside. Her stomach fluttered. Not scared, no. Eager.

He wasn't waiting in the foyer for her. She crossed

the faux-marble floor and peered through to the interior. The restaurant was sparsely settled, unusual for a Friday evening; Alex wondered if there was something she ought to have read in the restaurant reviews, like DELVECCHIO'S KILLS THREE WITH BAD MUSHROOM.

She couldn't see Gabriel Davies. That didn't bother her; it gave her the chance to take some deep breaths, wrestle her pulse rate down under a hundred. All the way over in the car she'd been in a locker-room pumped-up trance; here it was, the big one. Nobody had ever gotten an interview with Davies, not even when he was hot after the Broward case, or hotter with the publication of the book.

A word occurred to her, bright and shining as a brand new bar of gold. *Exclusive.* What a sexy word. She mouthed it lovingly, just for the taste, and smiled.

She pulled the door open and walked in with the confident step of a winner, a World Series veteran taking the field. On the other side a maitre d' slumped behind his reservation stand. He gave her a professional, tired smile, a man with nothing to do, still overworked.

"I'm here to meet—" She stopped. She had no idea what name Davies was using. "—somebody. Can I just look around?"

"Certainly," the maitre d' said. As she scanned the room, he pointed. "Try the back."

Davies had picked the booth for ambush. By the time she saw him through the gloom, his eyes had already focused on her, the way a tiger's focused on something live and moving and vulnerable. His face was empty, quiet, interested without showing a trace of recognition.

She came toward him with a reporter's trademark *I'm-busier-than-you-are* steps. She expected with each one to see his face lose that tiger look, to see him smile and look away and make her feel comfortable. Maybe he didn't recognize her in the low light. Maybe his eyes weren't so good.

By the time she'd reached the booth, she'd run out of explanations. His expression never changed, not even as she sat on the seat across from him. The thinning velvet upholstery held her back like an outgoing tide when she slid over.

"Thank you for meeting me," Alex said briskly, and leaned forward with her hands folded on the table. Earnest, that was the look she wanted. Honest. Trustworthy.

He continued to watch her, unblinking. He had a long-range stare, the kind she'd seen on soldiers coming back from war, and God, she hated feeling it crawl over her face.

She could *not* lose control of the situation, not this quickly. She managed to get her lips to curl into something like a smile and stared back. And back. And back. His irises were dark gold, blotted with a huge black hole of pupil. She felt her eyes start to burn and forced herself not to blink.

My God, she thought. *What if he's dead?*

She forced herself to stare at his chest until it rose and fell. Not dead.

Not physically, anyway.

"Mr. Davies?" she asked. He smiled, a thin stretch

36

of lips like a rubber band pulling. Nothing happened to his eyes.

She had to blink. Her eyelids fluttered, and dark blurred his image. The cool relief lasted only a second, and then the discomfort came back. He was still staring.

Maybe if she did something—by the time she thought of it, her fingers were rummaging in her purse, searching for her microrecorder. She watched him out of the corner of her eye; as far as she could tell, he never glanced away.

She set the tape recorder in the no-man's-land of white tablecloth and sat back to wait.

Davies reached out, without looking away, and picked up the recorder. He turned it over in his strong, thick fingers, examined the buttons with delicate touches. He put it back on the table, where she'd left it.

Alex had the suffocating feeling that she was back at the zoo again, and somebody had let her inside the tiger cage and forgotten all about her. Except the tiger.

A waiter came within waving distance, and she flagged him down. It gave her a reason to avoid looking at Davies for a minute, to pretend he might actually be looking away from her. As the waiter approached from behind Davies, she sensed some of his attention leave her, like a battlefront searchlight moving off to light up a flank invasion.

Still, his eyes stayed aimed at her. Unblinking.

She ordered coffee with extra cream. The waiter turned expectantly to Davies.

"Coffee's fine," Davies said. His eyes were wide

and gold and sucked her courage away like leeches. The waiter, writing on his pad, never even noticed. He just nodded and went away.

Alex wanted to yell at him to come back, but knew it wouldn't do any good. That's what *he* was waiting for, a clear crack he could stick a knife into.

Wasn't it?

"You've been reading the book," Davies said. She flinched and her arm knocked a glass of water; it jittered and settled as she reached for it. The cold sweat on its sides made an icy tattoo on the back of her arm.

"How did you know?"

He didn't answer. She concentrated on the glass, on the thin trickle of water slipping down the side. She could almost feel it whispering down her spine. Her peripheral vision told her he still hadn't looked away.

Damn it, that's enough, she thought angrily. *I'm here to interview him, I'll interview him. End of story. What to talk about? The casebooks. He's already mentioned them.*

"Speaking of the book, why didn't you sue omega, or at least Haley Landrum?" She winced; it sounded feeble, an amateur's question. "I mean, it was stolen material. Or if you didn't want to sue, why didn't you at least make a statement that it was faked?"

The waiter returned with their coffee. Davies didn't answer for so long that she was sure she'd failed, again—but as she pulled her coffee cup closer, she saw him move to get his, too, so he was responding after all.

"They weren't faked," he said. She reached for the cream and opened three of the little cups; the white swirls disappeared into the black of her coffee, misted back up. She picked up her spoon.

Across the table, Davies reached for the cream and meticulously opened three. He poured them into his coffee and stirred, then put his spoon back down and waited. Watching.

"That's all you have to say?" she snapped. "Jesus, I thought you'd be a little more interesting."

"Oh, I am," he answered. His pupils were wider now, sighting blood. "You have an interesting past, Miss Hobbs. The Carla Jenkins story, 1988. When your editor found out you'd plagarized, you threw a computer at him and broke his two front teeth."

There was no reason to feel violated. It was public record, easy to find out. She opened her mouth to tell him so.

"Was it true you did it because you were too drunk to write something original?"

It was a neat, surgical slice, right below her ribs, right through her falling stomach. The pain welling up was warm, like blood. She looked away so he couldn't see the damage in her face.

She could still feel his gaze, hot and intent, licking up her pain.

"It was no big deal," she muttered. She knew she shouldn't be answering, shouldn't be feeding him, but it was the only way to get him to talk. He wouldn't play her game.

She had to play his.

"Of course," he said. He didn't believe her, and didn't care. "Sugar?"

She reached out mechanically and got two packets. She glanced at him as she tore them open and saw him, still watching her, reach for the sugar. His fingers explored the contents of the bowl and found two.

He tore both of them open at once, just like she did. After she'd poured them into her cup, he followed suit.

She couldn't believe what she was seeing, or thinking. *He isn't doing what I do, is he? Is he?*

She picked up her spoon and held it in trembling fingers.

He didn't move.

She stirred her coffee, spoon hitting china in drowned clinks. She glanced down into her cup and saw her face reflected back in ripples, scared.

She took a deep breath and started to look up.

Across the table, she heard a spoon clinking on china as he stirred.

He hadn't looked away from her. His eyes seemed to have focused differently, though; not on her face, now. A little lower, around her neck.

What the hell was he looking at? She wasn't wearing a necklace. Her sweater didn't have any patterns to it. There was nothing, nothing to make him look there.

Yes, she realized. There was a hole in her sweater, right at the neck seam. Funny, she'd forgotten about it, but now she could feel the cool air through the ravels, feel him looking at it. She was open. Vulnerable.

40

She felt a sudden tightness in her chest, a phantom pain down her arm. She fought the urge to gasp for breath and forced herself to sit still. The game was still on.

"What do you want in return for the tape?" he asked. She kept watching him, feeling the pressure like a balloon filling in her head. He wanted her to look away, because this was the moment when she might win.

She swallowed and kept staring. He was still watching the hole in her sweater, targeting. Veins were under there, she knew. Vulnerable places.

"Exclusive," she said. Her voice sounded flat and certain, not scared at all. "I want to know what's happened to you since you left Chicago. I want the story of these bodies you talked about. I'll give you plenty of time to get out of town before I print, if you want."

The pressure was blinding. Her eyes ached, burned, trembled with the effort. He shifted his gaze again, minutely, and she got the full force of it.

"I won't be leaving town."

Fucker, she thought in a white fury, and blinked. The pressure deflated to a dull ache behind her eyes, and she saw him smile again.

She reached out and picked up four more sugar packets. She shook them and emptied them, one by one, into her coffee. Stirred.

She looked down into her cup and listened to the crisp tearing sounds as he opened packets. Four. A soft hiss as he poured the sugar in. The spoon, clinking.

The bastard *was* imitating her.

41

She put her cup to her lips and pretended to swallow. As she did, she glanced over the rim at him. He reached for his cup and lifted it, never looking away.

He made a face at the taste, but when she took another fake sip, drank again.

She swallowed a dry, frightened laugh.

"If you don't think my offer is fair, tell me what is," she challenged. He set his cup down and leaned back, head resting on the high cushioned back of the booth. He looked relaxed, except for the eyes.

"The baked ziti is fair. The lasagna is quite good," he said.

She nearly, nearly laughed. The silence dragged on. To prove her command of the situation again, she reached for more cream and poured it into her coffee.

As he reached across for more cream, she smelled his aftershave, and something crisply unpleasant underneath it. He smelled slightly burned, as if he'd dried his hair too long and crisped the ends.

They fell into another abyss of silence.

The waiter bore down on them, coffee urn as highly polished as his smile. Davies shifted his attention again without shifting his gaze. The waiter handed him a menu. He put the menu aside and folded his hands in front of him, right over left, on top of his knife and fork. Watching Alex.

"Coffee?" the waiter asked her, and splashed some into her cup without waiting for her answer. He added a dash to Davies' cup, too.

The menu the waiter had handed her felt slick and useless in her hands. Alex put it aside and leaned forward, taking advantage of Davies' distraction, however slight.

"I can't help you if you won't help me," she said. The waiter was forgotten even before he walked away, and Davies studied her again with all of his attention. She resisted the urge to throw coffee in his face, scream, anything to make him blink.

"What makes you think I need your help?" Davies asked. It was a blunter question than before, not so surgical. She smiled and felt the pressure building on his side.

"You're here."

He blinked. By God, he blinked. But after that, it was the same, the same stare, the same expression.

"Let me hear the tape."

She indicated the recorder with a be-my-guest gesture. His fingers explored it, lifted it up so his peripheral vision could identify the controls.

When he played it, her witness's voice sounded flat and elongated, slurred with too much booze. Next to it, her own sounded nasal. Alex stirred her undrinkable coffee and waited.

Gabriel Davies watched her throughout the tape. She couldn't tell if he waited for her reactions or just stared in concentration, and she didn't actually care. Her skin felt hot now, sunburned from his stare. The skin revealed by the hole in the sweater was probably blistered.

"A woman," he finally murmured. "Seems unlikely."

"He sounded pretty sure to me."

"Miss Hobbs, statistically speaking, women don't shoot other women in the head. The body, maybe, not the head. They generally hate to disfigure each other." Davies pushed back in his chair and sipped his coffee again. "Are you looking for a logical motive? There's nothing logical about displaying a body in this fashion. She, if it is a she, did it because she liked it."

"Or because somebody told her to do it," Alex countered.

"That someone would usually be her lover or husband."

"Serial killer, do you think?" Alex asked. He shrugged.

He didn't answer. He stared.

"You talked about other bodies. Is this part of a pattern?"

Gabriel Davies' lips smiled again.

"You don't like me very much, do you?" she demanded. It was the stupidest thing she'd ever said, or ever imagined herself saying. She felt an urge to put her hand over her mouth and forced herself to sit still, to keep looking at him. Davies' smile dissolved back into his mask and his eyes opened wider, drinking in her discomfort.

"On the contrary," he said very slowly. "I like you quite a lot."

She hadn't wanted to hear that.

Davies played the tape twice more, rewinding to listen to certain phrases or inflections. When he was done, he put the recorder back on the tablecloth, took a last sip of his coffee, and threw two dollars on the table. He had already risen and walked three steps away before she realized he was leaving, and she grabbed for her things and ran after him.

"Hey, we made a deal. I go with you, right?" she asked, as they passed the maitre d'. Davies shook his head.

"No, I'm going home now," he said, and politely held the door open to the street for her. They stepped out into the humid night, and Alex fumbled her tape recorder as she jammed it into her purse. It was city-dark outside, night but never really black. The streetlights were a kind of odd yellow-orange to the west, but on this block they were brilliant blue-white, like spotlights. She resisted the urge to shade her eyes and wished there were people here, passing strangers, witnesses.

"Where do I meet you tomorrow, then?" she asked, and plowed through the chaos of shapes in her bag to find a pen and paper. Gabriel Davies turned, and she saw the first real smile from him, a slice of darkness. His eyes looked too wet in the glitter of streetlights.

"Oh, I'll find you," he said. She froze, watching him. He walked away, quietly, unthreateningly.

She found she was holding her breath, and very carefully let it out. The flutter in her stomach had changed to a heavy pounding in her head.

He never looked back.

Chapter Six

She slept badly, but deeply. She woke to a scream, on-off, on-off, and struggled up and out of a mound of covers. She'd beaten the alarm clock senseless before she realized it was innocent.

The phone.

She lunged into the kitchen to get it and realized the sun was up and bright, splashing messily all over the apartment. Gee, it made the place look homey. *Jesus, she was late.*

Her frantic gaze finally settled on a clock across the room as she picked up the receiver.

Oh, God, she thought. *It's eleven. I have a one o'clock deadline . . .*

"Hobbs, you have a one o'clock deadline." a voice snapped on the other end of the phone. Alex cleared her throat, tasted fungus and fuzz in her mouth. She cradled the phone on her shoulder and picked up an abused last-Sunday's paper to rustle the pages.

"Yeah, yeah, Wheaton, I know. Just reviewing the copy. I've been up all night working on it," she lied.

"I'll have it there in—ah—an hour. Maybe an hour and a half."

"Make it an hour, I got enough trouble with Herman, that dirtbag. I told him to write a *conservative* opinion, didn't I? Didn't I?" Wheaton Sinclair III, who in no way resembled his name, didn't wait for her contradiction. She heard cloth stretch on the other end of the phone. All of his shirts looked like they'd been made for someone with a triangular neck. "Reactionary liberal bullshit. I'm busting my hump to get the damn thing rewritten. Don't make me come after the story, Hobbs."

"Have I ever?" she asked. He grunted. "Listen, I'd like to take some more time for the body on Meadow, okay? Put it in next week's issue. I'll have something really juicy by then, worth the wait. For now I'll just put in an 'under investigation' blurb, right?"

"And what the hell am I supposed to fill the page with?" Wheaton nearly shouted. She could hear his breath rasping as his asthma cut in. There was a distant hiss as he used his breather. "What are you trying to do to me, Hobbs? Kill me?"

"Nah, I need the paycheck." Alex coughed, buying a couple of seconds while her brain woke up. "How about a nice story about that guy who mailed his wife her lover's penis? Good angle. Sex *and* violence."

Wheaton was silent. She could hear him chewing over the idea, going over his memorized catalog of file shots and graphics. She shifted the phone to a cradle between her ear and shoulder and opened a cupboard. Ah. Coffee.

"Keep it in good taste," Wheaton finally snapped,

and slammed down the phone. Alex blew a kiss into the receiver and hung it up.

She'd already written the story. It was two years old. A little updating wouldn't hurt anybody, since she'd kindly elected to withhold the names of the guilty and innocent. And she'd never been able to sell it.

While the coffee was brewing she printed out the story, colorfully headed SEX IN A SMALL PACKAGE! It wasn't one of her better efforts, but what the hell, it was better than nine-tenths of the crap Wheaton accepted. He'd take it and slobber on it when she wasn't looking.

She called up the Davies story. It was going to be good, really good. Way too good for the *National Light.* Gabriel Davies was big-time—national press, big-money magazines. Movie rights.

She felt a distant stirring of anticipation as she saved the story again. Of all the people she'd investigated, Davies was probably the creepiest, the strangest, the most potentially dangerous.

But, in a very odd way, the most vulnerable, too.

They were the best ones, the vulnerable ones.

"Shit," Alex mumbled, and slammed the door be hind her. Her apartment looked like a reminder of all the things she hadn't done in the past six months. She dropped her gym bag on the floor and collapsed into a chair. "Life is shit."

She had nothing in her refrigerator but some crappy frozen lasagna, and she wanted nothing to do with Italian food, not after DelVecchio's and Davies. Pizza wasn't Italian, really. And they delivered.

As she reached for the phone, it began to ring. Alex drew back her hand and watched it narrowly, as if it were a bad-tempered pet. She picked it up on the fourth ring.

"Alex?" Wheaton. She let out a loud gusty sigh of relief. "Where the hell have you been?"

"Busy," she snapped. "I don't work nights, Wheat."

"Crime doesn't sleep." *You geek,* she thought. "That friend of yours, Rangel, the camera guy, he called. There's a murder down at Myrtle and Varansas. He says it's big, and to get your ass down there." Wheaton coughed. *"I'm* saying to get your ass down there. I need a decent story next week."

"Christ, that's two stories in two days—"

"I don't care if it's two in an hour! Get it!"

Alex winced at the crash of his phone slamming down.

When she topped the hill four blocks from her destination, she saw the Las Vegas display of blue-and-reds. The streets were, predictably, blocked off.

She was late to the party.

The scene looked like a carnival, complete with floodlights and overdressed TV reporters and harassed cops, all flashing red and blue and white, like a patriotic parade. The night smelled of exhaust fumes and sweat, but every once in a while she caught a whiff of something darker hiding in the air. Cordite? Blood?

Alex fought her way to the scene tape and found a friendly face to give her the basics. The victim was a man, mid-fifties, probably a businessman. Killed in his car, a sweet-looking metallic silver Jaguar XJ9.

The TV crews scented a to-die-for opportunity. A man driving a car like that was probably from the Emerald Lake end of town, richer than Midas's banker.

Punctuating the steady glare of TV lights were the flashes of still photographers. Alex followed the strobes, and found the one she was looking for.

Rob Rangel looked contented, like a rat-fed cat. His camera hung limply around his neck from its colorful embroidered guitar strap, and he smoked a cigarette as he leaned bonelessly against a handy TV van.

"Was it good for you?" she asked.

"You're late. I have got," Rob said in a rich and satisfied voice, "the most in-demand pictures of the year, babe. Full color. Man, they're as good as anything the cops have. I got a great closeup of his face—well, hard to tell it's a face, but it's a closeup, anyway. Looks like three-day-old raw meat."

Alex made a sarcastic retching sound. He pointed to the car, which gleamed a serene and creamy silver. A typical rich man's toy, she thought; sunroof, power everything, window tinting dark enough to keep the plebecite from staring in.

"Like the tinting?" Rob asked. She shrugged and craned her neck as she caught sight of Therese Villarreal doing a walk-and-talk across the way. Therese didn't look so good, which made Alex feel warm and cozy inside.

There was a tall guy standing on the opposite side of the scene tape, hands thrust in the pockets of a raincoat. His face was hidden by a gimme cap.

"Yo, Hobbs, you with me? Tinting on the windows?" Rob pressed. It took her a second to work it out, and she forgot all about the guy at the tape. She took another long look at the Jaguar, at the black windows.

"That's blood?" she asked, and Rob grinned. *"All* of it?"

"Like it was painted on with a sprayer, sweetheart."

"Who's been working the crowd?" she demanded. "Jesus, somebody must have seen something! Does Villarreal have it?"

"Villarreal's got nothing except a bad case of tummy trouble again. Nobody's turned up anybody yet, but you know, it takes time." Rob took a last drag on his cigarette and crushed it out. When a uniformed cop nearby glared at him, he picked up the butt and, after looking for someplace to put it, tossed it underhanded behind him. The cop, distracted by a pushy onlooker, didn't notice. "Jesus, I need a beer."

"Have you run the plates yet?" she asked very softly, the better to avoid any sharp-eared bystanders. He held out a palm to her. Alex sighed and dug in her purse for her wallet, found a twenty, slapped it into his hand. He kissed it in her direction.

"Don't have anything," he said sweetly. He looked so goddamned cherubic.

"Come on, Rangel, help me out. I gave you the son in the Croker case last month."

"Ooh, some help, the little brat took me for fifty before I wised up. Okay, okay, Charlie's getting it for me. Hang out for a minute, he'll be back. Hey, is it true you had a date last night?"

She looked at the guy in the gimme cap again. His face was all in shadow, but she had the nagging sensation he was staring at her, that he knew her. Rob nudged her, not too gently, to put her back in the conversation.

"What? No. Are you kidding? I get fewer dates than a mortician."

"Right. So who is he?" Rob's semifake good nature vanished. His eyes looked cool and silvery. "A big story? You holding out on your buddy?"

She flipped him a bird. Rob just grinned and popped the back of his camera, removed the cartridge, inserted another. It started loading the film with an annoying *whirr.*

Rob's gopher Charlie wandered over and passed him a slip of paper with the kind of slick misdirection usually reserved for stage magicians and dope transactions. Rob passed him back a twenty— Alex's—and Charlie wandered off.

Rob unfolded the note and read it. His smile oozed over, blissful and sated. He held the paper out to Alex. She squinted at the spidery writing.

"Verdun," she said aloud. And said it again as the name rang bells. "Verdun. Jesus Christ, you've got to be kidding. *Harry* Verdun?"

"You expected some homeless guy, driving a thing like that? Baby, I'm set. A couple of photos of the old Verdun hacienda with the security guards in front—modeled after the White House, you know?— put them next to the closeups—editors are going to kiss my fucking ass. They love it when the rich get smoked, lots of high-visibility shit. Hey, Hobbs, you coming? Get an interview with the maid or something?"

She shook her head, distracted. The guy in the gimme cap had moved away from the area where TV lights glared, was making his way closer. She squinted her eyes but couldn't make out his face, the bill of the cap was pulled too low. White guy, though.

She could have sworn he was looking at her.

"Your funeral, Hobbs. I'll see you later at the morgue," Rob said. She felt the van shift against her back as he pushed off and walked away, but she didn't watch him. The guy in the cap disappeared behind a knot of uniformed cops.

Well, whatever, she didn't have time for that. She looked around the site for good copy: a couple of bored cops, but no Markovsky; a bribable forensic tech; a few loiterers who would probably be good for local color, if nothing else. She probably wouldn't find an eyewitness, but the good news was that nobody else would, either.

Harry Verdun. Holy shit. She had enough old society photos to fill up a whole issue on the man.

The coroner was taking an unpleasantly long time crouched over the corpse, trying to count the number of wounds. She wished she could get up closer, get a good look, but that was a slim-to-none chance without Markovsky. She'd have to wait for Rob's pictures.

The guy in the gimme hat had settled in about ten feet away from her. His head was turned in her direction, and the streetlights picked out the JUST DO IT slogan embroidered on the cap.

A camera flash lit him up from chin to eyebrows. His eyes were huge and fixed on her.

Oh, God, it was Gabriel Davies. She felt it as if he'd touched her, a stinging surge of heat and a following wash of fear. He began walking toward her.

I could run, she thought very clearly. *I could make it to my car. I have a head start.*

Harry Verdun had been in his car. She pressed her back against the cold metal van and waited.

"Don't you ever go home?" Davies asked, and walked on past her. Hobbs found herself following him, not exactly willingly. Her legs felt numb, but they kept walking.

"No," she said, and thought, *not anymore.* "So what brings you here? Professional curiosity?"

It seemed to her that, in the liverish glow of the streetlights and the weak moon, he looked pale. Unsettled. She hesitated over the observation until a passing car turned and washed bright light over him.

Pale, all right. She caught an odor from him, a sweet scent of soap and water and fresh aftershave. He'd just had a bath. It was almost enough to cover up the ozone smell.

"As one expert to another, Miss Hobbs, who's in the car?"

"Well, the live one is the coroner," she said, and Davies stopped so suddenly she heard the *scritch* of gravel as he slid. His face didn't change at all.

"Please don't joke with me, Alexandra. I'm really not in the mood for it. Who is it?"

"Harry Verdun."

"Oh," he said, very softly, and his eyes slowly closed. His face looked terrible, pale and old. "Oh."

Alex didn't say anything at all, just stood looking at him. After an eternity, he opened his eyes again. They looked feral, all pupil.

"Harry was with me three hours ago," he said.

Chapter Seven

"You," Alex said, as she blew steam off of her coffee, "are dead. As soon as they trace him back to you—and you can bet your ass they will—there's nothing I can do to help you."

"I didn't do it," Davies said. He watched her take a sip and reached for his own cup. She'd only put three sugars in her coffee this time, and now there were six torn packets in the space between them. Since she hadn't ordered cream, neither had he. He didn't seem to notice the difference, though the coffee tasted sour and burned on her tongue.

She pretended she didn't care that he was still watching her.

"You know for sure you didn't do it," Alex said, and made it sound as if she believed him. His pupils contracted a little, but he didn't look away. "I think you ought to talk to Markovsky before somebody comes who won't be so nice."

"I haven't killed anyone."

Yet, she thought. *Hope I'm not the first.*

"You were with the man before he was killed.

You *know* what the cops think about you and the casebooks. Unless you've got an alibi, I think you'd better talk to Markovsky." He wasn't taking the suggestion very well. She wished he'd stop staring, wished that there were more people nearby so she'd feel more confident. Alex caught the eye of the late-shift waitress, who leaned wearily against the counter. The waitress put on a stubborn look and pretended not to notice her. Jan's House of Pancake Delights was having a slow and surly night. "You *do* have an alibi, don't you?"

"Do you think they'll believe I was taking a two-hour shower?" Davies asked. She took too big a sip of coffee and swallowed what felt like a thick lump of molten lead. The roof of her mouth simmered. She gagged and ripped open another sugar packet, dumped the contents in her mug. Davies took one, too, then felt around the rim of the coffee cup with his fingers to guide in a spoon.

The spoon clinked, lonely.

"You were taking a two-hour shower?" she repeated. He shrugged.

"Yes. I often do."

She had a skin-tightening vision of him standing in the spray, naked, open-eyed, open-mouthed. Mindless.

"I don't think they'll believe that unless you can prove it," she said slowly. He let his head drift over to one side.

"I don't normally shower with witnesses," he said. Alex decided it wasn't a joke, and didn't laugh. "I suppose you're dying to ask me about my relationship with Harry Verdun."

Dying, Alex decided, was not the verb she'd have used.

"Don't," he said. Alex blinked, but let it go. His eyes were glassy, as if the light hit some thin shell right under the surface and reflected off. He wasn't really watching her anymore, just scanning for movement. "There wasn't a relationship, as you would describe it."

"Excuse me, but a little while ago you looked pretty upset. Better get your facts straight before the police come knocking, friend, because they'll knock you down like a straw."

He'd taken his hat off, and she noticed that the ends of his hair were still wet, and waved slightly. The smell of his aftershave warred with the smell of spilled pancake syrup. There were tight little lines around his eyes, as if his skin had been put on un-ironed.

"Harry Verdun knew me from college. He brought me news, sometimes. Things I wanted to know," he said. His voice sounded like something dragged over concrete. Alex took a sip of coffee to steady a flutter in her stomach. The cup stuck to the table, courtesy of a SuperGluelike veneer of spilled syrup, and she slopped a few drops over the side as it jerked free.

"I can't imagine somebody as rich as Verdun being anybody's messenger. News about what?" she asked.

He rested his elbows on the table and pressed his fingertips lightly against his temples. He massaged his head in slow circles.

His eyes never left her at all.

"He brought me news about my family," Davies said very quietly. "My wife. My son."

58

Alex paused, cup halfway to her mouth. She must have looked as stunned as she felt.

"It's amazingly boring, Miss Hobbs. My wife divorced me. I haven't seen my son Jeremy since. Harry came to bring me a picture." Davies reached in his pocket and opened his wallet, slid a photograph across the table to her. "Harry might have been rich, but he remembered his friends."

Her instincts prickled, and she wondered how much of it had been friendship, and how much blackmail. Was Davies a blackmailer? Could he do anything so relatively nonviolent?

The picture was of a boy, ten or eleven, sitting beside a miniature stone castle and waving. He had Davies' face, altered a little by higher cheekbones and a sharper jaw. No smile. A shadow slanted across the grass toward him—the mother?

Nobody, including Alex, had ever known Gabriel Davies had a wife or a son. Whoever Davies' wife was, she'd covered her tracks like someone accustomed to hiding.

"There are three possibilities," Davies said as she handed the photograph back. "One, this murder is a totally unrelated incident with no connection to me at all."

"In that case, you are having one phenomenal run of bad luck."

"Two, someone killed him because he knew me."

"Unsettling. And three?" Alex prompted. He looked through her again, and his eyes were luminous, rapturous.

"Three," he said, "I killed him. I think that covers it, don't you?"

Chapter Eight
Davies

From *The Casebooks of Gabriel Davies.*
Published.

July 27, 1986

I've left the water running in the bathroom. Sink. No, it's in the bathtub, lower-pitched. I don't remember why it's running; I suppose I meant to take a bath. I would like to be clean.

There is a copy of the Free Press *from two weeks ago on the corner of my desk, the last time Barnes Broward's personal ad appeared. The paper is yellowed; in a month it will look ancient. The ad has taken on a dusty sense of antiquity.*

No one else thought it was strange. I wonder why I did.

Single white male, 32, he described himself. Loves every part of pretty ladies. He didn't like women; I think he wished he did. He never picked up the replies to his ad. I've read through them— poor, sad, lucky women. I suppose I should write to them and tell them how close they came to dying.

No one thought it was strange that Barnes brought a sleeping little girl to the company picnic, either. Oh, he had a good excuse—such a little girl, his niece, so tired from her plane ride, sedated because of her broken arm.

They all signed her cast. He must have had a felt-tip pen with him, or they would have heard the hollow tap of the ball point, and known there was no arm inside. Caroline Pitney, abducted from the south side. The cast contained nothing. Barnes had already begun to dismember her.

Water is pouring over on the bath rug. Cascading. After the first muffled splashes it takes on a moist, fleshy sound, like rain hitting the earth.

I should do something about it, but I can't go in the bathroom, where the mirrors are. Yesterday I saw Barnes's eyes looking back at me, blue where mine are brown. My mouth looks different, too; it seems fuller now, wetter.

I am afraid to tell anyone that I'm infected with him.

I think it happened when he stabbed me in the first struggle; I still wonder why he stabbed me instead of little Shalanna North, already tied down and waiting for him to love every part of her. Were my eyes already like his? Is that how he recognized me?

Carpet next to the bathroom is now a dark, creeping brown. The stain spreads toward me.

Stains down my shirt, spreading on my pants. Pain where Barnes stabbed me, stains left on the fence where I climbed it, stains on the lobby carpet of the

Montroy Hotel. On the roof. Anthony Lipasky was so angry I hadn't waited for him.

I remember Barnes's voice clearly. He knew me, he said. He'd seen me following him.

He said he knew I understood.

The knife felt so good in my hand, once I'd taken it away from him. I suppose he knew in that moment of looking into my eyes that I did understand.

He got the knife back again, somehow. I remember the hot drip of blood down my side, a second hand ticking away my life. He waited for me to come to him.

He looked surprised when I pushed him over the edge. I wonder if I looked surprised, too. The knife shimmered one last time, sliced into my left arm, a parting gift from him as he left.

The carpet is soaked in a section long enough for me to lie down in now. How would that feel? How did it feel to Barnes, lying in his own blood?

I remember the knife shimmering quietly on the pavement beside him, like a little piece of mirror. I wanted it, but it was too much trouble to go downstairs, and to visit the little girl Barnes had left behind for me.

Anthony was afraid of me. I saw it in his eyes when he arrived.

Shalanna's parents sent me her first grade school photo, as a gift. She wears a faded smile, an expression I sense she's had to work hard to relearn. I keep the photo in a frame on my desk, and when I touch the glass it feels warm and vibrant.

It's my piece of Shalanna. I should send it back. But I don't think I can.

My left arm seems stronger today. The stitches will come out soon, and with time the doctor thinks I will make a full recovery. My side bothers me, now and then.

The doctor told me not to take a bath, I remember. Stitches.

Did I start the water? Or did Barnes?

Chapter Nine

Alex had just hauled on one running shoe when the knock came at the door. The apartment management, ever thoughtful of her personal security, had recently put in a peephole viewer, set precisely one foot above her eye level. She dragged the stool in from the kitchen. The fisheye distortion made the man standing on the other side look wider than he really was. *Objects in this mirror may be closer than they appear,* Alex thought. She jumped off the stool, kicked it out of the way, and opened the door with an irritated, careless jerk.

She walked back to the couch without waiting to welcome him inside.

He came in without formalities, just politely closed the door and leaned against it. Alex glared at him, a familiar surge of anger in constant counterpoint to an equally familiar riptide of hormones.

"Why didn't you tell me to go home?" Rolly Eastfield asked, and she resisted an urge to find her other shoe and throw it at him. Not a good idea. One, it was assault. Two, it was a bad precedent, throwing clothing at this man. You never knew where it might lead.

He was not drop-dead gorgeous, too thin, too dark, too narrow-eyed. None of that mattered. He was as fatal to her self-control as a bottle of cyanide. His charm was his absolute surety that she would, eventually, do what he expected her to do.

"What is this, an interrogation? Thought you were an exterminator, not a cop," she said sweetly, and yanked the laces too tight on her shoe. She loosened them with meticulous concentration, ignoring the way he watched her, the way he smiled.

"If *you'd* asked, it would have been an interview."

"If I'd asked, I'd get paid for it. Why *don't* you go home, Rolly? I told you, I'm through with you. Done. Finished. Which of these did you miss in vocabulary class?" she asked, and heard her voice echo high and shrill. She made a deliberate effort to calm it. Deep breaths, which wasn't easy to do while bent over tying a shoe. "What do you want?"

"You. I've missed you, Alex."

It was that simple, that brutal. There was no seduction with Rolly Eastfield. It was something that she adored and loathed and needed, and today more than most times it appalled her. Alex Hobbs, well-adjusted woman, begging to be used. Rolly watched her with those quiet, dark eyes, and didn't move at all to come after her or stop her as she stood and walked unevenly into the bedroom.

She shut the door, locked it, and sat down on the bed. Her other running shoe was on the floor, aqua blue stripes cheerfully bright on the plain white leather upper. The soles weren't so pristine. It was the fate of soles.

Alex felt Rolly Eastfield's presence on the other side of the door, like a weight smothering her. If she let herself, she could imagine the way his hands would feel on her, his lips, his skin whispering over hers in smooth slides.

Her hands made fists. It was not enough to stop herself from getting wet thinking about him. It was a goddamn Pavlovian response.

"Go home to your wife, Rolly," she said in a perfectly normal tone of voice. The whole apartment breathed around her, waiting.

After a very long couple of minutes, the front door clicked closed. Alex sat on the bed for a long time, staring at the worn sole of her running shoe, picking sharp pebbles out from between the wavy lines of tread. Her eyes strayed to her dresser, where some photographs sat haphazardly around.

There, under a yellowish veil of bad housekeeping stood Rolly, caught in a rare laughing moment with a hot dog in one hand and a bottle of suntan oil in the other. He looked good in a swimsuit, all a uniform olive color, muscled like a grayhound and about as fast in the right circumstances.

Mrs. Rolly Eastfield (Susan) had apparently never remarked on Rolly's tan, or the sand in his shoes, or the American Express bill on which he'd charged their plane tickets to Mexico. Mrs. Rolly Eastfield obviously did not know. Or did not want to know.

Alex had never quite had the strength to demand that Rolly tell her. Rolly knew her too well.

She got up from the bed, dropped the running shoe

on the floor, and kicked the other one off, too. She turned the lock on the bedroom door and opened it.

Rolly Eastfield sat on the couch, reading the *National Light* and smiling slightly. He looked up as she approached, dark eyes kind and sweet. She hated him for pretending to be kind and sweet, hated herself for believing it.

She sat down on the couch next to him. Rolly put the paper aside.

"I never fall for that goddamn trick," she told him, as he eased her back to the soft chintz cushions, warmed by morning sunlight. His lips were soft and very, very demanding.

"I know," Rolly murmured. She strained against him.

Her body hummed in the warmth, like something plugged into a wall socket at a very low current. It felt like every cell in her body was shaking in disbelief at her stupidity.

Next to her, Rolly was sleeping. He had a scar high up on one cheek, courtesy of a graze by a knife in a barroom brawl. He was as secretive in sleep as in waking, not snoring, not even drooling. Composed.

Alex stretched her arms over her head, watching the pale globes of her breasts roll slightly with the motion. Her body tingled again, especially in her pelvis. Her vagina struggled to readjust from the shock. She lifted her head slightly to look down her naked body and saw dampness glittering in the net of dark hair at her crotch. Time to wash off.

In the shower, it occurred to her, as it always did,

what Mrs. Susan would think of her. To wash the thought away, Alex stuck her face under the needle-sharp spray of hot water. Her sinuses reacted with knifelike twinges of pain. After the first shock, the pain crept away and left only a distant pressure like a damp wind.

When her whole body felt numb, all tingling gone, she finished and dried off. As she was twisting the water out of her hair she heard the bed creak.

Though she took a long time in the bathroom, he was still there when she came out. He was fully dressed, tie perfectly knotted, shirt perfectly pressed. It was like the whole hour had never happened.

His eyes were still pretending to be warm and kind. As she passed to pick up her scattered jogging clothes, he caught her hand and kissed it. The rasp of his beard tickled her deep down around her pelvis.

"Alex, why don't you ever want to trust me?" he asked. She shrugged and reclaimed her hand. She found her sports bra draped over the lamp.

"I don't know, maybe because you're such a god-damn liar. I make it a policy not to believe liars."

"Only to sleep with them."

She whirled on him, full of rage and tears and things she didn't even understand, but all of that vanished at the sight of him. She couldn't make him angry. She could only smash herself apart on his thick shield of calm.

"Get the fuck out of my house. Go home to your *wife,* Rolly," she said, in a shaking voice. He nodded, slowly, and stood up. She dumped her clothes on the damp sheets and refused to watch him go.

The door clicked. This time, it wasn't a trick.

She wished to God, as the tears started, that it was.

Her crying jag was just tooling up from zero to sixty when another knock came at the door. She crumpled up her tissue and tossed it with its abused neighbors on the coffee table, thought about ignoring the summons.

Another knock put the brakes on self-indulgence. She padded in her socks to the door and leaned against it, too exhausted to drag the stool over and look out.

"Who is it?" she yelled. She felt a freezing half-second of fear that the answer would be *Gabriel Davies*. Or *Rolly*, God forbid.

"Phone company, ma'am." The voice was female, sounded as tired as Alex felt. She braced the door with the side of her foot and the heavy security chain and slid it open just about two inches.

Through the gap she saw a tall woman dressed in a plain work shirt, unflattering male-cut blue jeans, a tool belt stuffed with bulky metal things riding low on her hips. The phone lady accepted the scrutiny with a patient bovine stare.

"Let me see some ID," Alex demanded. And, like magic, a GTE badge with the woman's stare duplicated on it appeared at close range.

Alex unhooked the chain and swung the door wider.

"I didn't call—" she began. The phone lady went from bovine to bubbly, the poster child for customer service.

"Sorry to bother you so early, ma'am, but the phones are down all over the building," she said, and gave Alex a big, friendly smile. Not too bright, Alex thought, but happy. Like a golden retriever. "I'm trying to get a reading on where the break is. Can I come in and check your outlets, see if they're active?"

Alex could have done that by picking up the phone, but she knew there wasn't any use arguing. She shrugged.

"Sure, come in." The phone lady grabbed a bulky toolbox and took a purposeful step forward. Alex got out of her way. "The phone's in the kitchen."

The phone lady clumped across the room and unlatched her toolbox with the urgency of a paramedic going for an IV. She gave Alex's ancient princess phone a suspicious look, unplugged it and plugged in something that blinked quietly to itself.

There was nothing to do but wait. Alex poured herself a cup of coffee and sat down. Her eyes still felt puffy and grainy; she hoped they didn't look as bad as they felt. The phone lady, after frowning solemnly at the readings on the blinking box, unplugged it again. She unscrewed the face plate and poked around in the nest of paint-splattered wiring.

"Want some coffee?" Alex asked. Now that she had company, she was glad to have something to think about other than Rolly. The phone lady gave her a grateful smile and nodded. "At it early, aren't you?"

"Well, there was a big cable problem this morning, and they called us out special to relieve the last crew. I think we're close now. Hey, thanks for the coffee." The phone lady accepted the cup and sipped at it. Her pupils widened, and she gave Alex another polite smile, several watts dimmer than the last. She took another sip, for politeness' sake, before setting it aside. She took a little metal clip out of her toolbox and hooked up a big sturdy-looking telephone to two of Alex's wires. There was a clicking sound. "Beautiful place you have here. Cozy, like. You knit that afghan?"

"No, my sister did." Small talk. Alex had lost the art of it, in the last few years of being a muckraker. She watched, mystified, as the phone lady poked around some more in the wires.

"I used to have the pattern for that one. Never could quite get it right. You tell your sister I said she did a good job. Darn!"

"What's wrong?"

"Oh, I'm sorry. Do you have any other phones?"

"Yeah, there's one in the bedroom."

The phone lady got up and moved briskly off in that direction, tools chiming. Alex sipped her coffee and watched her; a big, sturdy woman with long faded-blond hair, braided tightly back in a rope down her back. Alex wondered what phone ladies did in their spare time. Hobby electronics? Horseracing? Ballet?

Might be a story in it, she supposed. PHONE COMPANY FEMME FATALES. Something like that.

The phone lady reappeared and connected something arcane to the wiring, slapped the face plate back on. She sat back with a triumphant ear-to-ear smile.

"Got it. You sure got some cute things here. I like that little cat with the feathers at the bottom—I used to have one like that. Hey, that picture in the bedroom, that your husband?" The phone lady hunted in

71

her tool box for a screwdriver. "Sure is a handsome man."

"Oh. No." Alex felt her cheeks reddenning. "Uh, boyfriend."

"Well, that's great. Caught a real nice one, I hope. No kids, then?" The phone lady found her screwdriver and brandished it triumphantly. "I just love kids. Got a son. Fifteen."

"Congratulations," Alex said, and wondered if she sounded as stupid as she felt. What did socially adept people say to something like that? Probably asked what school he went to, what he wanted to be when he grew up.

The phone lady muscled screws back into the wall until they ground little plastic shavings out of the face plate.

"Thanks. You're all fixed up here." The phone lady plugged the phone back in. She had a distant look on her face now, kind of worried. "Wish I could see my boy again. Hard, being away from your kid."

"Is he with his father?" Alex guessed. She was getting the hang of this small-talk thing. The next question would be about the school, definitely.

The phone lay holstered her screwdriver with a firm gunfighter's snap of the wrist.

"Yep. I worry about him, sometimes. Lots of bad people around, always ready to teach him wrong. You gotta keep them clean, kids. They're always getting dirty."

The school question no longer seemed appropriate. Alex just looked at her. The phone lady turned around and looked her full in the face. Smiled.

72

A hard-looking woman, late thirties. There was something wrong in her eyes.

She picked up the receiver of Alex's princess phone and held it out. Alex put it to her ear.

Dial tone.

"See?" the phone lady said. "Won't have any problems now."

Chapter Ten
Davies

From *The Casebooks of Gabriel Davies.*
Published.

May 5, 1987

Anthony is gone, and I am still shaking with rage. I dump papers off on the littered floor; a piece of glass glitters on the corner of the desk. I can't remember what I broke. There must be glass everywhere.

I left Shalanna's picture untouched, of course. And Barnes Broward's framed personal ad.

Thank God I still know not to hurt what I love.

I let Sam Quintus Valentine beat me. Never should have happened. Not him, that idiot-savant of murder. I expected so much more from a man so focused, so directed. I thought he would be so elegant, so perfect, so intelligent.

Just a fool. Below-average intelligence. A butcher. Simpleminded enough to fixate on the number five.

Why not his mother, or his father, or his pet dog? Five. What a ridiculous answer.

Ridiculous that I missed it, in my search for higher motives. Five victims. Aged in multiples of five. Bodies separated into five pieces—sloppy, but consistent. I'm sure that once we do numerical analysis of the victims' birthdates, we'll find they add up to some number of cosmic significance to Sam Valentine.

Probably five.

His apartment smelled of decaying garbage, cordite, a subtle perfume of blood. Huge seeping hole in his chest, souvenir of his suicide attempt with the shotgun lying beside him. Hands trembling uncontrollably. He foamed red at the lips, too, eyes half-open and showing hemorrhaged whites. Every twitch sprayed blood over the soaked carpet.

Dying unconscious, quite peacefully.

He looked so stunned when I woke him up. Anthony, I think, tried to stop me. There's a bloody handprint on Anthony's shirt, the exact size of my hand, where I must have pushed him away.

Sam Quintus Valentine died messily, and was awake for all of it. And still I'm angry, still shaking.

He didn't deserve to win.

Chapter Eleven

Alex sat in the offices of the *National Light,* which consisted of a stucco building converted from a garage behind Wheaton Sinclair III's dilapidated home. Her chair, which once upon a time had swiveled, now squealed annoyingly and rocked unsteadily back and forth. Somebody—not Alex—had soldered the base onto the chair, so it no longer turned, but didn't support too well, either.

She would have called it a worker's compensation claim waiting to happen, except that she knew Wheaton would never pay one.

She popped a disk into the computer and watched the virus protection jealously look it over. She'd save her Davies article as BOOK REVIEW, that was safe. Nobody in the *National Light* office read so much as the comics page, except when they had to or there was money involved.

She copied the file over and watched the screen flicker. Across the room, Wheaton had an epileptic fit over the article modemed in by his new conservative opinion-writer. Nobody was conservative enough for

Wheaton. Hitler had been a liberal. The opinion page, apparently, was to be a castigation of the environmental movement, and Wheaton's new word for the day was "eco-freak." Alex looked through the yellow sticky notes scattered over her desk, most with Wheaton's all-but-unreadable scribble on them.

MORE VERDUN! said one of them. She intended to, but not for the *National Light*. DO A SERIES ON TITTY BARS said another. She *never* intended to do that one. I NEED AN ECO-FREAK STORY THIS ISH. said the last. She looked at if for a few seconds, then shrugged and stuck it up on the computer screen; it wouldn't go under her byline, anyway. The *Light*'s most popular reporter was John Van Crest, who existed nowhere but in Alex's imagination. He handled all of the truly stupid work.

Stuck on the side of her computer was a note with her own handwriting on it. It said WHERE DOES HE LIVE? WHAT DOES HE DO?

She knew who she meant. Alex played with the paper, transferring it from one finger to another. The tacky glue pulled at her skin like a little finger massage. What did Gabriel Davies do when he wasn't making her life interesting? How did he make his money? He'd never been rich, and he hadn't made a dime off of the *Casebooks*.

Maybe he'd blackmailed the publishing house. That was possible. Or maybe he was blackmailing somebody else, like the late great Harry Verdun. That, too, was possible. Alex made a note.

Across the room, Wheaton had reached a boiling point—not *the* boiling point, just a preliminary one. He could do several in the course of a single conversation. His face, as she turned to look, was the exact shade of his beet-red tie. He pushed the telephone receiver closer to his mouth—any closer, she thought, and he'd leave teethmarks in the plastic.

"Look, you liberal jerkoff, just write it like I want it, okay? It'll be more—what? *What?* Conscience? I don't give two shits if you're a member of Greenpeace, buddy, you write this the way I want it or you're out, understand? OUT! No dinero, comprende?"

Wheaton leaned the phone into the permanent crease between his shoulder and ear, pulled at his collar with his free hand. Whatever the writer on the other end said, it caused Wheaton's face to turn from beet-red to oatmeal-white. Alex briefly wondered if she should call 911. Or, if she should, she *would.*

"Oh yeah?" Wheaton said belligerently. His mouth worked for several seconds, chewing up words and swallowing them. Sweat beaded on his forehead in little salty pearls. "That's what you—okay! Okay, fine! Whatever! Just get it here in the next twenty minutes or you're gone!"

Wheaton slammed the receiver down, then picked it up and slammed it down again. He caught Alex staring at him.

"What?" he snarled.

She just kept staring. He growled and picked up a stubby blue pencil. He slashed through the first page of copy on his desk. Alex hoped it wasn't hers.

"Goddamn nosy reporters," he muttered. "Hobbs, remind me again why I write you a paycheck. Where's my eco-freak special for the freak insert?"

She picked up his sticky note and displayed it on

her fingertip without a word. He glared at her and went back to playing editorial samurai. The telephone was blissfully silent, recovering from the shock. Wheaton's pencil-scratch took on a soothing, if sadistic, rhythm, and Alex let her eyes drift a little, toward the drooping houseplant on the end of her desk.

In twenty-five minutes she—or rather, John Van Crest, ace investigative freak reporter—had concocted a purely mythical story about a half-man, half-snake found in the rainforests of Brazil. She matched it with a file photo of a belligerent rattler and a fairly good retouch of an obscure sci-fi movie snake-monster. She paperclipped the whole mess and put it on Wheaton's desk. He glared as if she'd dropped a giant turd in front of him. His glasses slid down his sweat-oiled nose. He smelled of garlic and some terrible sickly sweet aftershave, the kind that came sprayed inside cheap magazines.

"What about the sidebar, Hobbs? Where's the fucking sidebar?" he demanded. She looked innocent.

"Sidebar?"

"Give me an *organization*. Like PETA. Like Greenpeace. Anything, make it up, whatever. Christ, do I have to teach you the business?"

"Then I can go, right?" Alex pressed. Wheaton glared at her.

"Go where?"

"To do my other story. My feature for next week."

Wheaton thought about it for a full minute, unblinking, then shrugged and went back to line editing. Alex sat down and banged out, in ten minutes, a nefarious organization by the name of PEST, the Planet Earth Strike Team. It meant absolutely nothing, but

79

by the time Alex was finished they'd blown up three power plants and were known to dig booby traps along jungle trails, the better to trap corporate exploiters. And they'd kidnapped the Snake-Man.

She crossed her fingers and hoped that Wheaton wouldn't think of that obvious ploy, the "interview" with the PEST leader. He didn't. John Van Crest made a note to do it for the next issue.

Free at last.

Under Wheaton's glares, she started with the phone book, that useful tool, but of course Gabriel Davies was not living under his own name, or his number was unlisted. She tried making a list of every male with the initials G.D., but that proved time-consuming, and besides, she didn't believe for a minute that he'd be that stupid. She shoved the phone book around with the eraser on her pencil for a while, then picked up the phone and dialed Information in Chicago.

She had a truly interesting picture in her private files, of a confused and disoriented Gabriel Davies huddled under a Chicago detective's raincoat in the pouring rain as the detective, Anthony Lipasky, whirled in fury on the photographer. Friends, she'd thought instantly on seeing the photo. Brothers. *Something.*

Her call to the Chicago Police Department informed her that Detective Anthony Lipasky was still on the force, in the Crimes Against Persons division. She made a note of the number and hung up. It would, Alex thought, be interesting to have a talk with Detective Lipasky, who might have a great deal to tell about Gabriel Davies. But it wasn't as important as the fact that the game was still being played on Gabriel Davies' half of the court. Alex needed the home-team advantage.

Assuming that the meeting in the bar that first time had been accidental (and she couldn't see any reason why it wouldn't have been), Davies either lived, worked, or had business in that neighborhood. No, wait, what was it he'd said to her on the phone?

Because this isn't the first time a body has appeared near where I'm staying. That's what he'd said. *Near where I'm staying.*

How near? There were a hundred buildings in walking distance where he could be "staying." Apartment buildings. Lofts. Hotels. Flophouses.

Alex called a realtor friend and had the names and addresses of nearly every apartment possibility in fifteen minutes. Unfortunately, there were about sixty of them. She stared at the lines of type scrolling off the fax machine and cursed softly, very softly, to herself. She *hated* footwork. It was one of the (very few) things she loved about writing for the *National Light*—no fact-checking. No facts.

She'd brought a picture of Gabriel Davies with her from her files, something more innocuous, almost pleasant. He was waving to the camera, smiling. It looked like it might be the photo of a friend. Good enough to make an ID from, she figured—if she could think of some inventive way to bring it up.

As she picked up her purse, Wheaton dropped his pencil—loudly—and rolled his chair backward with a screech. She grabbed her picture and shoved it in her carry-bag. Wheaton blocked her way to the door.

"Better not be a personal thing, Hobbs," he said,

and she grinned at him. He didn't grin back, didn't even look inclined to.

"I got you the severed penis story, didn't I? Who else could have come up with that one?"

Wheaton was not mollified, but he didn't have much of a choice. He shrugged and got out of the way just as the phone rang. To get back in his good graces, Alex grabbed for it.

"National Light," she said cheerfully. There was a short silence, broken by the crackle and hiss of a mobile phone.

"So who's the stiff, Hobbs?" a tinny voice asked. She frowned and shifted the phone to her shoulder.

"What? Who is this?"

"Who the hell do you think it is, Santa Claus? It's me, Alex. Rob. Robert Rangel, you know, the one you *owe*, right? So who's the guy you're seeing?"

Rangel sounded strange, and it wasn't just the weird distortion of the carphone. His voice was too high, too tight. Wired. Scared? She had no idea, and didn't want to; she shifted from one foot to the other and glanced at Wheaton for support. He wasn't paying any attention. He never was, when she needed him.

"You'd better check your sources, Rangel. Sorry to disappoint you, but I don't get dates. Must be the wonderful reputation of the *National Light,"* she said, and listened. He didn't go along with the joke, didn't even notice it.

"Man, Hobbs, don't be stupid. You don't know what you're getting into," he said. Traffic hissed by behind his voice. Static cracked. "There are *pictures.*"

She just stood, frozen, lips parted. Her blood felt thick in her veins. Nothing about it seemed to make any sense, like a conversation heard in a foreign language. Rob had *pictures*.

Of Davies? Was he blackmailing her to get in on the exclusive?

"Look, Rangel—" she said cautiously. Her voice sounded too shaky. She made an effort to steady it. "Rob, man, it was just some guy, okay? So why the shit? It's not like we're—"

She faltered to a stop. He didn't say a thing, but she could *hear* it rattling the cable between them, breathing from the plastic in her hand like oily fumes.

"Get rid of him, Hobbs. I'm warning you," Rob said.

He went through a cellular dead spot, severed, disconnected. She felt that, too, a cold, physical sinking that left her weak and dizzy. Alex slowly replaced the receiver on the phone and looked over at Wheaton.

He wasn't paying any attention at all. He was bluepenciling her PEST sidebar.

What the *hell* was Rob doing?

The aging, sagging sign in the thick-lettered style of the '70s read *The Biltmore*. It had never borne any resemblance to anything so fancy. Alex thought of it, unkindly, as the *Bile*more, since the management had chosen to paint it a color she associated with dirty diapers and nasty half-digested pieces of vegetable. The Bilemore had about sixty units clustered around a potholed parking lot. Not potholes. Sores—deep, crumbling oil-and-water–filled pustules.

Even leaving aside the parking lot, it wouldn't end up as the centerfold in any apartment guide. The landscaping consisted of dumpsters tastefully dotted around the hole-mined lot. Every one of the dumpsters was full to overflowing, and as Alex opened her car door the fruity rotten smell blew toward her and reminded her gratefully that she hadn't eaten lunch.

Something crunched underfoot. She looked down as she locked the door and saw a nice glittering spray of square-edged safety glass from a previous visiting car. Not a good sign.

A beer can, lonely, rolled metallically across the ruts and found a pile of its friends, some of whom had been there long enough to attract the enthusiastic attention of ants and flies. Somebody—probably one of the residents—ambled out from the other side of a dumpster with a rusting shopping cart filled with tattered clothes and assorted mechanical junk. He looked her over. Alex was glad she'd dressed in the same sloppy jeans and torn sweater that she'd worn to the office. Of course, in this neighborhood, she looked prosperous.

The man's shopping cart hit one of the "potholes" and dropped more than a foot. He mumbled something and hauled ineffectually at it. Alex gave him a wide berth on her way to the door that read OFFICE; she reached it with a sigh of relief and satisfaction. A blast of too-warm air hit her as she opened it, along with a sour smell of sweat, smoke, and old, unwashed clothes.

The "office" was one room, stripped of furniture

except for a beaten desk and a ratty-looking guest chair. The leasing agent sat crouched in a chair on the other side, wreathed in smoke, and as Alex let the door close behind her he coughed and stubbed out his cigarette.

"Help you with something?" he asked, a monotonous drone that didn't sound very interested in the answer. Alex eyed the guest chair and decided to stand.

"Uh, yeah, I'm looking for an apartment. One bedroom. Nothing fancy," she improvised. Well, that was safe enough. There surely wasn't anything fancy here at the Bilemore.

The leasing agent looked as seedy as his property. He ran a nicotine-stained hand through his greasy hair and smiled at her. His teeth looked unnaturally perfect, and were the exact shade of brown eggs.

"Sure, sure, got just what you're looking for. Your name—"

"Sandra," Alex said briskly. "Sandra King."

"Yeah, Sandra, the rent is two-fifty a month, deposit is fifty. You get it back if you clean." He smiled again, as if they both understood what a crock of shit that was. "I can show you a vacancy."

I can see one, Alex thought, *in your eyes.* "Sounds fine. Listen, I was referred by my friend, and I thought maybe you had some kind of bonus program for him, you know? Like a gift or something?"

"What friend?" he asked, still smiling. She made a show of searching for a name.

"Well, his first name's Gabriel, I don't remember his last name—here, here's a picture of him." She laid the photo in front of him. He glanced at it. No reaction.

"No bonus whatsis. Besides, he don't look like none of my tenants. You want to look at the apartment?" He smiled so widely that his perfect teeth, mulelike, looked capable of snapping off a finger. His eyes shone wet and oily, like the potholes outside.

It didn't appeal to Alex to be stuck alone with this man. She looked around, desperately, but there was nothing to look at.

"Ah—amenities?" she asked. He frowned.

"A-what?"

"Pool, hot tub, tennis courts, anything like that?"

He rolled his eyes. "What you see is what you get, lady."

"Fireplace?" she asked. He grinned again.

"I got enough trouble meeting the fire code. No fireplaces. Look, you want to see it or don't you?" he demanded impatiently. "I got my lunch in ten minutes."

She breathed a sigh of relief and got to her feet.

"No, sorry, got to have a fireplace. It's a must. But thanks anyway."

"Crazy bitch," she heard him say as she slammed the door. She stood there breathing for a minute, then the wind shifted and blew a rich rotting whiff of *eau de dumpster* her way. The shopping-cart man had made it halfway across the lot. She hurried back to her car—the windows were still intact—and drove away.

One down.

Fifty-nine to go.

By the time she'd knocked her list down to forty-seven left, it was five-thirty and her chances of catching a working leasing agent were getting slim. She checked off *Woodbridge Terrace*—no wood, no bridges, no terraces, and no Gabriel Davies—and looked at the next name on the list. And looked again. The blurred fax print looked like *Asylum*, but it was the misspelled *Alysium*. She tapped the paper with the tip of her pen and thought about it. She had things to do—groceries, laundry, pay bills, call her sister—but one more stop wouldn't hurt.

Alex put the car in gear and drove out onto Crowelly. *Alysium*—or *Asylum*—was listed at the corner of Crowelly and Sixteenth, a slightly better neighborhood than the Bilemore's and the others she'd spent the afternoon checking.

She turned into the parking lot and was stopped by a set of intimidating-looking gates topped with curving spikes. *Like a prison,* she thought. *Or an asylum.*

There was a slightly-used metal panel on a pole at her drivers' side. She pushed the button labeled RENTAL CENTER.

Unlike the other apartments, this one had a perky, happy woman at the other end. Her charm practically oozed through the speaker at Alex as she declared herself to be Lisa, and asked could she be of any help?

Alex allowed that Lisa probably could. And the gates magically broke in half and opened. She felt like Moses at the Red Sea. She drove on through and thought that, in spite of the gates, *Alysium* might be closer than *Asylum*. The apartments weren't upscale, but they were nicely constructed and decently maintained, freshly painted and landscaped—with plants, not with dumpsters. The dumpsters were barely visible in little slots off the parking area.

The lot was smooth, even, and freshly striped. Alex parked in front of the Rental Center, which proved to be a huge two-story building with enormous windows and, astonishingly, a chandelier. Alex straightened her torn sweater and went in. The air inside tasted of potpourri. The furniture scattered around the huge room was of the latest sleek designs, the carpet a huge expensive Persian thrown casually over equally classy terracotta tile. Alex was lost in contemplation for a minute, thinking of her own old dingy apartment, and turned when she heard the businesslike click of approaching low-heeled shoes.

Lisa proved to be a tall, perky woman of about twenty-two, with scads of curling brown hair and a figure that made Alex cordially resentful. She chatted on about amenities (*she* knew what it meant) and apartment size and deposits and resident activities (which did not include shopping cart races from dumpster to dumpster). She offered Alex coffee.

There was a bowl of Andes mints on the corner of Lisa's washed-oak desk. Alex took one, sighed at the taste, and took another. Lisa returned with her coffee on a little bamboo tray, complete with real cream and her choice of pink, blue, or sugar.

Alex began to feel *very* comfortable.

Lisa did not seem concerned that it was nearly six o'clock. She urged Alex to take a look at the one-bedroom model apartment, and Alex, bemused and mellowed, handed over her driver's license for identification and followed.

"The pool is heated," Lisa said, and they walked

around the three-level fountain-fed thing that looked more like a water sculpture than something you swam in. Alex was used to plain old pools, the serviceable kind. Lisa pointed past it to something giving off wisps of white mist in the twilight. "That's the hot tub. We keep it running all winter."

Alex was aghast, but in the sneakily admiring sense, the way she was shocked at how much rich people spent on air-conditioned doghouses. But she didn't think Lisa would understand or appreciate it if she mentioned that, so she nodded, wordly wise, and they rounded the corner and left the pool behind.

"Now, over here is the picnic area—we have barbecues in the summer—and that's the laundry room. But we have full washer and dryer connections, of course."

Alex had never owned a washer and dryer in her life, and the thought of doing laundry in her own home sounded vaguely sybaritic. Lisa walked her through another gate, down a pansy-lined walkway and up a flight of stairs.

Vaulted ceilings. A fireplace. A *trash compactor,* for God's sake. Alex began to feel as if she'd been snatched by aliens from the planet Westinghouse.

"How much?" she asked bluntly. Lisa-the-Leaser didn't look offended at the mention of filthy lucre, and brightly handed her a list of prices.

Alex sat down in one of the model-home-provided overstuffed chairs. A misprint. It was a misprint. The price could not possibly be five dollars *less* than her rathole of an apartment.

She wanted to cry.

Lisa-the-Leaser thoughtfully handed her a blank application form and a pen.

It took only a minute. Alex felt, as she handed the paper back, as if she'd started sliding downhill into yuppiedom. Next, a washer and dryer. She'd figure out how to compact her trash. She'd *recycle,* for God's sake.

This was not her career plan.

The sunlight hit her like a splash of acid, glittering off the pool, hissing off the hot tub's simmer. She blinked back tears and followed Lisa's swaying grace through one gate. There was the laundry room, familiar with the smell of fabric softeners—a man stepped out of the door with a load of laundry in his arms, and Alex came to a polite halt.

It wasn't until he stopped that she thought to look at his face.

It was Gabriel Davies. His golden eyes widened, his pupils flared. But his expression didn't change at all.

In spite of the warm blanket of the sun on her shoulders, in spite of Lisa waiting just beyond him, Alex felt cold. His eyes spoke to her.

You're all alone, they said.

"Welcome," he said softly. His voice sounded sharp to her, avid. Alex resisted the urge to blurt out an explanation he wouldn't listen to. Behind Davies, Lisa-the-Leaser had acquired a new uncertain expression, reacting to whatever fear was showing on Alex's face.

"You two know each other?" Lisa asked, not very boldly. Davies' attention snapped around toward her, dismissed her in a flicker. He continued to stare at Alex, to strip her to the bone.

"Oh, yes," he said, and his tone was very pleasant. His eyes were not. "I'll be seeing you soon, Miss Hobbs."

"I—"

Gabriel ignored her faltering beginning and pushed past her. He walked quickly away, trailing a smell of freshly washed clothes, fabric softener, and a peculiar hint of harsh ozone.

Alex took several deep breaths and smiled weakly at Lisa.

"How long has he lived here?" she asked, hoping it sounded casual. From Lisa's still-unsettled expression, it didn't.

"About six months, I think. Look, is there some problem?"

"No, nothing like that. It was just a surprise, that's all. I thought maybe he lived here, but I hadn't gotten around to asking." Alex was coming out of her shock, and her heart was starting to pound. It wasn't good to surprise someone like Davies. She'd never intended to come face to face with him. "Old boyfriend, you know how that is. Uh, nothing weird. Really. We just didn't expect to see each other."

"Okay," Lisa said doubtfully. "Well, do you still want the apartment?"

She said she'd think about it. As she walked past the three-level heated pool and the steaming hot tub, she saw Gabriel Davies standing on a second-floor balcony, watching her.

Always watching.

Chapter Twelve
Davies

From *The Casebooks of Gabriel Davies*.
Published.

January 4, 1987

The dream came again last night.

It's been fuzzy before, out of focus. Sharper, this time. Tastier. I drink a cup of hot tea with lemon to kill the flavor, but it lingers in my mouth like cancer.

The cup is smooth in my fingers. It is a gift from someone I've forgotten. It's of a popular blue, deep and watery, and I can see the outlines of things hiding at the bottom.

The lemon tastes flat and strange.

In the dream, I am young, small, five or six. It is night, and Maxi, the dog, and I are supposed to both be asleep, but we're not. Maxi looks bigger in the dream. He is mean, like a wolf.

He lopes across the lawn, hunting by the moonlight. He has surprised something small. A cat. The cat sees him too late. Tries to run.

Maxi's teeth flash. Disappear. The cat shrieks, and Maxi's head shakes. Drops of black spatter the side of the house and the window. I look at the moon through the filter of them. It is red.

The screams go on. I hear my heart beating quickly. Wet snapping sounds as the cat's bones break. Maxi's teeth tear at raw flesh.

He whimpers. He sounds happy.

I watch the moon. It flies apart into pieces, and the pieces become flesh, and drip a red rain as they drop down toward me. I lift up my hands and touch the drops, and the warmth of it soaks deep inside of me and stays, like a stain.

That is the end of the dream.

I sit here with my hot tea, the taste of lemon flat on my tongue. I don't think what Maxi attacked was a cat. My sister Viva went to the hospital, and there was blood on the side of the house that Father sprayed away with the garden hose.

They had Maxi put to sleep after that. I never saw him again.

Of course, they couldn't put Viva to sleep.

Too bad.

Chapter Thirteen

Alex knew better than to try to check any books out of the library. So far as she knew, they had an outstanding book warrant on her for the seven novels she'd borrowed in February 1991 and had piled under her bed like pirate treasure. In fact, she was more than half-afraid that some alarm might go off as she went through the smuggled-book detector; maybe it was really some kind of identification device in disguise. It probably sent a flashing picture of her to all of the smiling librarians, warning them to call the SWAT team and slap a clip into their Uzis.

Alex knew she was paranoid. She didn't mind it at all.

She had to study the map to find the periodicals section, and it took a little time figuring out the microfilm machines, but in a very short while she'd found what she was looking for. The *Chicago Tribune*. It wasn't much of a feature, tucked in the center of the paper after bigger atrocities—the discovery of the first victim of Barnes Broward. She printed it. The next article was dated three weeks later, and the headline was at least three points bigger. One dead child was a tragedy. Two were news.

Three were a goldmine. She located and printed all of the original articles, then searched out the endless stream of "explanatory" articles—interviews with psychologists, crackpots, grieving families. She saw a couple of her own bylines, but skipped over them; no sense in copying what she already had. Still, it gave her a funny feeling to see it, proud and angry at once.

No problem. She'd be on top again, after this.

Her bill came to fifteen dollars and seventy-three cents. She took the copies to a big empty table and spread them out in consecutive order, then reshuffled them according to topic. Facts, there. Opinions, there. Tabloid, there.

She wondered which pile her story would go in.

Gabriel Davies' name appeared in only two articles before Barnes Broward's death. One, a hard-nosed just-the-facts-ma'am piece mentioned him briefly as being present with Detective Anthony Lipasky. There was an accompanying murky photo with Davies' face ghostly in the background. The other article was more ambitious, linking Davies with important past cases, playing up his uncommunicative attitude, the screaming sensationalism of the crimes. There was a hot-looking photo of Davies in this one, obviously not posed, but more effective for all that; the photographer had caught him coming out of fog, and the eerie misty quality fit perfectly, even without planning. She checked the byline.

Landrum. Jesus. No wonder. He'd gotten fascinated with Davies, and gone on to steal the casebooks. After publishing them he'd moved to Europe.

She read the article two or three times, but it didn't tell her anything she didn't already know. Landrum had persevered, but he hadn't gotten close until, for some reason, Davies had handed over his casebooks. Flattery? Bribery? Or just carelessness?

She shuffled the articles together and put them in her briefcase, together with her dog-eared copy of the *Casebooks*. Then she went to the True Crime section and found three books written on the Broward case, one of them complete with gruesome body-discovery photos and family photos of the children. There was Caroline Pitney, plump and pretty in her mother's arms. There were the two oldest boys, Charlie Cassetti and Jason Gardner, best friends. The last photo was of Shalanna North, the sole survivor of the ordeal—with the exception of Gabriel Davies.

The latest novel had written Davies into the Broward investigation, all right, delicately implying that wasn't it *convenient* that Davies found Broward first, and wasn't it possible that Davies and Broward were—partners?

Alex had already thought of that one. It wasn't even a very well-written piece of muckraking. She reshelved it and sat down to read the other two. Interesting, the thing about Davies' sister, Viva. Permanent vegetative state from a childhood dog attack. Davies had been described as "devoted to her." Offhand, Alex couldn't imagine Davies being devoted to anybody except himself; she made a quick pencil notation, *Viva Davies, Collins House, veg. Trace Davies from there? Get picture of sister?*

She felt a prickling on the back of her neck, like

sunburn. When she looked up, she saw someone disappearing around the stacks.

The feeling of being watched persisted, distracting her so thoroughly she found herself losing her place every time she checked over her shoulder. She put the book aside and stood up to stretch.

Someone was looking through the shelves at her. She froze in mid-stretch, arms raised as if to surrender. The eyes were there for only a second, then were gone. Steps thudded on the other side of the stack. Alex hurried around the end, but there was nobody there, nothing to see. She stood on a chair and scanned the area.

Nothing. In the distance, people sat at study tables and stared curiously at her. A librarian, frowning deeply, started in her direction. Alex hastily came back to floor level and sat down to read her book.

It had been such a flash that she hadn't seen the color of the eyes. Gold, maybe?

Maybe not.

Her midday run hurt, and hurt badly. It wasn't exercise, it was an exercise in masochism.

Alex reached the end—not of the run, just of her endurance—and leaned against a lamppost. Her lungs felt like wet leather, and her legs felt like wet spaghetti, and the rest of her just felt wet. She'd run too hard, too long, but that had been a kind of punishment.

As usual. *Jesus,* she thought, *what a pathetic loser I am. What a stupid bimbo.*

Either the thought or the run made her feel nauseated. *The truth shall make you throw up.* She ducked her head and wiped at her face with the sweatband around her wrist. As she looked up, blinking away sweat and black dizzy stars, she saw a man seated on the steps in front of her apartment.

He was reading a paper. Well, that wasn't so sinister.

Alex straightened up and coughed. That didn't help. The pain from her lungs spread out over her chest like a thick, wet blanket. As she coughed she kept her eyes open and on the man on her doorstep.

He put his paper aside and got up, walking toward her. Overheated though she was, she felt a chill hit her hard.

Gabriel Davies had found her. God, she didn't like that. At all.

But she'd be damned if she'd let him see her scared. Alex lifted her chin and wiped sweat from it, then nodded to him as he stopped a few steps away with his hands in his pockets.

"Nice work, detective," she said, and that was all she had time to say. He reached out so quickly she wasn't even able to flinch before his fingers—those thick, strong fingers—closed around her arm and jerked her forward, off balance. She slammed into his chest and looked up, shocked, into his eyes.

They were as vacant as a doll's. Alex opened her mouth to scream, but his eyes widened, and she knew somehow that she'd better not.

She'd better not do anything.

"Come on," he said in a shockingly normal tone of voice. Something about him overwhelmed all of

Alex's smart survival instincts. He'd kill her, she knew. For anything. For nothing.

She let him lead her away, hand tight around her arm. He led her up the stairs and held her there while she fumbled for her key and opened the entry.

"Don't do this," she finally was able to say, as he pulled her down the hall toward her door. "Oh, man, don't do this. You don't have to do this."

"Be quiet," Davies said, still very calm, still conversational. "Open the door."

Her fingers didn't seem to want to fit the key into the lock. He took the jingling keys away and slid the right one smoothly in, turned. The door swung open.

She stumbled forward under the force of his shove and caught herself on the smooth cushions of the couch. The door snicked shut behind him, reminding her of Rolly and all of her sad, pathetic guilts. The deadbolt rolled closed. A chain rattled as he slid it on.

Her decision-making problem had been reduced to two clean, clear alternatives: keep her back to him and hope it was sudden, or turn around and see it coming.

When she turned, he looked completely different. He was smaller, not so threatening, and he hadn't moved away from the door toward her. In fact, after a silent second, he smiled a little.

"I'm sorry, Miss Hobbs, but I couldn't be sure you weren't in danger on the street. I needed to get you inside."

Bullshit, Alex thought swiftly. *He got off on frightening me, but he doesn't want to take it too far. He's afraid of letting go.*

The thought was strangely steadying.

"Next time, just ask," she said breathlessly, and remained where she was. He walked over to a chair and sat down unasked. "You've got ten minutes. What the hell do you want?"

"Your opinion on something," he said. He glanced around, once, a comprehensive and unnerving judgment of her apartment. She felt naked here, ashamed of the unwashed dishes, the laundry dumped in the chair, the unmade bed in the next room. *You want him to like you,* she thought. It sickened and frightened her.

"If someone is stalking me, it stands to reason that it's someone I know or have seen, correct?" he asked. She sank into the soft, comfortable embrace of the couch. Her fingers ached from the way she'd been clenching them, and she rubbed them against her sweaty fleece pants.

"You're the famous detective." He stared at her. She coughed and swallowed what felt like a mouthful of blood. "I guess so. Unless it's some psycho who read the book and fixated on you."

"That's possible," Davies said, and sat back in the chair. If he was making an effort to look relaxed, it failed. "What about you?"

"Me?"

"Don't you ever worry about people coming after you for the things you write?"

Alex stared at him in amazement. He seemed perfectly serious.

"Who, Elvis? Alien visitors? Look, most of what I write these days is crap. It's fiction. My serious work was—the same time as yours."

"Then why are you writing about me now?"

"Because—because you're what I need to get me *back*. Where I was."

Gabriel smiled. There was nothing spontaneous about it, nothing genuine. His eyes had taken on that long-range stare again, focused, targeting.

"I see," he said, and laced his fingers together in front of him. "In other words, I'm a good story."

"Of course you are."

He leaned forward, eyes wide-open, strange molten gold in the sunlight.

"And how far would you go for the story?" he asked, very low in his throat. She blinked once, twice, and somehow managed to not look away from him. The sweat cooled her skin and made her shiver. She tried for a stubborn, aggressive look, and hoped he wouldn't notice her goosebumps.

"I'm going about as far as I'm willing to go, buddy, and you'd better back off or you're out there on your own, understand? The cops are going to figure you out soon. Do you really want to be kicking your only friend at a time like this?" Good, she thought, good. Her voice had just the right mixture of sarcasm and anger.

Oh, God, she hadn't meant that, had she? *Friend?*

It was Davies' turn to blink. He didn't.

"It was odd, the timing of it. You came along so suddenly, Miss Hobbs. As if you'd picked your moment very carefully. I've been thinking that if someone is, as you've said, setting me up, perhaps I'd better look at the people with the best opportunities and motives to do that." He put his hands in his pockets and rustled through them intently. He found a photograph and pulled it out, but he didn't hand it to her, just glanced at it and kept it casually at his side.

He was trying to drive her crazy. She could see it coming.

Alex decided it was time to take control of the situation, if that was at all possible. She got up and walked away from him, into the kitchen. She opened the right-hand cabinet by the sink and took down two chipped coffee cups, then got the coffee beans from the freezer. The grinder's shrill whine was a kind of cathartic scream.

Her hands were reasonably steady as she poured the brown powder into the coffeemaker. She was not surprised to find that Gabriel Davies had followed her into the kitchen as far as the dividing line where the cracked linoleum met the matted carpet.

The coffeemaker gurgled contentedly to itself, like a full belly. She could feel him watching her.

"If you thought I was setting you up, Gabriel, you'd have come out and said so. You're not exactly a subtle person when you're pissed off, are you?" she asked. She slid the right-hand drawer open to take out two spoons. She left it open a little, so she could get to the long bread knife she kept there.

Gabriel Davies stood there, photograph still held in his hand as if he'd forgotten it, and watched her. He didn't say anything at all. Alex felt stupid conversation bubble up in her throat and swallowed it, swallowed until she thought she'd gag. She reached up in the right-hand cabinet and got down packets of sugar.

"How did you find my apartment?" he asked. She shrugged.

"I looked. I showed your picture around. Simple enough, any cop could have done it, and I guess you found me the same way."

He didn't answer. The silence dragged.

"So, besides me, who else have you got that might know enough about you to set you up?" she asked. No answer. The coffeemaker gurgled out enough for two cups, and she poured. The drop or two of coffee that fell on the burner made a smell like rancid caramel.

Gabriel Davies went past her to the refrigerator, where he removed the milk and smelled it mistrustfully. He shrugged and gave her a polite questioning look. She nodded, and he poured a dollop into her cup.

God, she thought, *ain't we just fucking civilized?*

She passed him sugar packets. He still took six. He'd taken up a station just about two feet away, and she leaned casually against the counter and the open drawer with the bread knife. Could she get to it before he slammed her hand in the drawer?

Maybe. If she threw her coffee in his eyes.

If he didn't throw his first.

They both sipped and watched each other. The coffee was hot and sweet and creamy. It tasted like woodsmoke.

"Lipasky," Davies finally said. Alex tried to look blank, as if she hadn't already dug the photograph of Lipasky and Davies out of her files. "Detective Anthony Lipasky. You remember him."

"Sure," she said. She remembered Lipasky pretty well; she'd interviewed him, or tried to. A slow-talking sort of guy, mistrustful, the kind of cop who had no comment, no matter what and no matter who.

The coffee seemed to have mellowed Davies. He was a little less on edge, though no less ready to move. He held the cup just below his chin, smelling the rich vapor, sipping occasionally but never looking away from her.

"Detective Lipasky would know who else has shown an interest," he said. Alex tapped her fingernails on the blue ceramic of her mug and watched the tan surface of the coffee wrinkle and ripple.

"What about your ex-wife?"

A flash of something that might have been amusement, now. "No. She doesn't know where I am, and doesn't want to know, I imagine. Only Lipasky knew where I was and—other details."

"He knew about your problems, then? Before the books were published, or after?"

"Lipasky's known me for a long, long time, Miss Hobbs, longer than you'd believe. Lipasky helped me arrange my relocation after the casenotes were published."

Alex thought about that as she sipped the coffee, and her eyes drifted down to the picture he still held in his left hand. She couldn't make much out of it, just that it was some kind of a head-and-shoulders shot. Dark hair.

"So why suspect him?" she asked. Davies shrugged.

"I don't," he said. "I suspect you. And your lover, perhaps."

She took too big a mouthful of coffee and swallowed a burning gulp. His eyes had changed again, hardened.

"What are you—"

"You know who I mean," he said. He delivered it very calmly, but the look in his eyes—she jerked and felt hot splashes of coffee slide over her fingers, down her arms. "Perhaps you've forgotten which one. The *married* one, Miss Hobbs."

"My—married—" Alex's voice ran out of steam. She felt weak at the knees. "You've been watching me. Watching my apartment."

Since before she found his. Rolly had been here before that.

Gabriel Davies came a step closer. He set his coffee on the counter. She tightened her grip on her cup and set her left hand on the drawer. Her fingertips brushed the wooden handle of the bread knife.

"His wife's name is Susan," he said. He flipped the photograph at her; it slapped against her chest and slid down to the floor. "I thought you'd like a picture of her. Perhaps you'd like to frame it and put it on your bedroom wall."

"You son of a bitch!" Alex screamed. The rage that swept over her was liberating, rage she couldn't vent to Rolly, rage she couldn't drown in a glass of bourbon anymore. She grabbed for the bread knife.

He launched himself toward her. She had the knife only halfway out of the drawer when he slammed his weight against it. The blade bent at the impact, snapped with a musical *ping*.

He knocked her coffee cup away with one casual slap as she tried to throw it at him, and held her hands tightly in his. The cup spun across the linoleum, coffee spiraling out of it in brown splashes. *So close*, she thought. *I could have made it.*

Davies held onto her for what seemed a very long time, not speaking, not moving. He just watched her while she began to tremble.

"Don't be stupid, Miss Hobbs. Get rid of him."

"What the fuck makes it your business?" she spat. He smiled slightly. The burnt smell of him was chokingly strong, mixing now with her stale sweat.

"You do. You're the one who wanted to get close to me. *You* offered *me* this. Now you'll have to play by my rules, in my game." Davies let her go and picked up the photograph from the floor. It had some drops of coffee on it. He wiped it off on his coat and handed it to her. "A woman was driving the van, Hobbs. This is Susan Eastfield. The Eastfields have a van."

"Van?" she repeated. Red van. The faceless woman, lying on the sidewalk. Rolly. No. "No."

"Safer to assume a yes." His eyes narrowed. "Just get rid of him. I don't like him here."

Alex's heart stuttered in her chest. She watched him as he picked up her fallen coffee cup and put it in the sink. It had a large crack in it.

"I'll get you another set," he said. When she didn't respond, he went out of the kitchen, to the door. He looked out of the peephole before he opened it.

"Your fucking ten minutes are up. Stay out of my life," she yelled at his retreating back. He never even looked back, just closed the door behind himself, very gently. She flew across the room and slammed the deadbolt closed, then the security chain. Her heart was pounding painfully in her chest, and she slammed the flat of her hand hard against the wood. Before the shock could numb her skin, she did it again, and again.

"How dare you?" she screamed, and hit the door one more time, for emphasis. The locks rattled. "It's *my* life, mine, you don't even know me! How dare you—"

She ran out of words for the fear that kept bubbling up inside of her. The photograph of Susan Eastfield was lying on the kitchen counter, where he'd left it; Alex glared at it, noting and then ignoring the similarities between herself and Rolly's wife.

She turned on the front burner on the stove. Blueflame gas shot up, and she held the picture over it until the paper bubbled and crinkled and burned. Susan Eastfield's face leprosied and decomposed.

"Fuck *you*, Gabriel. Nobody tells me what to do," she muttered, and wiped at her tears angrily. "Nobody. Nobody."

The day, such as it was, passed. Alex kept the door locked and cleaned, dusted, vacuumed, and moved furniture, because it gave her something physical to do to keep the ghosts away, out of sight. But then, eventually she got tired. And the ghosts laughed at her, creeping around behind her, seeping inside of her like poison.

She needed Rolly. That was it.

Rolly's office didn't know where he was. She left him a message, which he didn't return. She flipped through the phone directory and found a listing for an R. R. Eastfield, and she wrote it down on the pad next to the phone. She got to seven digits before hanging up.

The night passed like the day. Emptily. She stared at the television and understood nothing on it. Somebody knocked at her door, and she leaped up to climb her stool and look out, but it was a kid selling candy, nobody to help her. After he'd gone, leaving her two candy bars poorer, she felt more alone than ever.

By midnight Alex felt empty and flaccid, like a burst balloon. She couldn't stop thinking about it. *He's violated me,* the thought kept circling. *He's watched me. He's been in my house.*

God, she needed somebody. Not Rolly. Somebody who could—would—help her hang on.

God, she needed a drink.

A late movie started. Alex's fingers trembled as she flipped through her address book. It was a pathetic enough list: her sister Katrina; her father, out in Minnesota; her cousin Gregory, in New York; a few casual acquaintances; a few bosom college buddies who'd long since gone on with their lives and left her at the crossroads.

She stopped in the R's. And dialed.

"You'd better be giving me money," a thick voice on the other end mumbled. Alex opened her mouth, closed it again. "Hello? Anybody home?"

"Rob," she said softly. There was a brief, telling silence. The voice, when it came again, wasn't thick or slow.

"Hobbs? Damn, woman, it's after two in the morning. What's up?"

She couldn't tell him. The words crowded around in her throat, banging loudly on the roof of her

108

mouth, but she couldn't let them go. *He's mine,* she thought. *Gabriel Davies is mine, and I can't let him go.*

"Hobbs?" Rangel asked again, softer now. "Alex?"

For a stupid, frightening moment she felt her stomach lurch, her throat lock up. Tears? Not in front of the competition.

"Rob, I need you," she said in a rush. "Please. Come."

For a wonder, he didn't make a single sex joke. He waited, plainly stunned, while she gulped down breaths that, like her dinner, threatened to vomit back out.

"You okay?" his voice whispered, such a long distance away. She closed her eyes to tune it in like a psychic wave.

"No." She was still having trouble breathing. Her rib cage hurt with the effort not to hyperventilate. "Look, I'm sorry to call you. I shouldn't have bothered you."

He was uncomfortable now, uncertain. They had never traveled this ground before, and it was full of sinkholes and land mines. "No, you aren't bothering me, it's just, you know, late. Are you sure—"

No, she wasn't sure. Her world had changed, subtly, drastically, and she wasn't even sure of her own reactions now. Maybe Davies hadn't meant anything threatening. Maybe she was overreacting.

Maybe not.

"Alex?"

"I'm here. I'm—" *I'm in trouble. Say it.* "Do you want to come over?"

He was quiet again. In the background she heard something click, like a light going on.

"Say that again," he said.

Jesus, what am I doing? she wondered, and felt panic pinch her stomach. "I mean, would you come over? Please?"

The hesitation went on just a fraction of a second too long. She heard the whisper of fabric moving against fabric on the other end of the phone, and Rob cleared his throat.

"Sure," he said. "Uh, now? It'll take me ten minutes or so."

"Thank you," she whispered. "Thank you."

The phone clicked and she was alone again, disconnected, separate. And the apartment seemed dark and foreign and chilled. The TV flickered meaninglessly, sound muted, perfect company for her autistic mood. *Coffee,* she thought. *I should make coffee. Rob likes it.*

For no reason at all, she thought of bourbon. She had a bottle in the cabinets, pushed all the way to the back. A cheap brand, her poison of choice. There were cold Cokes in the refrigerator. Bourbon and Coke. She could almost taste it.

It was one or the other, then. Rob, or the bottle. Rob, or oblivion.

How pathetic.

She couldn't move, even to make the coffee or take another look at the dusty bottle of bourbon. Her muscles felt thick and heavy and uncontrollable. She rubbed her swollen eyes and wrapped up in the heavy afghan on the couch. The steady quiet hiss of the TV soothed her like a monotonous lullaby.

Rolly hadn't called her back. The bastard.

With no feeling of transition, the world was dark and warm and quiet.

Chapter Fourteen

She woke to the warm breath of sunlight across her face, and tried to wipe it clumsily away. Her arms were tangled in the afghan.

The sun dazzled her, made her eyes narrow painfully when she pried them open. As she clawed her way out of the afghan she felt a chill; her skin was sweaty, overwarm. Alex squinted through the morning toward the avocado-green kitchen clock.

Someone was blocking the way. She gave a wordless *whoof* of surprise and kicked off the couch, ready to fight, ready to run.

It wasn't Gabriel Davies. It was Rob Rangel, asleep, head tilted back against her leather armchair's high back. He looked as if he'd just rolled himself out of a warm bed—sloppily wrinkled sweats, hair mashed unevenly, a too-thick growth of stubble. He'd thrown one of her spare blankets over himself, but he couldn't have been too comfortable with his head at that neck-breaking angle.

Alex resisted the urge to shake him awake and went to check the door instead. The deadbolt was locked. She slipped the chain on, too, and went into the kitchen to make coffee.

The whine of the coffee grinder brought him straight up out of the chair, but he flopped back into it just as quickly. She dumped the powder into the coffeemaker and heard him let out a low, heartfelt groan.

"You could have found some nicer way to wake me up, like a cattle prod. Jesus. I'll never sleep again."

"Not in my chair, you won't," she agreed. She came out of the kitchen and faced him, arms folded. "How the hell did you get in?"

"Key," he said, and held it up. "Remember? You gave it to me last fall. I watered your plants for two months."

She was almost sure she'd asked for that key back, and gotten it. It didn't surprise her that he'd made a copy, though. Sneaky, thorough bastard.

"Why didn't you wake me up?" she demanded. He rubbed a hand absently over his bald patch and shrugged.

"You were sleeping so well. I just thought I'd hang around in case—you needed me."

He didn't look at her as he said that, looked anywhere but at her. At the table. At her dusty pictures on the walls. At her desk.

She felt a strange tenderness for him. When she needed him, he came. At two in the morning, without an explanation, without even a promise of getting laid, he came. And stayed.

"Coffee," she said quietly. He nodded.

They sat together at the breakfast table and sipped

coffee. No conversation. Every time Alex caught him looking at her she felt her face grow as warm as the coffee cup in her hand.

I'm acting like a thirteen-year-old, she thought. And wanted to laugh with delight.

"Nothing—happened to you, did it?" Rob finally asked, quickly, as if the question had been pressure-cooking for some time. Alex blinked and studied him for a full minute before she figured out what he meant.

Raped, he meant. Molested. Attacked. In hindsight, she supposed she was acting about that oddly.

"No."

"Oh." Rob fished around in his coffee with a spoon, hunting for sunken treasure. He glanced up at her, then down. "So, what's up?"

"You said you had pictures of me with somebody. Who?"

Rob heaved a great, guilty sigh and continued to slowly poke his coffee, submerging the spoon in careful little dunks.

"Him. The guy. The one you've been seeing."

Rolly, or Davies? Alex felt the flash of alarm again.

"What I do in the privacy of my own apartment is my own business," she said, a wild stab. Rob's lips tightened.

"Hey, no contest. It's just—he's married, you know. This buddy of mine, he was hired to get pictures of the two of you. By, you know, the wife. Mrs. Whatsis."

Pictures? Detectives? Mrs. Susan Eastfield hadn't ignored the American Express bill, after all. Alex felt

114

a sick sensation in her stomach, as if she'd swallowed something live and squirming. *Divorce court, here we come,* she thought. Ugly. Nasty.

Of course, there was nothing about the whole affair that hadn't been ugly and nasty. She knew that, knew that was, in effect, why she'd done it.

"I bought them," Rob said in another gush. He reached in a pocket and pulled out a thick, crumpled yellow envelope. "Photos and negs. He let me have 'em cheap, 'cause I did him a big favor once. Here. Burn them. Whatever."

Alex slowly eased the envelope open and took out the sheaf of prints. Grainy black-and-white, nasty, recognizable. She felt dizzy and hot, and closed her eyes.

So incredibly ugly, seen this way. The way Susan Eastfield saw it.

"Thank you," she heard herself say. Rob grunted. After another minute of avoiding her eyes, he got up and wandered into the living room. She heard the TV go on.

She pushed the photos around with her fingertip, blindly, and then stuffed them back into the envelope. They didn't quite fit. She shoved it in the pocket of her robe and felt all of it hit her again, a slap that made her veins squeeze tight and her heart thump with panic. Rob wasn't watching her. She blinked back the tears and swallowed the last of her coffee, a hot, choking gulp.

She went into the living room and sat down on the couch. The news was on. Rob looked a lot more interested in it than he had any reason to be, except that it was something to look at besides her.

They were sitting close together, not touching. In time, he'd probably forget about the pictures. And she'd forget about Rolly.

"Slow news morning," Rob said, and jerked his chin at the footage rolling on the screen. Hastily shot footage, underfocused. A fire, with something metallic blazing at the center like a hard, rotten core.

"Shhh," she whispered. It had once been a truck or something, but now it was so twisted and blackened that it was tough to see any details. The footage had been shot at night, so some of the quality was lost, too.

The reporter did a rough voiceover, shouting to be heard over the wail of sirens and hiss of fire.

"Dead at the scene are two unidentified victims, male and female. The police aren't releasing the details of the accident at this time, but witnesses say that a late-model car apparently rear-ended the van and drove it headlong into an oncoming semi. The car left the scene at a high rate of speed. Once again, a tragic scene on Highway 30 where two people are dead at this time in a hit-and-run—"

"Christ," Rob moaned, "I missed good, crispy pictures. Now I gotta bribe that asshole Jerome to get in, and somebody else already got the scoop—"

"Sorry I ruined your evening," Alex said. He slid her a glance.

"You want me to go?" he asked. She shook her head, still watching the TV screen, an eerie feeling creeping up her back.

"Not yet. Let's do a movie, okay?"

"That's four more hours."

"Enjoy it."

* * *

Alex had an overwhelming urge to do laundry. As she stripped the sheets off of the bed and stuffed them into the basket, she heard the doorbell buzz, like a nearly dead fly on a windowpane. It was followed by a thick, forceful knock. Rob appeared at the bedroom doorway and gave her a mute look of inquiry. She was still carrying a pillowcase and saw Rob's eyes flick toward it. It had some curly black hairs on it.

Obviously, not hers. She pushed by Rob and through the living room.

She opened the door and looked at Detective Markovsky, who swayed back and forth, heel to toe, and glared at her. She felt a chill come over her, and wrapped her hands in the pillowcase to keep her fingers from shaking.

"How's it going, Hobbs?" Markovsky rumbled. His thick-set little dark eyes were bright, intent, absorbing the lines in her face and her uncombed hair and the way she stood, fists clenched in the pillowcase. "You gonna let us in?"

Davies, she thought. *They'll want to know about Davies.* Alex didn't want to, but she stepped back and Markovsky pushed by. He was followed by another detective, younger, female. She had the same eyes, though. Quiet, knowing eyes.

What had Davies done?

They both stopped when they saw Rob Rangel sprawled out on the couch, reading a magazine. He sat up and gave Markovsky a grin.

"Yo, man, didn't know you were invited. Come on. Sit down."

Markovsky and his partner looked at him with identically empty expressions, assessing, cataloging. Markovsky slid a quick look at Alex. She was lost, and knew it showed.

"Coffee?" she asked, just to have something to do. Markovsky nodded. The woman signaled an emphatic no and walked over toward the bedroom. Alex forced herself not to watch her. Coffee. She went to the kitchen and took down two more cups—no, no, one more—and poured it full. Markovsky had followed her in, trying to distract her from what his partner was doing.

God damn it, why were they here?

"Laundry day?" he asked, and pointed to the pillowcase she'd laid out on the counter. She handed him the cup, and he took a cautious sip. "Thanks. Nice. Too early in the morning for this shit, Hobbs, I ain't gonna beat around the bush. Rangel been here all night?"

She looked at him. Past him, at Rob, who nodded his head very slightly.

Not Davies, then. Rangel. She had to pull Rangel's nuts out of the fire, the stupid asshole. She had to, because she'd called, and he'd come.

"Jeez, Markovsky, what do you think?" she snapped. "No crime, is it? I'm legal, so's he. Far as I know, we didn't violate the Penal Code."

"That's a good one," Markovsky said, and smiled. He looked smooth and easy, smooth as glass, smooth as a knife-edge. "You writers, always with the jokes. I like you, Hobbs. I really do."

118

His partner came out of the bedroom carrying a dusty picture frame. She held it carefully by the thick cardboard stand part. Markovsky leaned over and looked at it, then raised his eyebrows at Alex. She waited, frozen, for someone to hand her the script for whatever scene they were playing. Which picture was it? She didn't have any pictures of Rob, no framed pictures of Gabriel Davies.

Markovsky dug some cheap little reading glasses out of his pocket and put them on to peer at the photo. "You take this one on vacation? Looks like you get around."

Rolly. In the sand. On vacation.

Rob had gotten up from the couch and positioned himself in the doorway, tall, lanky, innocent-looking. He leaned over the woman's shoulder and studied the picture himself.

"Yeah, what's his name, Rolly. Alex used to see him," he said, deliberately casual. Alex stared at him.

Even Rob knew the script. She felt adrift, floating, lost. Scared.

"Who asked you?" Markovsky snapped without taking his eyes off of Alex's. "Shonberg, why don't you take his statement someplace else?"

The woman took Rob's shoulder and steered him toward the bedroom. He went without protest, but there was a tenseness in his back that made Alex nervous. What was he going to say? Or, more important, *not* say?

The thick package of photos in her robe pocket felt as heavy and hot as molten lead. What about Rolly? What had he done?

"I used to see him," Alex said. "Sure. You want to tell me why you're here, Markovsky? Just for fun?"

Markovsky sipped his coffee.

"Sure," he said. "Mr. Rolly Eastfield and his beautiful wife Susan Eastfield got themselves scattered all over Highway 30 last night. Somebody ran them head-on into a semi. Next thing I know, I get a call saying you were banging the guy, Hobbs, and his wife was gunning for a divorce. I leave anything out, or is that pretty clear for you?"

Alex felt nothing. Nothing. She remembered the TV footage, flames, sirens, the crumpled wreckage of a van. Head-on collision.

"Rolly," she said, a single sharp whisper.

"Glad you remember him, Hobbs, thought for a second there you were too busy. How long you known him?"

"T-two years. He exterminated my apartment." What a stupid Penthouse Letter kind of thing to say. *He exterminated my apartment, I love a man in uniform and let's just do it, I'm so hot*—Alex felt sick, really sick, and pressed her hand to her mouth. "Jesus, Jesus, I didn't know."

The questions went on. She answered them the best she could; *no, she'd never been to his house. Never seen his wife. Yes, he'd come here.* She looked over at the pillowcase, which hunched like a dead thing on the counter. *No, she didn't run them off the road.*

Markovsky's partner came back to the kitchen and pulled him out for a little conversation. Alex waited while their voices rumbled and buzzed. Rob sat on the couch, looking white and scared.

120

Markovsky came back to thank her for the coffee. He asked for the picture. She let him take it.

They showed themselves out.

Alex closed her eyes and heard footsteps, felt Rob's hand pat her shoulder, light, tentative, distant. Like a murmur on a phone line.

No more Rolly Roy Eastfield. No more greyhound-slim body. No more smile, no more kisses, no more. Gone.

Alex opened her eyes to look at Rob, who faced her with a half-worried, half-fascinated expression. She searched his eyes for some hint of what she should feel.

"You missed your crispy pictures," she heard herself say. He flinched away from her, hooked his foot on a chair and almost fell. He dropped into it instead and scooted it forward in a screech of metal on cracked linoleum.

"God damn it, Alex—" he said. She just turned away, back to the still-blaring TV, where they were telling her that she could have a body like Cher's for $49.95 a month, plus tax.

Crispy. She felt crispy, too.

Rob moved, and now slid his hands warmly around her back. She felt that distantly, as if someone had wrapped her skin in plastic.

Davies, she thought for no reason. *Davies didn't want Rolly here.*

That had been last night. Another morning. Another day.

Rolly was dead.

Davies didn't want him here.

Rob's warmth seemed so far away. Her body

ached, under the plastic. Her head pounded. Her eyes felt red and swollen, but not with tears, with anger.

After a decent interval, five or six minutes, she picked up the phone and dialed. Rob asked her a question, some meaningless babble she couldn't hear.

She called the number of R. R. Eastfield. Just to be sure.

Rolly Roy Eastfield's voice answered, mechanical, frozen.

"Hello, we're not able to answer the phone right now. Please leave your message at the beep."

Rolly Roy Eastfield wouldn't be able to answer the phone, not ever again. She replaced the phone quietly in the cradle.

"How did you know?" she asked Rob calmly. His round eyes asked her what she meant. "You were already covering up even before you knew what Markovsky wanted. Why? What did you do?"

Please, she thought, *please don't say you did it. Please don't say that.*

"I didn't do anything," Rob said. "But I figured you did."

She started to laugh, a high, thin giggling that shattered into sharp-edged tears. He patted her back anxiously, trying not to force the sobs back in, or make her choke on them.

"Alex, come on, you call me at two in the morning in a panic and you won't tell me what's going on and then the Homicide boys show up? What am I supposed to think? I mean, the pictures—I thought you killed the missus. Susan."

Of course he did. She took the pictures out of her pocket and shook them out on the table, still crying, still giggling. She chose one of Rolly, her back-door man, straining at her back door. Her tears fell on the shiny surface and made little cruel magnifiers.

"Did you?" Rob asked. She thought of Davies, of his taut, pale face, of his wild eyes.

Of the picture of Susan Eastfield.

"Yes," she murmured.

It was easier to tell, once she'd broken that wall. Rob listened without comment until she handed him her dog-eared copy of the *Casebooks;* he opened it and turned to the grainy black-and-white photos in the center of the book. Gabriel Davies, shielding his eyes from camera flashes at a news conference. Gabriel Davies, streaked with blood, standing over the sheeted body of Barnes Broward.

The Broward house. The Broward utility room. School photographs of the children.

One fuzzy photo of the remains of Kevin Reynolds, the third victim. Rob studied it intensely.

"I remember this guy," he said. She wasn't sure if he meant Davies, or Broward. "Big, big story at the time. Haven't read the book, though."

"Go buy it," Alex ordered, and got her copy back before it disappeared into his pocket.

"So where's he live?"

"As of two days ago, the Alysium Apartments. Now—who knows? He's good at dropping out, probably as good as anybody he hunted down." Alex smoothed the embossed cover and turned it over to study the picture of Haley Landrum, the man who'd stolen the *Casebooks* and published them. Haley looked worried.

She'd have been worried, too.

"You think he did the Eastfields?"

She gave him a shrug for an answer. It wasn't what she perceived as Davies' style, but he was intelligent and unpredictable, and sticking to his style had probably never stopped him from doing the expedient.

"I don't think he has a car," she said. She hadn't thought it through, but it made sense. Cars required licenses, insurance, registrations, tags, things that you needed an address for, and things that formed a permanent trace. He was too smart for that. "The Alysium was in walking distance of the bar off of Meadow. Also close to the second crime scene."

"So he's striking close to home, from necessity," Rob said, and crossed his arms over his chest. "Could have done Verdun, sure. Verdun gives him a ride, Davies blows him up and walks home."

"Davies doesn't have a washing machine. He has to use the apartment laundry. You think he'd take a chance coming home bloody to a busy apartment complex and washing his clothes? Nope. Don't think so." Again, it was an instinctive response. Alex felt him stirring inside her, fighting his way to the surface. She was beginning to understand him, to reason like him. She closed her eyes against the morning glare, Rob's peaceful presence. "He can't ditch the clothes on the way, too dangerous. So what does he do?"

"Go home, stuff the clothes in a garbage bag, take a shower," Rob said, and stuffed a thick chocolate candy in his mouth. He tossed the wrapper onto her coffee table. "Then come back to enjoy the show."

Jesus Christ, it fit. Dumpsters parked in discreet little sidelots at the Alysium. Easy to tie the bag and toss it, and the next day the evidence is on its way to the city dump along with the trash of a thousand other apartment dwellers.

She saw him again, in her mind's eye. His hair, wet at the ends. He'd taken a shower.

"And the body on Meadow?"

"Dunno. Maybe not related." Rob chewed on his candy, smiling contentedly. "Or maybe he just wants in your panties, Hobbs."

The thought, frankly, made her shiver. She threw a pillow at him and picked up a pad of paper. She drew little circles on it, like spreading raindrops.

"He's been watching you," Rob said more seriously. "You know that. He knew all about you and Rolly. Maybe he's still watching."

"I have to assume he's not going away," Alex agreed. "So what do we do now? Run?"

"Fuck no, Hobbs. Markovsky and his guard doberman were here to take a little peek, see if you were properly upset about the event. You know how it works. Look at the spouse; if it ain't the spouse, look for somebody else the victim was screwing. *Then* look for another motive. You make a strange move, Alex, and you'll be calling your lawyer from downtown at four in the morning and sleeping in a cell with a biker mama." Rob didn't look all that discontented with the idea. "But since I was here all night—"

"How long do you think that one will hold up?" Alex sighed. She made an X through one raindrop, then another. "People saw you leave your place, saw you arrive here. Saw you sitting at stoplights in your car. Rob, you wouldn't believe how much Markovsky can find out about your movements from ten to ten if he's interested."

Rob picked another piece of chocolate out of the box on the table and mashed it between his teeth. He spat it quickly back out onto his palm and looked at it as if it might squirm away.

"Goddamn creams," he said, and held it at arm's length while Alex got a paper towel for him. He wrapped it up and dropped it in the trash. "Jesus, doesn't this thing have a map or something? I'm gonna get poisoned. Hey, did they look at your car?"

Alex stared at him. He grinned, teeth brown-streaked.

"Front end damage."

"They didn't ask."

"Means they already checked it out and you're clean. If you'd had some fresh dents, they'd have marched you down there to explain it. Great, that means whoever did the Eastfields didn't bother to frame you for it."

She felt sick and clammy. She got up and walked to the kitchen counter to pour herself another cup of coffee, her fourth, and knocked the pillowcase off the counter. It fell slowly, spreading out like wings. She bent and picked it up and pressed it against her nose.

She could still smell him.

Rob didn't say anything. He pretended to hunt through the box for a safe nut cluster.

"If it *is* Davies, I have to do something to show him I'm not a victim."

"Anybody can be a victim, to somebody like Davies."

"I know that, damn it, I'm talking about *percep-*

126

tions, about how he views me. If I run away, if I cover my eyes and pretend he's not there, if I whimper and whine, I'm a victim." Like Barnes Broward, she thought. "I can't afford that, not with him. He has to see me differently."

"How?"

She stared off into the distance, the lingering scent of a dead man rising from the pillowcase to remind her of the line, of what could happen when she crossed it. Or didn't dare to try.

"You in?" she asked. Rob blinked, chocolates forgotten. The blue eyes weren't friendly anymore, weren't vague or cute or anything like that. They were satanically exultant.

"You bet your fucking ass, Hobbs."

"Then get me some boxes."

At nine o'clock, when her apartment manager answered the phone, she gave an immediate move-out notice. By twelve she and Rob had made a huge pile of trash. Clothes. Shoes. Files. Anything she no longer had a use for. She packed the rest. When she was done, she had enough to fill about twenty boxes.

She called a mover. Within six hours, she was packed and ready.

Lisa at the *Alysium* remembered her and was happy to hear that she'd decided to take the apartment. Yes, she could have it immediately. No problem. Alex said she'd bring her the deposit and sign the papers.

"Hobbs, I wish I understood what the hell you think you're doing," Rangel said, as she drove down Grove, heading toward Meadow. "Don't you know how Markovsky's gonna see this?"

127

"I left Markovsky a message on his machine. Gave him the new address. Look, people in grief do strange things, and the fact I didn't try to hide it will make him think twice about suspecting me."

"He'll go through your trash."

"Let him. Shit, we left him about ten bags full." Alex turned the wheel, blew the horn at a punk kid who was tinkering with his stereo at a green light, and turned into a parking lot. "It's junk, Rangel. He won't find anything to incriminate me, because there *isn't* anything."

"Sez you. My bet is, he'll haul you in just to see you sweat a little. Hey, where are we?"

Alex popped her door and got out. He followed her.

"My bank."

The teller wasn't very happy about letting her draw out five thousand six hundred eight-seven dollars, or to hear that she was closing the account. Alex made it clear that she was not put on the earth to make the teller happy. Rob stood by, mystified, while Alex signed the appropriate papers and got the money in cash, thanks, no cashier's check.

"What the *hell* do you think you're doing?" he asked her as she made room for the bills in her purse. She didn't tell him.

By the time they got to the Alysium, her movers were there and waiting. She signed the lease with Lisa; sat through the usual bullshit of apartment rules and pet regulations and lots of speculative looks at Rob Rangel, who was looking speculatively at Lisa; and got her keys. While the movers were carrying in

128

boxes, she left Rob to supervise and went up a flight of stairs to an apartment overlooking the pool.

No answer. He wasn't home.

"Well?" Rob demanded when she got back. "What the hell are we doing?"

"Not being victims," she said, and took a look around at the assembling chaos. The movers were about halfway done, big, hefty men who thought twenty boxes was a joke. "If Gabriel Davies wants to watch me, I'm going to be looking back."

Chapter Fifteen
Davies

From *The Casebooks of Gabriel Davies.*

TO: Detective Anthony Lipasky

FROM: Gabriel Davies

DATE: April 14, 1987

SUBJECT: Transcription of crime scene tape

As you requested, the following is a verbatim transcription from my tapes of the crime scene at 1284 Royal Park Drive on April 12.

Tape begins.

Lipasky:	*"Someone she knew. The door wasn't forced. The mailman found it open and ajar."*
Davies:	*"Anything on the mailman?"*
Lipasky:	*"No. We've run him through. I've got him downtown if you want to talk to him, but he never got inside, just swung the door open."*

Davies:	"This is a policeman's house, isn't it?"
Lipasky:	"Patrolman George Salerno."
Davies:	"Okay. This inside light here was on?"
Lipasky:	"Yes."
Davies:	"He turned it on. It's a bright day. She had the blinds open. He wanted more light."
Lipasky:	"Sounds right."
Davies:	"Blood trail starts here, six feet from the door."
Lipasky:	"Shot her in the back as she turned to run. Probably shot her again here, at the foot of the stairs."
Davies:	"She was still standing when he hit her here. Going upstairs?"
Lipasky:	"Yeah. You can see the smear on the wall where she fell."
Davies:	"Handprints."
Lipasky:	"Grabbing the wall, trying to get up. Don't touch the banister."
Davies:	"Bloodstains up—to the landing."
Lipasky:	"Crawling. He probably shot her again here on the landing, see?"
Davies:	"Not so much blood up here on the upper steps."
Lipasky:	"That's because she was practically empty by the time she made it up here. Nothing above this step."
Davies:	"This is where she stopped." (pause) "She has two more wounds to the head."
Lipasky:	"Mmm-hmm."

Davies:	"Why the eyes, I wonder?"
Lipasky:	"I think she was past wondering. You coming?"
Davies:	"She was probably dead when it happened."
Lipasky:	"Yeah, I'm liking that thought, too. Nothing here, she never made it up this far. Okay. Hallway."
Davies:	"Strong smell of urine."
Lipasky:	"It's the kids. On the left, the baby's room."
Davies:	"One shot."
Lipasky:	"Christ, I hope so. Never moved the kid, as far as I can tell. She was probably asleep."
Davies:	"No."
Lipasky:	"Don't tell me that. We know he was here for a couple of minutes at least, because he did this."
Davies:	"Interesting."
Lipasky:	"Okay. Next door. Two boys."
Davies:	"The urine smell comes from here."
Lipasky:	"Yeah, I'm not surprised. Oldest kid looks to be about twelve, the younger one is five."
Davies:	"He used the gun on the wife and baby, not these two. Why not?"
Lipasky:	"He was nicer to the women. Hey, you see that? What's that?"
Davies:	"Scratches. Deep ones. On the younger boy's upper arm—appears to be bruising as well, finger-shaped."

Lipasky:	"Somebody dragged him out from under the bed, kicking and screaming."
Davies:	"Notice the spacing of the stab wounds. He was fighting hard when he was being pulled out. That's why the initial wounds near the face and chest are so ragged and close together, and the ones on the lower extremeties are more careful."
Lipasky:	"I hate it when you're right."
Davies:	"Don't take this personally, Anthony."
Lipasky:	"What?"
Davies:	"It was someone who knew these children. Someone who knew exactly where the children would hide. He never tried the ground floor. He never looked in the back yard, or in the parents' bedroom, or in any other room of the house. Look, the older one has similar bruises to the younger one. They were both under the bed, and that's a deep bed, difficult to see under. It isn't the first place to search in this room, either. These closets are more accessible."
Lipasky:	"Maybe they made noise, he heard them."
Davies:	"Maybe, but I don't think so. I think he knew them well enough to tell them what to do in case of trouble. To tell them exactly where to hide."
Lipasky:	"Like a parent."
Davies:	"Where is Salerno's partner?"

133

Lipasky: *"Christ, you've got to be kidding."*
Tape ends.

Sincerely,
Gabriel Davies

Addendum to the typewritten report, written long-hand in Gabriel Davies' journal:

Lipasky has arrested Ernesto Salerno, brother of patrolman George. Ernesto has no apparent motive. I don't believe he acted on his own; George Salerno had a hand here, I can feel it.

This is so familiar to me, so personally instructive.

Like Maxi, sometimes the worst monster is the one who lives in the house.

Chapter Sixteen

Wheaton Sinclair III was not amused, not at all, with her lame excuses. Alex hung up the pay phone very gently, concerned for its blasted speaker. She rubbed her ear absently and fished in the silver slot for her coin, but the telephone gods had not blessed her.

"Well?" Rob asked, from where he sat on the laundry room steps.

She shoved her hands in her coat pockets and walked past him. There was a noisy scrape of shoe leather on concrete as he lurched to his feet and followed.

"He didn't fire you, did he? Hey, if he did, no big thing. You can get another gig."

Alex stopped by the hot tub, an alchemical fountain of steam in the cool air, and dipped her fingers in. Hot enough to boil.

"Can't you?" Rob finished. He wasn't quite as firm as he should have been.

"Sure," Alex said, and turned to look at him. "As soon as I find an editor who didn't hear about me throwing a computer at Ben Hughes at the *Times,* or who happened to miss the pictures of me getting thrown out in the street, blind drunk and puking. Sure, I can get a job from one of those guys. They're probably putting out *Pravda* now."

Rob was one of those friends who, when faced with an insurmountable problem, just pretended it wasn't there. He grinned and sat down next to her, so full of energy and enthusiasm she fought the urge to punch his lights out.

"Alex, that's old news. Nobody's going to jerk you around for that, not after five years. You've been doing good work."

He simply didn't understand that the work she'd been doing was schlock, that she ached to be welcomed back to the *Times* and Ben Hughes, who'd had his teeth capped and looked almost as good as new. That there was only one road back uphill.

Davies.

Rob, next to her, shifted uncomfortably at her silence. He squinted his eyes against the sun to peer through the windows to the leasing office, where Lisa perched in her long-legged glory, waiting for a fly to drop into her web. His expression was wistful and a little blank.

"Think she ever comes out to the hot tub?" he asked. Alex took her numbed fingers out of the water and watched them steam in the cool air.

"Am I crazy?" she asked him quietly. Rob blinked and looked at her. "Do you think I'm crazy to be doing this?"

"Would it piss you off if I said yes?"

"Yes."

"Then you're not crazy." He stared at her for another few seconds. "But maybe you're crazy if you don't—you know, take some precautions."

Visions of condoms and spermicidal jellies danced in her head. She just shook her head.

"No, man, really. Some simple things, like duplicating your tapes and notes and sending them to me. I can go to Markovsky if something weird happens."

"No," she snapped. Rob was a friend, but he was out for money just the same. She wasn't as naive as Gabriel Davies. Not about stuff like this. "No, I'll think of some other way to do it. Put them in a safety deposit box or something."

He drew back, hurt or faking it well. She refused to look at him and watched the steam rising into the thin, cold air. It smelled metallic, like aluminum. *Jesus,* she thought. *People get in there and breathe this shit.*

"Do you have a gun?" Rob asked. She hunched her shoulders and shook her head. "You're a goddamn stubborn stupid bitch, Hobbs. Get one."

He turned and walked away, around the pool, under the protective flapping canopy. Heading for the leasing office.

And Lisa.

If Davies came after her, would a gun help her? Would she be able to find it, use it, kill him before he got to her?

If Davies killed the woman on Meadow and Harry Verdun, he had a gun, too. And he wasn't afraid to use it, or to get messy doing it.

Gray brain fungus, pushing through a hole where her eye had been—

Alex took a deep breath and turned in the direction of her new apartment. Someone was leaning over a third-floor balcony, watching her.

It was a woman, middle-aged, wearing a polyester floral print shirt and stretch pants. She realized Alex was looking back and hustled around quickly, busy, too busy to pay attention to other people. The patio doors slid shut with a bang.

Alex looked over three apartments, to where Gabriel Davies lived. His patio doors were shut and curtained.

Alex trudged up the concrete steps to her metal door and fished her keys out of her pocket—new keys, bright, scratchless. She unlocked the deadbolt and fit the second key into the knob lock.

A hand fell on her shoulder. She jerked away and slammed into the stucco in her haste to turn; she didn't have time to scream, though she had plenty of energy. A hand slammed down over her mouth and silenced her.

The smell of hot ozone and cologne crawled up her nose.

"I'm sorry," Davies said very quietly. "Be quiet. We don't want to alarm the neighbors, do we? We both have to live here. Quiet. I won't hurt you."

He let go of her just as suddenly, and the flow of blood back into her arm and the skin around her mouth felt like an embarrassed blush. She stayed where she was and darted glances up and down the narrow concrete hall, the stairs, out to the pool area. No one around. Rob Rangel was halfway to paradise with Lisa-the-Leaser by now, as unreachable as Mars. Davies had drawn back two steps, but he was near

138

enough to keep her from going for the steps, if he wanted. Or to push her down them, head first.

"You son of a bitch," she hissed.

"You're one to talk, considering my provocations," he said mildly. He crossed his arms and leaned back against the wall opposite her, with her apartment door between them to one side, the steps to the other. Two avenues of escape, both covered. "I trusted you, you know. I'll be very disappointed in you if you turn on me."

Something went through Alex painfully, like an electrical current, like a high-tension wire snapping. "Turn on *you?* You self-centered crazy bastard, who do you think you are, anyway? *I* trusted *you,* you fucker. *I* trusted *you.*"

She was dangerously close to tears, to a screaming blue fit of rage. She went for her door again and shoved the key into the doorknob. Davies didn't try to stop her.

The door sighed open, puffing out smells of wet clean carpet and new paint. She went inside and began to slam the door closed on him, but the sight of his face stopped her.

"Please," he said to her through the narrow crack. He straightened up now, and he brushed self-consciously at the maroon sweater he wore, the faded blue jeans. "Please talk to me."

"Rolly Roy Eastfield," she said flatly. His expression didn't change. "He's dead. But you knew that, didn't you? You ran him off the road. Him and *Mrs.* Eastfield."

There was no way to fake the expansion of his pupils. He hadn't known. His face went a sallow color, unhealthy, and he looked away from her at the bland stucco wall.

"I'm sorry," he said, but he wasn't. He was afraid. Alex watched him for another minute and let the door swung wide.

"Inside," she ordered.

He came hesitantly, like an animal walking into a particularly vicious trap. She stayed well away from him as he circled around the small apartment, touching the sparse furniture, looking at the boxes stacked unevenly against the walls. He looked into the bedroom, where her brand new bed leaned against the wall still in its plastic wrap. The ultimate in safe sex.

"I see you've settled in nicely," he said, but there was no bite to it. Alex moved a stack of books from one chair and gestured to it. He didn't move to sit down, just stared at it.

"It doesn't have spikes or anything," she said angrily, and sat down in it herself. Davies picked an empty section of wall and settled himself against it. He slid down, slowly, to a sitting position.

"Did you ever realize," he said, "that you can't really tell from a photo if someone is alive or dead? They might have been dead a while, posed for the picture. There's no way to tell."

He looked down at the clean, springy carpet and ran his fingers idly through it. She tried to follow his thinking and gave up in agitated disgust.

"Did you kill Rolly?" Alex demanded, and then belatedly, "and Susan?"

"Of course not," Davies said, and looked up to stare at her. "Don't be stupid. You said they were run

140

off the road, how did I do *that,* with my bare hands? I don't even have a car."

"You could have stolen one."

"Could have, could have, I *didn't.* Why would I? Don't be stupid enough to think I was jealous of you, Miss Hobbs. I have no interest in you except where you can help me survive. If I wanted you to be suspicious of Eastfield, it's because I'm *trusting* you. I can't afford to trust anyone else by extension." Davies propped his head back against the wall, eyes half-closed. She freeze-framed the image in her mind. Yes. He could have been dead. *We only prove we're alive by moving,* she thought.

"Then who killed them?"

"There's random violence in this city five times a day. Why does it have to be related to me, or to you? Drunk drivers kill any number of people." He paused to look at her. "Is that why you moved here? To confront me for your dead lover?"

Let him wait, she thought. *Let him guess.*

"Or because you think I'm stalking you?"

A chill worked up and down her spine, climbing hand-over-hand on her vertebrae. His eyes narrowed.

"If I were stalking you, Miss Hobbs, you wouldn't know the first thing about it until it was too late," Davies said. He sounded wounded by the insult to his professional ability. "I don't want to hurt you. I need you to help me."

"Help you what?" she shouted. "Help you cover your tracks with the cops? Help you kill somebody?"

"Help me before anyone else has to die for me!" he shouted back, and clutched at his head as if something had broken. Sweat shone in a crown at the top of his head. "That woman on Meadow died for me. Harry Verdun died for me. It's possible even Rolly Eastfield died for me. No more, Alex. You have to help me make sure there won't be more."

"The easiest way to do that is to put a bullet in your head," Alex heard herself say, and felt a twitch of surprise and shame. His head jerked up, eyes wide.

"Do you think I haven't considered it?" he asked. "Putting suicide away for the moment, Miss Hobbs, I think our best option is to just *find* her."

"I'm not the cops."

"I'm sure if you need one, you know one."

Alex fiddled with a ragged fingernail for a few seconds, watching him, waiting. It was her specialty, waiting. It was one thing she was good at and other people weren't. Of course, it was his specialty as well. She hated the way his eyes watched her, the way he automatically picked at his own fingernail, aping her. Waiting, too.

"I hope I can trust you, Miss Hobbs," he finally said. She smiled.

"As long as there's a story in it for me, yeah, you can trust me. But if I find out you're fucking me around about Rolly, you'd better kill me, too, 'cause I'll find a way to get to you. You think Landrum fucked you on the *Casebooks,* baby, you ain't seen nothing compared to the ax job I'll do on you in every major newspaper, magazine, and bookstore in the country. You won't be able to find a place to lay your head, not in any country that I can get foreign publishing rights to. Are we clearly understood?"

He smiled, a tiny, unwilling smile, the most natural

one she could recall seeing from him. He inclined his head, and his eyes looked weary and swollen.

"One more thing," he said. "Be very, very careful. If the deaths of Rolly and Susan Eastfield were not incidental, someone knows you as well as me. And is watching you. I can take care of myself, Alex. But I may not be able to help you, as well."

She shrugged, indifferent. No one had ever promised her safety. Once she'd hung from a rope over the edge of a building with Rob Rangel, shouting questions at a demented would-be jumper who'd taken his daughter out on the ledge with him. Rob had taken the pictures.

Alex remembered that sensation of swinging in the wind, helpless.

"Tell me one thing," she said, and that same feeling welled up in her stomach again, of arrested falling. "Can you swear to me, absolutely swear, that you've never killed anyone?"

His smiled vanished. There was nothing in his face, nothing. His eyes were flat as glass and his muscles were neither tight nor loose, just there. *Dead,* she thought again. He looked dead.

"Of course," he said.

She knew he was lying.

"We're being sued," Wheaton Sinclair III growled at her, as she dropped her purse on the floor and reached for the button to boot up her computer.

"What? By who? The Presley Estate?"

"Get serious, Hobbs. No. By—" Wheaton grubbed through a pile of newspaper clippings and found a sheet of severe-looking letterhead. "The People's Evangelical Society of Tampa."

"What did we ever do to Tampa?" Alex asked. "Recently?"

"Nothing." Wheaten chewed on his fingernail. "It seems that they've gotten some unpleasant mail about springing the Snake-Man from Brazil."

"Oh, Christ, you've got to be kidding. Somebody actually named their organization PEST? What are they, crazy?"

"They're *evangelical,* Hobbs."

"How much?" she sighed. Wheaton flipped to the second page.

"Whereas, the *National Light* has damaged the credibility of the People's Evangelical Society of Tampa, and permanently impaired its ability to collect funds for public works"—public, my ass—"the People's Evangelical Society plans to file a suit in the amount of one million dollars for damages—"

"That's all?" Alex interrupted. Wheaton lifted an eyebrow. "Shit, you had me scared for a minute. Very funny."

"Yeah, I thought so. I'll stick it with the others."

He opened a file drawer crammed with severe-looking letterheads, some of them dating back six or seven years. To date, none of the letters had actually resulted in a suit, though two or three had come close enough to make Wheaton sweat. That, of course, was the game. Insult people, but not enough to make them spend money. Never insult anybody with truly limitless funds. That's what the *National Enquirer* was for.

"Where's my titty-bar series?" he asked. Alex looked blank.

"You never gave me a note on it. Was it for this issue?"

"Damn it—" Wheaton sighed. "Yeah. For this issue."

"Then you'll get it as soon as I get the expense money."

They exchanged glares until he unlocked his desk drawer and pulled out a small cashbox. He peeled three hundred off and handed it to her. She signed the slip he passed across and stuffed the bills in her pocket. They were old bills, limp and greasy, perfect for passing in a topless joint.

"I'll modem it in," she said, and checked her computer for messages. Nothing. Wheaton had put several more sticky notes around her workstation: WAS VERDUN A MOBSTER? NEED ANOTHER FEATURE ON SNAKE MAN. BREAST AUGMENTATION PIECE TO GO WITH PENIS ENLARGEMENT STORY.

And the last, which Alex picked up and read with a sense of unsettling déjà vu: WHAT HAPPENED TO GABRIEL DAVIES?

Who'd sparked his memory? Rob Rangel? Was Rangel planning on cutting her out?

Alex crumpled up the sticky note and dropped it in the trash. She popped her disk into the computer and copied her Davies file under BOOK REVIEW. It was up to twenty pages now, good, solid work, salable work.

If she lived to sell it.

"Hey, Hobbs, I got a call from Ben Hughes at the

Times," Wheaton said from behind her. His chair creaked as he leaned forward, and a pencil scratched. "Fucking asshole. Just wanted to find out if you were still here. You planning on breaking his teeth again?"

"Not particularly," she said, and felt a little bright star of heat bloom somewhere under her breastbone. It felt like hunger. "I just sent him a postcard to let him know I was still alive."

"Don't worry, he'll never forget you, not considering his dental bills." Wheaton's voice was cool and calculated. He knew something was up; she wouldn't drop a line to Ben Hughes just to say hello. "Just remember who pulled your fucking butt off the street when nobody else would, Hobbs. Hughes threw you away like yesterday's ground round."

"Whereas you recycle people like yesterday's toilet paper."

"Very funny, Hobbs. Watch it. He'll fuck you over."

She finished at the computer and turned it off. Another squeak and rustle told her Wheaton was leaning back in his chair, tottering precariously.

"Hobbs," he said. She twisted to look. He was leaning back, all right, listing at an alarming rate. "I want *change* back from that three hundred."

She flipped him the bird and bolted while she still could. Instead of hiking through the dilapidated garden, she went out through the garage. Her car sat forlornly at the curb, abused and used. As she approached it, she saw a van sitting three cars back, on the other side of the residential street. It was an old van with round windows high on the sides. Not

146

red, though. This one was primer gray, with tinted windows.

She unlocked her car and got in. It was a good day, and the poor thing turned over on the third try. She slipped it in gear and pulled away from the curb. She adjusted the rearview mirror and told herself she was imagining things.

The van glided out after her. She stopped at the light and watched it pull in a car length back. The light turned green. She took a right.

The van took a right.

"Jesus Christ," Alex breathed. She nudged her speed up a little; the van fell back, but not very far back. She turned right again, then left.

There was no sign of the van for several blocks. Then, in the distance, she saw it turn in behind her again.

She felt her stomach go light again, hanging suspended by that fraying rope. Except that Rob wasn't hanging with her this time, snapping pictures, cracking jokes. She couldn't feel his warmth at her back, his arms ready to catch her.

She was flying all alone.

Chapter Seventeen
Davies

An excerpt from the diary of Gabriel Davies. Not included in the Omega Press publication, found in the effects of Haley Landrum, deceased.

Unpublished.

February 14, 1988

As I write this I'm sitting in the chair next to Viva's bed. She doesn't know I'm here. She never does.

I don't know why I keep coming here. Her face is lumpy and vacant, tumorous. Her eyes are barely visible, mostly whites, and they roll constantly. I don't know why I must come here and hold her hand. Maybe Viva is alive, thinking, screaming. It's cruel of me to think so.

I wonder why something tells me she's better off like this. Does Viva hold the key to something I can't understand?

I shall be leaving Chicago soon. I've asked Anthony to help me, and he has, in spite of what he must suspect. He has never said so, but I'm sure he checks every possible police report for a match to me. To my obsessions.

I am holding Viva's limp, puffy hand. The sun has not touched it in twenty-six years. She looks like an old woman, shriveled and yet somehow bloated. Her hair is gray now, her eyes milky and blind.

Maxi. Maxi and the cat, and my father hosing blood from the side of the house near my window.

I must remember, I must, for Viva, for myself. I must dream the dream again.

It's morning, now. I must write, and I can't, I can't think. But I have to. For Viva. For myself.

Father, angry with her. Father in the shadows, watching. Letting Maxi off the chain. She tried to run but she was too little, like a cat, a helpless, mutilated cat. And I watched.

So did he, my father. Wet eyes. Angry eyes.

My father hid in the shadows and watched. Why didn't he save her?

It replays in my mind, and I cannot stop it. Maxi tears at her, whimpering. Father crosses the yard and picks up a piece of wood. He grabs Maxi's collar and tries to pull him off Viva. Maxi won't let go. Viva has stopped screaming and now dangles limp, one bloody arm still in the dog's mouth.

The first blow falls, then the second. They both miss Maxi.

I can hear the thick crunch of Viva's bones. The wood makes a wet sound against her head.

Blood against the house, splattered like red angel wings. Father's blow finally falls on Maxi, equal punishment for victim and killer. Maxi's bones sound different.

Father looks up from the dead dog, the silent daughter, and sees me in the window. His face is red and streaked, and through the red veil on my window I see the light in his face.

It is not a dream, was never a dream.

I am sitting beside Viva again, poor pale, lumpen Viva, a cancerous growth put here by my father. Why didn't I scream? Try to save her?

I have left fingerprints on her pallid skin where I held her hand.

There is more. I know there are more horrors in the dream, more demons to be found. More pain.

I, like Maxi, am guilty.

Chapter Eighteen

"Good afternoon, Collins House, how can I help you?"

"I'm looking for a former patient of yours who was moved somewhere else about—oh, five years ago."

"Name?" A rustle of paper on the other end.

"Vivian Anne Davies, or Viva. Age, about thirty-eight. She's in a permanent vegetative state."

The rustling stopped. "I see. And you are—"

"Her cousin Rhonda."

"One moment." The nurse's voice had gone from cheerful to guarded. The phone line clicked temporarily dead. On hold. Held where? Alex fidgeted until static on the other end told her the nurse was back. "Rhonda what?"

"Rhonda Davies," Alex guessed. There *was* a Rhonda Davies, or had been. Pages flipped.

The silence stretched on too long. The nurse wasn't going for it.

"I'm sorry, ma'am, but I'm not authorized to—"

"I have permission from Arthur Davies, her father," Alex interrupted. More silence.

"You do. Well, I'm sorry, ma'am, but Arthur Davies is specifically excluded from any information regarding Vivian Davies. It's at her brother's request. You'll need to bring permission in writing from Gabriel Davies before I can release any information about her transfer. Thank you, and have a good day." The nurse hung up with a polite but firm click. Alex stared at the receiver in her hand, stunned, and gently put it back in the cradle.

Gabriel wouldn't let his own father know where Viva was. Why? What was so important about *that?* She'd wanted to take a look at Vivian just to complete her picture of Davies, but that didn't look feasible now. But why was it so difficult?

Reporters. They must have been all over Vivian during the feeding frenzy, snapping photos of her staring gap-mouthed into space. DAVIES' DROOLING SISTER. Oh, yeah, that must have been lovely.

Maybe, Alex thought cynically, if I tell him I'll only take *one* picture—

She picked up the phone again and dialed Chicago information. There was no listing for Arthur Davies, or for his wife, Gwen. Alex dug in a dusty box of notes until she found, scribbled in the margin of a manuscript page, the Davies family number.

Doo-doo-doo. *That number has been disconnected.*

She tapped her pencil against the phone, impatient, getting angry. They'd moved. Vivian had been moved. She had nothing, except Davies himself, and that was not enough. Not nearly.

She went over her yellowing notes. Father, Arthur

Davies. Mother, Gwen Davies. Sister, Vivian Anne Davies. Cousins Rhonda, Sean and Jeanine Davies, on his father's side. On his mother's, nothing.

Aunts. Uncles.

If he was worried enough about Viva to move her from Chicago, and prevent his own family from visiting her, why would she be far away from him?

Alex flipped open the yellow pages. There were seventeen possibilities.

The sixth rung cherries.

"Vivian Anne Davies? Yes, she's a patient here."

"No visiting restrictions?" Alex hoped. The nurse rustled paper.

"No, ma'am. No restrictions. Visiting hours are from nine in the morning until three in the afternoon, and from six in the evening to ten. You'll need to sign in at the desk."

"Of course." Alex hung up and gave the yellow pages a big, fat smack. She'd kissed worse.

It was six o'clock. She grabbed her purse and headed for the door. The phone rang behind her, and she hesitated, one hand on the lock.

She could never resist a ringing phone.

"Alex Hobbs," she said, and shoved hair back from her face as she reached for her pencil. No answer on the other end. "Hello?"

Finally, hoarsely, an answer. A whisper.

"She was here."

The voice was threadbare, shocked, distant. Alex clutched the phone tighter and sank into a chair.

"Davies?" she asked. There was no answer. "Davies, where are you? Are you in your apartment?"

"No." God, he sounded half the world away, lost

153

in static and the phantom whispers of others' conversations. A ghost himself. "Need help."

"Where are you?" she almost shouted. More static. Car phone, she thought, because she thought she heard traffic. No. Pay phone, on the street.

"Don't—know. Can't see."

He was hurt, she thought. Stabbed. Dying.

"Look for a street sign. Tell me where you are." Alex heard his breathing now, fast and uneven. Traffic hissed behind him, menacing. She felt her hands trembling and wondered suddenly why she was doing this, why she even cared. Just a story, she reminded herself. Nothing special.

"Sixteenth and—Carlisle."

She had no idea where that was, but there was a map in the car. She gulped in a quick breath and wished she'd taken Rangel's advice and bought that gun. A big gun. With lots of bullets.

"Good, stay there, I'll pick you up. Don't move, okay? Wait for me."

"She was here," he said again, and he sounded so bewildered that she felt her heart lurch. He was cracking, right down the middle.

"Don't move, damn it! I'm coming!"

She hung up without waiting for his answer and slammed the door behind her. She took the steps three at a time, missed the last one, went crashing to one knee. The pain stunned her so badly she couldn't get up for a few seconds, but the knee worked, and the ankle held her weight. She limped out to her car and was out of the parking lot in less than ten seconds.

At the first long stoplight, she scanned the map

and found Sixteenth and Carlisle. It was a long way, too long for Davies to have walked it. Cab? Or bus? He'd been moving with a purpose, to have gone that far. She made sure her door was locked and her windows rolled up, and hissed orders for the light to change.

When it did, she raced through it and took a right onto the freeway. As she broke the speed limit and looked for her exit, part of her kept wondering why in the world she was racing to save somebody she couldn't even be sure wouldn't kill her when she got there.

In a romance, she thought, this would be the part where she ended up in bed with him. What a repugnant thought.

Sixteenth and Carlisle was an industrial district with security lights instead of streetlights. There weren't any businesses open here, with the exception of a convenience store on the corner that looked like it attracted more robbers than customers. Alex slowed and cruised. One pay phone in front of the store, its receiver swinging in the wind. One bored clerk visible through the plate glass window, and one of what in these politically correct times Alex figured she'd have to call the economically disadvantaged. He was picking through the dumpster for half-eaten daily specials.

No Gabriel Davies. She didn't feel inclined to park in the convenience store lot, too vulnerable, so she turned the corner and cruised down Sixteenth. Nothing. Nobody. Not even a stray cat.

A shadow flickered behind a building. She slammed on the brakes and stared. A man was standing there, his back to her. If she hadn't been looking for him, she wouldn't have glanced twice. She put the car in park and waited, but Davies didn't turn, didn't seem to notice she'd arrived.

She damn sure wasn't getting out of the car. She turned the window crank and let in about five inches of cool windy air.

"Hey! Davies!" He didn't turn. She wet her lips. "Let's go, damn it!"

No response. It was like talking to a zombie. She rolled the window back up and shut the engine off. The ticks as it cooled sounded like a bomb ticking down to explosion.

The first step was the most difficult. She felt exposed outside of the comfort of her car, aware that if he turned on her nobody would know the difference. She crossed the street and approached to within ten feet, and apart from tension in his shoulders, he didn't even seem to notice.

"Davies?" she asked again, more gently. "Are you okay?"

He turned, finally. His face looked bland, completely normal. He stepped aside.

"I think you know him," he said. She took two involuntary steps forward, eyes adjusting to the darkness.

He smiled at her out of the shadows, no, it wasn't a smile, his mouth gaped open, a dark cave. His eyes stared. He sat propped on a crate, head lolling bonelessly to one side.

Staring.

Staring.

There was something wrong with his head.

Staring at her.

There was no top to it.

His camera lay on the ground, smashed. A carrybag of film had been ripped open, and film lay strewn around like party favors after the guests had gone.

Flies buzzed.

Alex thought it was strange that she couldn't scream at all, couldn't get a sound past the blockage in her throat. She felt warmth at her back, knew Gabriel Davies stood there.

"His name is Rob Rangel," she heard herself say, instead of a scream.

"He was following me," Davies said. A longdistance whisper. She could not turn, to look at him, to see those eyes. "Taking pictures. He must have gotten a picture of her, and she couldn't let that happen."

Alex's hands wrapped themselves together, lifted themselves slowly to her mouth. She stopped the scream with a gag of her own flesh.

There wasn't any woman.

Only Davies. Only, always, Davies.

She felt his hand brush her arm.

"I'll call the police," he said then, softly, and when she turned he was walking away, head bent forward, shoulders hunched against a cold she couldn't feel.

She couldn't understand why he hadn't killed her. Why he hadn't even tried.

Didn't he understand that she *knew?*

Chapter Nineteen
Davies

An article written by Gabriel Davies for *True Cases* magazine, published in the Summer 1988 issue.

Nancy Hargrist disappeared early on a Sunday morning. Her car was found, driver's side door ajar, in the parking lot in front of a small neighborhood donut shop. Her husband led an impassioned search, posting handbills and even going on television to beg her captors to let Nancy go unharmed.

It was all good theater. My friend Detective Lipasky asked me to come with him to interview Richard Hargrist one last time, three weeks into the disappearance. Every other time Richard had come to the station, but Lipasky had a desire to look through the house again.

I waited all morning. Lipasky was delayed. I decided to talk to Hargrist on my own. Whatever blame there is rests entirely on my shoulders.

I should have waited on Lipasky.

I knocked, waited, while there was shuffling on the other side of the door and someone peered through the peephole. I was scrutinized. In time, the locks on the door clicked open.

Richard Hargrist had not borne the ordeal well. Thin and tall, he looked skeletal under his blotchy skin. His eyes were feverishly bright and yet somehow dim, as if he had polished them up with amphetamines.

The smell reached out for me, even on the doorstep. It crawled over me, a moist, clinging odor of decay that found its way into my throat and nested there on my taste buds. Richard Hargrist smelled bad, certainly, a man who'd gone unbathed for nearly three weeks. There were mounds of trash in his kitchen.

But there is no other odor quite like the one I smelled.

We sat down on the couch. It felt damp. I ran my hand over the cushions and wiped it on my pants; if there was any moisture, it didn't show. The smell there was strong, lingering.

We went over the story again. Nancy Hargrist, dressed in her blue sweatsuit, leaving the apartment. Never returning. The police had the car. There was no sign of her anywhere.

He seemed almost apathetic, weary with the whole business. When he spoke about Nancy, his eyes clouded over with tears that slid down his cheeks. He didn't seem to notice.

I asked if I could look around. He shrugged and sat there on the couch as if he were too weary to move.

The smell was everywhere, and nowhere. I looked in the closets, under the bed, in the cabinets, refrigerator, washer, dryer.

I went through again, one room at a time, methodically. The children's room. The toy chest. The closets. Every drawer.

Nothing.

Richard Hargrist remained where he was, on the couch. He had stretched out full length on it, staring at the ceiling. He looked dead himself, waxy. If it hadn't been for the flicker of his eyes and the rise and fall of his chest, I would have believed he'd committed suicide in front of me.

As I started to close the door, the presence seemed to swarm over me, pummeling, enraged. Don't leave, *it said.* Find me. Find me.

I went back inside and closed the door. I stood there staring at Richard Hargrist, who slowly turned his head toward me. He smiled.

It took all my strength to drag him off the couch. I threw him across the room; he hit his head on the wall and sat there, befuddled, while I tore the cushions off and found the hide-a-bed underneath. I pulled. It was stuck. I pulled again, and it glided out, sprouting steel legs as it did, unfolding.

Nancy Hargrist was a small corpse, but she made an unwieldy lump in the bed. She had rotted quite a bit inside the plastic drop cloth. The smell came again like a physical assault, green in my mouth like vomit.

Across the room, Richard Hargrist wailed, a terrible lost sound.

He was convicted and sentenced to fifty-seven

years in the state penitentiary, despite his rather novel claim that his wife must have somehow suffocated after falling into the hide-a-bed. His only crime, as he saw it, was to have tidied up and replaced the cushions.

I have no doubt that he believed it.

Chapter Twenty

"Detective Anthony Lipasky," Alex requested at the main desk. It was a madhouse. The uniformed sergeant gave her a weary once-over and checked his log.

"Yeah, he's here. Wait while I call him."

While she waited, Alex scrutinized the array of desperadoes waiting with her. Victims clinging pallidly to the arms of unfortunate friends or relatives. A few lawyers, nattily at ease in the midst of the confusion, reading magazines or notes or, in the case of one, a comic book. Their clients waited on benches with their wrists handcuffed behind them. Some of them looked rabid and surly. Alex was personally more nervous about the ones who looked like English teachers.

There were an unsettlingly small number of cops, considering the foot traffic.

"Hey! What's your name?" the desk sergeant demanded, and pointed a finger like a bazooka directly at Alex's forehead. She decided on the formal approach.

"Alexandra Hobbs."

The desk sergeant had a conversation with a telephone receiver and, when finished, gave her a long, measuring look. He fished a visitor's badge out of the mess on his desk and watched her clip it to her shirt.

"Wait here," he ordered. "Lipasky's coming up for you."

She nodded and moved out of the way of a very fat woman speaking firecracker-rapid Spanish. The desk sergeant listened to her just as attentively, if unhelpfully. Alex found a blank wall space and occupied it while she counted out the few dollars left in her wallet. Enough to get her back to the airport. Maybe. She might do better to cash in her return plane ticket and rent a car. Or to catch a plane out of the country and just never look back. Bermuda. That was an option she'd been thinking about a lot.

A tall stoop-shouldered man strolled through the confusion, eyes raking the crowd. She remembered his face, caught in the explosion of a flashbulb in 1985. He'd aged well; the lines on his face made him look softer than before, more approachable.

It was all a fake, she knew that as soon as she saw his eyes. The lines were a friendly trap. The gray eyes were empty, waiting.

"Detective Lipasky," she said, and stuck out her hand. He didn't take it. His lips thinned, and his eyes drifted half-closed. "Alexandra Hobbs. Maybe you remember me."

"I remember. Hit the road, Hobbs. I don't talk to the press." He started to turn, all elbows and sharp shoulders. She grabbed for an angle.

"Wait! I—I need to talk to you. It's important. It's

163

about Gabriel Davies." She felt flushed and a little dizzy after she'd said it, but Lipasky obviously found nothing spectacular about the revelation. His eyes remained half-closed, sleepy, giving away nothing. "Look, Detective, I'm not shitting you. I'm really scared. I need your help."

"That's too bad," he said as if he meant it. He reached out and plucked the visitor's badge off of her chest. "Have a nice day."

When she reached to stop him again, he came around fast, like Davies. She held her ground. "Damn it, I'm not jerking you around. I know where he is, I know what he's doing, and he's in trouble. So am I. *He sent me to ask for your help.*"

Lipasky stood quietly, watching her. Though she saw nothing change in his face, she felt he wanted to believe her. He took a minute, thinking about it, checking his physical boundaries with automatic glances right and left. He was looking left at a bench full of lounging suspects when he answered.

"Where is he?"

"Living at the Alysium Apartments about one floor up from me. Look, I'd rather not talk about it in the goddamn lobby. Let's find a quieter place, okay? Please?"

He let his gaze continue its patrol, back to the right, finally stopping on her face. She couldn't tell what he thought, but he shrugged. Gestured with a long jacketed elbow.

As he turned away, he tossed her visitor badge back over his shoulder to her. She clipped it on her shirt and hurried after him, down a dark, smelly hallway lit by guttering fluorescents. He turned right, down another hall. They passed a group of three men clustered around a clipboard; all three scanned her automatically and dismissed her once they saw the visitor's badge. Lipasky shoved a door open at the end of the hall and gestured her inside.

She took a few steps in and stopped. It was an interrogation room. She recognized the one-way mirror.

"Have a seat," Lipasky said. It wasn't a request. She circled the table. He stayed on the opposite side. There were two chairs, one on either side; they both looked equally uncomfortable. She put her hand on one, felt the metal sear her fingers with cold, and Lipasky stopped at the chair facing her.

"After you," he said quietly. His courtesy was deceiving, like the friendly lines on his face. He wanted her to sit first, to have to look up to him (God, didn't he tower over her enough already?) and let her know who was in charge. She pulled the chair out with a whining scrape of metal and stood there, hands folded on its rounded top. She did not sit.

She waited.

There was no clock, and she didn't dare look at her watch. She tried to keep count of her pulse, then her breathing, then just gave up and hung onto staring him down. After a long, long time, the gray eyes widened just a little, and she thought she saw a smile flicker through them.

"Alysium Apartments, huh?" he asked. He pulled his chair out with a sideways shuffle of his foot and sat, relaxed. Not admitting a loss. From his body language, they were cozy friends, old pals. He was glad to hear from her. "Come on, Alex, sit down. I hate looking up at people."

"You should get more practice," she said, but eased herself down. The chair was icy through the worn fabric of her blue jeans. She couldn't help but wonder about the last person to occupy the chair. Thief? Murderer? Rapist?

Funny, she thought, that she didn't think of *innocent person* until last.

"You fly down just to tell me Gabriel Davies is at the Alysium Apartments? Could've saved yourself a ticket and called," Lipasky said. He smiled now, fully. Fakely.

"If you'd have given me ten seconds before you hung up," she answered. He nodded as if she'd made a good point. "Look, I know you were his friend—"

Lipasky leaned back, eyes still at half-staff, studying her. She felt she'd made a mistake, didn't know how to correct it. She didn't like the room. Didn't like Lipasky.

"—And I know he trusts you. Maybe he's told you more than he has me, I don't know, but he says somebody's following him, and I *know* somebody's *killing* people." She waited for a reaction, didn't get any. She leaned forward and put her hands flat on the table. "Don't you care?"

"Davies told you somebody's following him? Somebody's killing people?"

"Yes."

He looked at her for a long, long time. She pressed her hands hard against the table, felt a sticky false veneer of old sweat and spilled coffee cling to them.

Lipasky slowly blinked and leaned forward.

"It never occurred to you he'd done it himself."

The woman, her head shattered by a bullet. Harry

166

Verdun, blasted to shreds of meat in his car. Rolly. Rob Rangel, head lolling, staring at her.

Alex felt a sudden sharp pain, as if Lipasky had reached across the table and punched her. She jerked against it and held rigid, waiting for it to pass. Every breath stabbed like a knife below her ribs.

"Of course it occurred to me, Lipasky, I'm not an idiot."

"Then why are you trying to help him?" Lipasky cocked his head, attentive, friendly.

She didn't have to think about her answer; it floated up like the surfacing of a drowned object.

"I thought for a while that he was—that he'd—but now I don't know. Besides, these people were shot. His weapon of choice would be a knife, wouldn't it?"

She'd surprised him. Lipasky's eyes flickered for a second, opened wider.

"How'd you meet him?" he asked. It sounded like the kind of question her mother would have asked, if she'd been stupid enough to bring someone like Gabriel Davies home. She felt a stupid compulsion to say, "Well, I saw him on *America's Most Wanted*—"

"In a bar."

"Not unusual for you, is it?" Lipasky murmured. She felt her stomach lurch and forced a smile.

"Do you want to hear it or not?"

"Oh, absolutely," he said insincerely. He checked his watch.

He wasn't checking it anymore by the time she'd described Davies at the murder site, or at the scene of Harry Verdun's killing. He was expressionless, all the false warmth gone. She'd surprised him again, she thought, by telling him the truth.

"You think this woman in the van is following him, maybe you."

"I *know* somebody in a van is following me. It isn't red, like my witness reported, but it's primer gray. It could have been stripped. And Davies said that this woman had followed him, and my friend Rob had taken pictures of her."

"Get anything off the film?"

"Nothing. All exposed."

"And you think you may be next," Lipasky finished. "Yes. Looks like you have some good reasons to think so."

Alex felt some of the tension dissolve in her stomach. It felt a slightly sick feeling she didn't want to identify as fear.

"Are you his friend? Really?" she asked. Lipasky frowned. She recognized with him that her voice sounded a little shaky.

Lipasky pushed his chair back and stood. He walked over to the mirror that wasn't a mirror, checked his face to be sure it wasn't giving anything away. He watched her in reflection.

Her reporter's instincts scented the temptation to lie.

"Gabriel Davies doesn't have any friends, not the way you understand the word. He has people who help him or people who don't. By that definition, yeah, I'm his friend. I help him."

"Why?"

He didn't like being questioned, certainly not by a reporter. He let his eyes drift half-closed again and turned back to face her.

"Why do you?"

She started to answer, stopped. He nodded.

"See? He isn't a likable guy, you've noticed that. And he's got so many lug nuts loose he could pop a tire off at any time. I shouldn't help him, and neither should you. Sooner or later, we'll be sorry."

"I'm already sorry," she said. He grinned.

"No, you're not. Okay. You've been straight with me, I'll be straight with you." That was a lie, she knew. If he showed her his cards, at least two of them would be up his sleeve. He settled on a corner of the table, staring off toward the far wall of the room where a rust-colored drip stain had conquered two feet of the paint. "I've known Gabriel Davies since 1983, before that Broward fuckup. He was always a little unplugged, but he was good. Really good. We kept running into each other on things. He was private, working for clients here and there, but most of the homicide stuff he poked his nose into for fun. Hell, I didn't mind. He was good at it, saw stuff we didn't. Some of the guys thought he was psychic."

"That good."

"That good," he agreed. His face had relaxed a little, the lines eased. He didn't look as friendly now, but he looked more honest. "He was usually right on the money. It got so we expected him around—and then it got so I called him when I had one he could help with. He didn't want to get paid, and we didn't have the money to pay him, so it was perfect."

"Except."

"Yeah, except. He started getting a little too much out of it. He liked looking at the bodies. He liked reconstructing the crime. It wasn't—normal. Putting him on the Broward thing was my mistake."

169

She stared, fumbled for a question.

"He solved the case. You said yourself that it would have taken four or five more victims before you put it together."

"I know what I said." He shoved his hands into pockets already baggy with the habit. "Gabriel's like a cruise missile. You turn him on, off he goes, and once you figure out something's wrong it's too late. He was a ghost. We couldn't work with him, he wouldn't talk to us."

"He talked to *you*, though."

"Sometimes. But he was too far gone. I thought for a while he was over the edge. I never counted on it doing that to him," Lipasky said. It was half to himself. "But he got the bastard."

"And afterward—"

"He went on. He was okay. I kept him away from kid cases when I could, when he'd let me. Still, it was in his eyes all the time, that look. It ate away at him until I guess he figured, what the hell, let this reporter Landrum look over his case notes. You know all about that." Lipasky paused to look her over again, what he thought about reporters chilly in his eyes. "I helped him get out of town. He asked me to, and I did it."

"Even though you knew he might kill someone later."

"I didn't know that. I still don't. Look, I've seen a lot of things, and I've never seen anybody fight like Gabriel. Every day it's a fight, and I've never seen him lose."

Alex thought about that. There was a lot of truth in

it—but she didn't believe, and didn't think Lipasky believed, that Davies was infallible.

"You weren't surprised he was living in the Alysium Apartments," she said, and he shrugged without taking his hands out of his pockets.

"He calls me. He has every day since he left Chicago."

Alex stopped dead, staring. Lipasky prowled around the room and waited for her to snap out of it; he shot her little glances, nothing intimidating, just questioning. She curled her hands into fists and felt her nails dig into tender palms.

"You're kidding."

"No, I'm not. Every morning about seven thirty, he calls. Either I talk to him or he talks to my answering machine; it doesn't matter much to him. He tells me where he is, what he's thinking, what he's doing. I know you were lying, by the way; he didn't say anything this morning about sending you to ask for my help. Hell, he doesn't need to send you. He could have asked directly and I would have been on the next plane," Lipasky said. Hobbs cleared her throat, shifted on her cold chair.

"I don't understand. What's he been telling you?"

Lipasky's smile this time was real, warm, and edged with triumph.

"Well, he's been telling me about this woman in the van, and how he thinks it might be one Alexandra Hobbs, who's been following him around and may be trying to kill him. That's what he says."

"That's a load of shit!" Alex exploded. Lipasky just shot her another sideways look, content. Alex stood up, sending the chair backward with a screech.

"He doesn't believe that. He *can't*. Why the hell would I come here if I were trying to kill him?"

"Now, that," Lipasky said quietly, "is a good question. And I have a good answer."

She waited. He leaned his shoulders against the wall and folded his arms over his chest.

"Either you have a gun in your nice big purse, Alex, or you've got a bullet waiting for me back home. Which is it?"

The laugh began as giggles, bubbling up her throat and exploding like burps. She clapped her hands over her mouth, but that didn't stop it, and her whole body began to shake. She collapsed back into the chair and leaned forward, elbows resting on the sticky table. For a terrible breathless minute she thought she might vomit.

He watched her without a change of expression. He'd probably seen murderers laugh like this, or vomit, or cry. This was the room for it. The giggling stopped as suddenly as it had started, and she felt safe enough to take her hands away from her mouth and rub at her cheeks with trembling fingers. They came away wet, but she wasn't sure if that was tears or sweat. Sweat, she thought; when she moved to lean backward she felt the drag of her blouse across her wet skin.

"Lipasky, he's wrong," she said wearily. "I don't want to hurt you. I think that if you don't help me I'll end up dumped on his doorstep like a dog run over in traffic. The worst part is, I won't even understand why. Please, Lipasky, help me. I'm scared."

It didn't sound convincing to her, and she felt sick again, the fear in her stomach crowding acidly up into her throat. Lipasky came back and sat down across from her. He leaned forward across the table and studied her with flat gray eyes.

"Yeah, I see that. You used to be a stone bitch. Surprising you've gotten so soft," he said. He rested his chin on his hand. "So what do you want me to do about your little problem? I'm in Chicago. You'll be on a plane out of here today. You want me to tell you to get as far away from Gabriel Davies as you can and you'll be all right? It's too late for that."

"Should I be afraid of him?"

Lipasky took a long time to answer, staring at her, through her.

"I don't know," he confessed. "He's strange when he talks about you. I admit, I don't think he really believes you're trying to hurt him—but if you do anything, *anything,* to convince him otherwise, you'd better be afraid. What he's been through in the last four years is enough to send anybody over the edge, and he was already there."

Already there, in the pages of his casebooks, for everybody to see. She closed her eyes and remembered him imitating her movements, watching her with those cold eyes. There were moments—long ones—where he dangled on the other side of the edge, on a fraying rope, just as she did.

"Has he told you anything about the dead woman dumped out of the van?" she asked colorlessly. Lipasky shook his head. "I got an ID from a friend. Her name was Dianne Gardner. From Chicago."

Lipasky started to say something, stopped. He waited.

"That means something, right? Everything comes

173

back here, to the Broward case. She was part of something here."

"She was the mother of Jason Gardner."

Alex remembered the photographs, the two smiling boys, best friends.

"Jason Gardner, Charlie Cassetti. Barnes Broward killed them together."

"Yeah," Lipasky murmured. "But Dianne Gardner didn't have anything to do with Gabriel. She barely talked to him."

"Maybe she was sleeping with him?" Alex guessed, and saw a weary distaste cross Lipasky's face.

"No," he said. He sounded too certain.

"Oh," she said, and followed with smooth skill. "I thought he was bisexual. Maybe he got interested in Dianne Gardner."

She'd hit him, she could smell the blood. Lipasky looked away.

"Not likely," he said. She tapped her fingernails on the table, watching him, waiting. "She wasn't his type."

"Were you his type, detective?"

"Shut the fuck up," Lipasky said sharply, and reached across the table to grab her hands. He nailed her in place with wide gray eyes, seared her with them. "You don't know what the hell you're doing. You're going to kill him *and* yourself."

"Dianne Gardner is dead, and you don't care!" she shouted back in his face. "Harry Verdun is dead. My best friend is dead. Did Davies have a sexual relationship with Harry Verdun, too? Is somebody punishing his lovers?"

Lipasky was pulling hard enough that she felt the squeeze in her shoulder muscles, but she didn't back off, and he didn't let go. He simmered with rage, but she wasn't afraid of him.

He wasn't anything like Gabriel Davies.

"You don't understand anything," he finally hissed, and shoved her backward. "If you believe all that, why are you so scared? *You* fucking him?"

She rubbed her wrists and didn't answer. Lipasky stalked around the room three times before dropping into his chair again, facing her.

"Gabriel Davies has never had a sexual relationship with Dianne Gardner."

"Or Harry Verdun?"

"Or Harry Verdun."

"Or you?"

"Or me," Lipasky bit off grimly. "You're getting it wrong. Whoever is after him, they're focusing on something imaginary, not something real."

Alex stopped drumming her fingernails.

"Then I *am* in danger."

Lipasky didn't say anything. She sat back in her chair and let her head drop against the cool metal. The detective's eyes were far away, unfocused, looking at something years away.

"Rachel," he murmured, and stood up. Alex stood up with him.

"Rachel Davies? His ex-wife? Do you know where she is?"

That brought him up short, not puzzled but angry. "He told you about Rachel."

"And about Jeremy. You bet. I think he's afraid to even try to find out if they're all right, because it might lead the killer to them. Do you know where they are?"

"Yes," Lipasky began, and stopped. Thoughts sped by in his eyes. "I've made it my business to know, but Gabriel doesn't know where they live. I don't think he really wanted to know. Rachel—"

"What?" she asked. He hardly seemed to see her.

"He calls me every day. He tells me where he is, where he lives, what he's thinking. He doesn't talk to anybody else." Lipasky rubbed his face. "He's been getting these letters—for years. At first they came to me, to be forwarded. Later they went directly to his addresses, wherever he was."

"What was in them?" She leaned forward, put her elbows on the table. "Do you have a sample?"

"If I did, I sure as hell wouldn't show it to you," he said. "It's just somebody obsessing on the Broward case. Press clippings. Bullshit."

"Bullshit that might drive him right over the edge."

Lipasky didn't argue that. He looked thoughtful.

"He doesn't give out his address to anybody but you?" she asked doubtfully. "No forwarding address cards at the post office? Nothing like that?"

"Nobody but me," Lipasky said definitely.

"Do you tell anybody what he tells you?" she asked. He shook his head. "Then you couldn't be responsible for the letters, for any of this."

He met her eyes, and she was shocked at the bitterness there, the anger.

"Yes, I am. He called me with his new addresses. Somebody tapped my goddamn phone."

* * *

Lipasky dialed the number and put it on speaker. Around them, other detectives took statements, spoke into their telephones, yelled questions across the room. Nobody paid any attention.

The line clicked and began to ring. And ring. And ring. Lipasky let it ring ten times, then quietly hung up. He looked up at Alex and shook his head.

"He's not home."

"Or dead," she said softly, and his eyes sparked impatiently, hating her for saying the obvious. "The only way to know is to get me back there."

"No," he snapped. "You're already being followed. He talked about you to me, and if they didn't have a line on you before, they've got one now. You go back and start poking around, and I'll be identifying you on a slab."

"Then what do we do?" she asked. She had to go back. She'd left four thousand plus dollars hidden in the bottom of her flour canister.

"Stall. You stay with me tonight, I talk to him tomorrow morning. If he doesn't call, we'll know what's going on. If he does, I can get him out of there after I clean my phones." Lipasky had lost the pinched, sick look she'd seen in the interrogation room; he looked full-bodied again, swollen with rage. She remembered the feeling she'd had after Davies had forced his way into her apartment. Violation.

Lipasky dealt with his the same way she did. Angrily.

"You married, detective?" she asked. He glanced up, gray eyes wary.

"No."

"Great." She grinned when he looked even warier. "No wives to explain things to. Don't worry, Lipasky. I'm a clean houseguest."

"You're not my guest."

"Prisoner?"

He didn't bother to give her a reply, just sat her down in his chair and stalked off in the direction of what she supposed was a captain's office. The blinds were drawn. If there was shouting, she couldn't hear it over the noise of the room.

A short young man in a wrinkled jacket stopped and put a cup of coffee on the blotter next to her elbow. She nodded her thanks and took a sip, then discreetly spat it back out into the cup. Day-old and burned to a crisp.

"It ain't for you, lady, it's for Lipasky," the man said. She smiled and put it back down.

"I'll be glad to give it to him," she said, sincerely.

Lipasky came back like a whirlwind, scattering people out of his way with singleminded determination. She handed him the coffee. He drained it in one mouth-singeing gulp.

"Let's get out of here," he muttered, and she just had time to grab for her purse before he took her arm and heaved her out of his chair. He stopped at a blackboard to draw a line through the next three days on the weekly calendar and write three V's on top of it. "Before the captain recovers enough to fire me."

She turned in her visitor's badge at the counter and had to run to keep up with Lipasky, who hadn't slowed down. He kept her at a jogging pace all the way downstairs to the police parking garage. He had a decent-looking car, sky-blue, with all the cushy extras. She sank into the passenger seat with a grateful sigh as he threw the car into reverse and narrowly missed two large Lincolns behind them.

"Why did you lie to me?" she asked him. The tunnel they were driving through was dark, and she couldn't see his expression. "About Davies?"

"I don't know what you're talking about."

"Are you that ashamed of it?"

"Shut up," he said, and they burst out of the dark into the surly Chicago twilight. "You talk too much, Alex. Bad habit for a reporter."

"He told me about you," she lied, and saw his face change. Suffering. As if she'd sliced him open. "About the two of you."

His fingers tightened on the steering wheel, loosened, tightened. His eyes were blank.

"Let me tell you something, about me and Gabriel," he said. He sounded tired. "It was after Broward, just before the casebooks were printed. Gabriel knew it was only a matter of time before something happened, and it was eating at him, sucking him dry. He started patterning—going certain places, doing ritualistic things, fantasizing. Driving past playgrounds. Past schools. He was scared.

"Every day, he came to my house and told me about it. Faithfully. It was like confession for him, you know, a way to get rid of the tension without doing the deed. And then one day he stopped coming."

She risked a sideways glance at him. He looked gray, fading with memory.

"I went to find him. I found him lying on his bathroom floor, all alone. He'd handcuffed himself to one

179

of those steel handhold things beside the tub, just enough slack that he could get to the toilet. I guess he was planning to just lay there and die like some sick animal. When I uncuffed him he just sat there, staring at me. Jesus, he scared the shit out of me. So I moved him into my house, and he lived there until Landrum published that goddamn book."

She'd looked too long. Lipasky shot her a glance, and the look in his eyes was full of pain. And hate.

"He tries, Alex. God, I've never seen anybody hang on like that. I wanted to check him into a hospital, but they wouldn't take him, he hadn't done anything and they were full up with assholes who had. He's all alone. I'm the only one he's ever had who trusted him—me, and you." The gray eyes, wide open now, studied her. "Don't fuck him up, Alex. Don't make it all for nothing.

She turned her face back to the passing Chicago streets. She couldn't promise that. She needed Gabriel Davies to pull herself back from the edge, and if he went over, well, that was life. She needed the story.

And now she needed Lipasky's story, too.

Chapter Nineteen
Davies

An excerpt from the diary of Gabriel Davies. Found in the personal effects of Haley Landrum, deceased. Unpublished.

August 17, 1988

I went to the playgrounds today, watched the children playing.

I'll need some way to dispose of the remains. Must not make the mistakes other have made.

Broward used lawn and leaf bags, dumped them casually wherever he felt was appropriate. Of course, he was lucky.

Maybe boxes, lined with plastic. I should call for prices.

Maybe instead I should go out and buy a gun and blow my brains out.

Mall. So many children, clinging to their mothers' hands, their fathers' legs, giggling with friends, run-

ning ahead, falling behind, so easy, so easy. My eyes hurt with the pleasure.

No control. None.

Anthony isn't home, and his answering machine can't order me home, can't save me.

She comes wandering out of the toy store for her appointment with me, lost. Six years old, if that. A pretty little Hispanic child. I wonder how many times her mother has told her not to talk to strangers.

I tell her lies. She puts her hand in mine, and goes with me, through the mall, past all those unseeing faces, gone, gone away.

I take her outside, into the dark. I can't get to the car, the pressure is blinding, killing me. I lead her to the darkness of an alcove where a generator hums, where the smell of urine is sharp and burning. This is a Bad Place, a Bad Man. Her eyes begin to leak silent tears.

I cry. So close to peace, now, thirty seconds away, I won't have to hurt her much, just a little, and I'll never hear her scream because my hand is over her mouth and her bright black eyes are wide and crying and I feel the vibrations of her screams through my hand and fingers wrapped around her small face—

The girl stops screaming against my hand. She is still crying, quiet tears that feel warm sliding down my skin.

I have not hurt her.

Have I?

Her arm is bruised and hangs at an odd angle. I run away, leaving her there alone in the dark, hide like a frightened animal in the safe womb of my car.

The next thing I remember I am at a traffic light,

182

almost home. Have I imagined this? Or have I done something—something terrible? How can I possibly know?

I do not dare tell Anthony.

The handcuffs he gave me sit in their usual place on the corner of my desk. They feel smooth and cold, the chain between the cuffs slippery. There is a place in the bathroom where I can fasten myself down, out of range of the mirrors that tell me my eyes are blue and my face changed. And there I will wait, until God decides my fate for me.

Chapter Twenty-Two

Lipasky was a good cook, something Alex was not. She relaxed at the bar with a hefty glass of diet soda while he sliced garlic with smooth, meticulous strokes of his knife. It was like watching a Japanese chef, she thought, only not so expensive. The sounds of chopping soothed her and made her eyes drift closed.

He was making an Italian dish, and the air smelled of warming spaghetti sauce. She thought of DelVecchio's, Gabriel Davies. Her eyes flew open again, and she watched Lipasky bend over the counter to count the number of garlic cloves he'd chopped.

"Tell me something, why is it every man in the Western world only knows two recipes, spaghetti and barbecue?" she asked. He grunted. "Shouldn't we be doing something about Davies?"

Lipasky swept the chopped garlic into a pot and stirred it. He turned to look at her as he tasted the sauce.

"Look, I can always take you to the Motel 6 down

the street, only they don't serve dinner. Don't pretend you're the only person worried about Gabriel, okay? I've called and he's not here. There's nobody else to call, and my wiretap guys won't be here until the morning. Just relax and pretend you're not a reporter, or I'll have to shoot you."

Alex smiled and rested her chin on her hand.

"Promises, promises," she purred, and watched his back stiffen. He didn't like being flirted with, which was why she continued to do it. Lipasky was an interesting guy. Her digs about his love affair with Davies had been half guesswork, half shock value, but she'd certainly hit a big mother lode of a vein. He wasn't gay, didn't fit the bill.

The fact that he was willing to let her *think* he was gay to spare an explanation of his relationship with Gabriel Davies—that was something.

"If I'm not a reporter, is this a first date?" she asked. He grunted again, but she thought she detected a little humor in it. "I've never had a cop cook for me. Well, Markovsky microwaved a burrito for me once, but that probably doesn't count."

Lipasky got out two shining light-blue plates and scanned a row of glasses. He picked a pair of light-blue mist-thin goblets to go with them. She noticed he overlooked the everyday plastic tumblers and cheap Wal-Mart special glasses to get to them, and raised her eyebrows. Next thing, she'd get the good silver, too.

She went around the bar and took the plates and goblets from him. He let her have them without comment; she set the table and examined the bottle of red wine sitting open on the sideboard. A good brand, for your average bachelor dinner alone. Unless he'd been planning on having guests, or had dragged it out of storage for her.

Damn, it *was* beginning to feel like a first date.

She shouldn't be drinking the wine, she knew. She poured a glass and took a deep breath of the rich, thick fragrance. It smelled good enough to make the diet soda taste stale and flat.

She carried it into the kitchen and handed it to Lipasky, who was busy chopping an onion. He took it without comment and sipped, very lightly.

"I can't drink wine, you know," she said. He looked over at her, eyebrows raised. "I'm an alcoholic."

"Oh," he said, and frowned. "Sorry. I forgot."

"Jesus, don't apologize, you're the first person I've met in five years who forgot. So, how long have you lived here?"

"Sixteen years. Bought the place with my wife, then she died in 1983." Lipasky tasted his spaghetti sauce again, all concentration. He added a splash of wine, gave her a guilty look. She shrugged. "It's a big place, I shouldn't have kept it, but I just never had the time to move. Kept thinking, someday I'd sell all this stuff and get an apartment, but I never have. You married, Hobbs?"

"No," she said, and thought about Rolly. "Had an affair with a married man. That was as close as I've been."

Lipasky didn't seem too shocked by the revelation, or too curious. He seemed more intent on the alchemical mixture of his spaghetti sauce than on her story.

186

"He leave you?" Lipasky asked quietly. She blinked and looked away. "You kick him out?"

"He's dead." The words sounded harsh and final, and he looked straight at her. He didn't have his professional face on now, and she could see why Gabriel Davies called him, depended on him. It made her a little ashamed to even be talking about Rolly. "Car accident a couple of days ago. Might have been murder."

Lipasky didn't say he was sorry, which she thought was strange. He just went back to stirring his sauce and sipping his wine.

"I didn't really love him," she said. "Not really." He just nodded.

"He used me, you know? And he wouldn't even tell his wife, wouldn't even pretend he was going to leave her for me. She hired this detective to take pictures, I guess it's only a matter of time before the cops find out about that. Do you think they'll believe I had a motive for killing them?"

Lipasky shrugged. He added some basil and covered the saucepan with a shiny copper lid. Alex watched him and felt absurdly sad, as if somebody had just told her about Rolly, as if the past few days hadn't even happened.

"No," Lipasky said. "No, I don't think so. Call up your friend, Markovsky. Tell him about the pictures. If they thought you were a serious suspect they'd already have taken you in for questioning. You thought Gabriel did it, didn't you?"

She could only nod. There were tears clogging her throat now; she had to tilt her head back to keep them from slipping out of her eyes and down her cheeks. Stupid, stupid. Always stupid.

"Gabriel doesn't love you, Alex, any more than you loved your married man. He isn't jealous." Lipasky turned and leaned against the cabinet, facing her. He took another drink of wine without looking away from her. "Do you feel guilty about his death?"

"Rolly's?" She shook her head. A tear broke free and started down her cheek; she intercepted it with a quick, trembling hand. "No. I didn't do it, I couldn't help it. It wasn't my fault."

"Sometimes that doesn't matter, Alex. I didn't put my wife in a convenience store at ten o'clock at night. I didn't go in there and put a gun to her head and blow her brains out. Sometimes that just doesn't matter," he said softly, and put the glass aside on the counter. She was transfixed, waiting. The silence grew and became uncomfortable, and he turned back to the stove to get away from it. "You want garlic bread?"

"Sure."

There was a picture of his wife in a silver frame on the sideboard, a pleasantly pretty woman, nothing special even when flattered by good lighting and makeup. There were no pictures of children.

She wondered how many nights he'd thought about it, all alone. Death didn't seem to make any sense, except to people like Gabriel Davies. She wondered how Lipasky grieved, wondered if he did it silently, wondered if he kept her things in boxes and took them out to touch, the way she'd smelled the pillowcase with Rolly's scent on it.

The sauce was popping and sputtering behind her.

She heard Lipasky lift the pan off the burner and set it aside on a hot pad. Another gas jet fired up for the spaghetti, another pot clattered.

She poured herself a glass of wine. Dipped her tongue into it, gently. The taste climbed into her mouth and seeped into her throat, rough, sweet, cool. The mouthful she took was better, and she let it simmer and hiss in her mouth for a few seconds before she swallowed. Heat traced an incision down to her stomach.

"Thought you were an alcoholic," Lipasky said from behind her. She let out a breath, tasted the wine again on her tongue.

"This is what alcoholics do."

By the time the spaghetti was properly limp, so was she. It had gone to her head faster than she'd believed possible. Her fingers felt clumsy and numb as she picked up the bottle to refill her glass.

Lipasky took it away from her and set it on the sideboard. She started to reach for it again, and he kept his hand on it.

"Who are you, my mother?" she asked, and the words tasted like good wine. His gray eyes turned sleepy again, distant.

"Your jailor. No more for you."

"You sure have forgotten how to show a lady a good time, Lipasky." He set her spaghetti down in front of her, a steaming mess of pale noodles and red sauce. The smell was wonderful, but she felt her stomach knot up. He set his own plate down and put the wine bottle on his end of the table, out of her reach. His goblet still had several inches left in it, she noticed.

He didn't make casual dinner conversation, just ate. She forced herself to take a bite and couldn't stop herself from cleaning the plate; she'd had next to nothing to eat for days, and not even the lure of wine could convince her she wasn't hungry. Lipasky watched her, now and then, with a slight smile on his face.

The garlic bread was thick and crunchy, buttery on her tongue. The rest of the wine washed it down.

He was a slow eater. She sat and watched him, chin propped on her hand, and wondered if Gabriel Davies had sat here like this, watching. Around Lipasky, Davies would be different. Not so alien. He'd copy Lipasky's casual movements, his sleepy stare. He'd be warmer, not so distant and cold.

She wished she'd known him in 1985, really known him, instead of hounded him for an interview. Five years had sucked the warmth away and left the shell.

"No dessert," Lipasky said, and drained his wine. He'd finished eating while she'd stared, but it hadn't bothered him to be stared at. Well, why would it? He'd known Gabriel Davies.

"Good." Alex sighed and found herself staring, not at Lipasky, but at the wine bottle. "Can I have another glass now?"

"No." Lipasky poured himself another, just to make her nuts. There was enough left for one more glass, just the right size for her. She watched him take a long, savoring sip.

"Shithead," she muttered, and picked up her plate and left the goblet. She was rinsing blood-red sauce

190

from the plate when a hand appeared over her shoulder, holding her glass.

He'd filled it up. She took it and turned, eyebrows raised; there was no special expression on Lipasky's face at all.

"Aiding and abetting?" she asked, and swirled the glass under her chin. The wine shivered and circled like a bloody whirlpool.

"I'm sorry your friend died," Lipasky said. She thought about it for a long minute as she lifted the glass and licked at a drop lingering on the rim. Her tongue funneled the taste up in a glorious burst.

"He wasn't my friend," she said, and took a deep gulp of wine. It burned. "He was an unfeeling, selfish bastard who used me just like he used his wife. In all the time I knew him he never told me one thing you'd tell a friend, never wanted to hear anything about me or my life. I have better friends."

She meant it when she said it, and then remembered. Rob was dead.

Who was left?

"What if he isn't dead? What if he's standing on your doorstep when you get home? You going to throw him out?"

"No," she answered truthfully, and watched his mouth curl up in triumph. "I'm too much of a masochist."

He looked at her for what seemed to be a long time, and she felt her face grow hot, her fingers tingle. His gray eyes were cool and steady and made her feel exposed, but she didn't want to look away. He wasn't like Davies.

Not at all.

"You don't know what a masochist is," he finally said, and moved her out of the way to rinse his own plate.

A shadow, standing over her. Alex yelped and lunged sideways, clawed at unfamiliar sheets and smooth blankets. A hand restrained her, held her down.

"Easy," the voice said, and she blinked away sleep and saw his face resolve in the spill of hallway light. Lipasky. He looked rough and exhausted. "Get up."

"Why?" she mumbled, but fought her way free of the tangled sheets and slid to the edge of the bed. The t-shirt he'd found for her was large enough, but pretty thin; the white fabric turned shadowy over her crotch and nipples, and she resisted the urge to pull the sheet back over her. Lipasky stepped aside and went to the window. "What time is it?"

"Three-fifteen."

"You've got to be kidding."

"Put your clothes on. I'm taking you to a hotel."

He was standing straight, and under the loose shirt his shoulders were tense.

"Did you talk to Davies?" she asked, and hunted on a chair next to the bed. Bra. Pants. Her shirt and, modestly last, day-old panties. Lipasky didn't look willing to leave the room, so she stepped into them and pulled them hastily over her hips. "What's wrong?"

"Nothing. Just hurry up."

She hesitated over the t-shirt, but his back was turned and he was steadfastly ignoring her. She

192

yanked it over her head and fumbled for her bra. It was inside out. When she tried to straighten it, the catches snagged in the lace. She cursed in frustration and peered at the tangle in the dim light.

"Goddamn it, hurry up!" Lipasky hissed. She yanked and heard nylon threads snap. The bra straps raked harshly over her arms, and she hooked it closed just as he swung around from the window. She couldn't see his face.

"Is somebody out there?" she whispered. She struggled into her blouse, hating the day-old smell, hating the painful jumps her heart was taking. "Jesus, she didn't come here, did she? Is she outside?"

Lipasky left the window and went out to the hall. His shadow paced, impatient. She pulled her pants up and jammed her feet into her shoes and stood there for a second, heart hammering, scanning the room for something she might leave behind. Just her stomach.

"Lipasky?" she asked, and looked down the hall. He was at the end of it, staring into a darkened bedroom. He snapped his head around toward her, scanned her quickly, looked away again. "What the hell is going on?"

He went down the stairs. She followed, one hand sweaty on the banister. He was digging car keys out of his coat pocket when she arrived at the bottom.

The phone rang. Lipasky froze, watching it, and let the keys drop on the table beside him. He picked up the receiver and held it to his ear.

"Lipasky." His tone was clipped and unwelcoming. When the answer came on the other end, he closed his eyes, sank down in a chair. In spite of the relief in his face, his shoulders stayed tightly locked. "Jesus, where have you been? No, never mind, don't tell me."

A short silence. Lipasky rubbed his face and looked up at Alex as she came a step closer.

"Yeah," he said. "She's here."

Davies? Alex mouthed. Lipasky didn't confirm or deny, didn't even seem to see her. His gaze wandered away to focus on a far wall.

"No kidding," he said dryly. "No, she's okay. I'm putting her on a plane back home this morning."

That wasn't the plan, Alex started to tell him, but shut her mouth as she remembered his suspicions about phone taps. She pulled out a chair and sat down opposite him, waiting.

"I'm fine. Really. Stay where you are—no, don't tell me where—and call me back at eight. Got it? Be careful."

Lipasky let the receiver drop back in the cradle and looked across at her, face expressionless.

"Is he okay?" she asked. He nodded. "We can't warn him about the phone."

"Not until my guys get here at seven-thirty and check the lines."

"Are you really putting me on a plane this morning?" she asked. He stared over her shoulder and nodded. "Even though I'll probably get killed?"

Lipasky leaned forward, rested his forehead on clenched fists. His voice, when it came, was muffled and weary.

"You can't stay here. You can't."

"Why not?" Oh, but she knew. She knew why he'd come and rousted her out of bed, frantic to get her

194

out of his house. "Because I'm making your uncomfortable?"

Uncomfortable. She hadn't meant to be so delicate. Lipasky laughed. His tense shoulders shook.

"No, you're not making me uncomfortable. You're driving me completely fucking insane."

It took a minute to realize she'd been right, but there was no doubt, once she got a clear look at his face. Her heart stopped its panicked beating and settled on an uneven, hop-skip sort of rhythm.

They stared at each other. His lips twisted in a smile.

"Well," she breathed. He shrugged.

"Forget it, Hobbs. It isn't going to happen."

"Why not?"

"Because I need to think about him, not you." His gray eyes were quiet, gentle, honest. "He needs me a hell of a lot more than I need you."

"Liar," she said, and stood up. "Tell me to go."

"Go."

If he was a liar, he was a damned good one. She reached across and picked up the receiver on the phone. Dialed information. Asked for a cab company.

She dialed six digits before he reached over and hung it up for her. His fingers rested lightly on hers, warm, so warm. She studied his face, the sharp cheekbones, the large eyes, and thought that he'd probably looked brutal next to all the angel-faced teenagers in high school. Sensuously harsh.

He still looked sensuous, but age had softened the edges. She smiled, and watched him struggle not to.

"What?" he asked. Her fingers curled around his, and she saw his pupils blow open. Oh, yes. Sensuous.

"The cheerleaders must have hated you in school."

"Hobbs, you were *never* a cheerleader." He paused, and she could feel his blood beating in his fingertips where they rested on hers. "I liked looking at you in the T-shirt."

She couldn't get up and go to him, and for now it seemed enough to just feel her pulse race and see the look on his face as her fingers slid over his skin.

"What now?" she asked him. Lipasky leaned forward and moved the telephone out of the way between them; he held her outstretched hand in both of his, fingers traveling slowly from palm to the inside of her arm. He had a very light, sensuous touch. She struggled to keep her breathing steady.

"Now, you go back to bed," he said. His voice had dropped lower, a rich thick baritone.

"So you can roust me out of bed again in half an hour? No, thanks. I'd rather stay awake."

"And make me uncomfortable."

"Oh, yes."

He studied her with those large, luminous eyes, and she understood why he kept them half-closed all the time. They were powerful, sinister eyes, glowing with wickedness. His fingers traced down the inside of her arm again, to the soft bend of her elbow, and she shivered.

"Tell me," he whispered. "Tell me why. Do you think it's because Rolly's dead?"

She had to shut her eyes for a second, to blot out the sight of him, to let her thoughts sink into order again.

"No. I think it's because you—you told me more about yourself in a day than anybody else has ever told me." She slid her fingers up inside his loose shirtsleeve, felt warm skin and crisp hair. His eyes seemed to darken as his pupils expanded again, blind with rapture. "If it's because Rolly's dead, that still doesn't change anything, does it?"

He shook his head. She unbuttoned his sleeve and let her hand follow the warm, smooth track of skin to his elbow.

"So, what now?" she asked.

"Tell me," he whispered again. She felt dizzy from the force of it, the permission he offered her. She felt her fingers tighten on his, tried to relax them. They were shaking. "Tell me what you're thinking, Alex."

"I'm thinking how much I'd like to come across this table."

"And?"

"And unbutton your shirt." It was as clear to her as if her fingers were there, working. She closed her eyes and smelled the heat of his skin. His fingers paused briefly on her arm, then continued their slow invasion. "And find out how your skin tastes."

"Where?" His whisper was faint and rough. She didn't open her eyes but she could feel him watching her, those huge pupils devouring her.

"On your neck. On your shoulders. On your stomach." Close, she was getting close, could feel the warmth sliding across the table now, could feel his fingers growing uneven as they traveled.

He was quiet for a while. She opened her eyes. "Is that why you were going to throw me out? Because you were thinking about me sleeping in the next room?"

His fingers slowed and stopped, became warm and then hot against her skin.

"Not quite. I started thinking about other things."

She breathed in and felt the air turn hot in her lungs, like blood.

"Tell me," she whispered.

Chapter Twenty-three

Sleep drifted away gradually, like snow blowing, soft and quiet. Alex lay still and listened to the distant sound of voices buzzing. She was warm and comfortable and oh, so very relaxed, and for a minute she even forgot to wonder where she was, and why.

Voices outside, men's voices, words lost in the distance. She turned over and looked at the other pillow.

Lipasky was awake, watching her. The sheets had slipped down over his long, sleek chest, all the way to his hips. There wasn't much light in the room, but his expression was easy to read.

He smiled.

"My friends from wiretap are downstairs," he said, and leaned forward. His lips brushed hers, and when she moved into it, molded tight. Funny, the kiss felt new again, as if she'd never tasted his mouth before, never felt his tongue touch hers. Alex shuddered and burrowed toward him under the sheets. His skin touched her breasts first, stroked them, burned into them. She hadn't been mistaken about what she saw in the shadows, under the sheet. His erection drew a hot line along her thigh.

He broke the kiss with a sound halfway between a gasp and a sigh.

"Did you go meet them like this?" she asked, and her fingers explored, following the arrow-line of soft graying hair down his stomach, tracing the thickness at the end of the journey. He put his head down on her arm and closed his eyes; his hair was tangled, gray and blond, streaks of light brown. He didn't look tired, even after the long night. He looked like a lion, resting.

"Of course," he murmured. "I can't stay here, Alex. They're waiting for me."

"So am I," she reminded him. He smiled without opening his eyes.

"I know. Don't move. I'll be back."

Because she had to, she let him slide away and reach for the thick bathrobe draped over the end of the bed. She wondered if he'd bothered to clean up her scattered clothes from the living room before he let his friends in. He was discreet, she thought. Careful.

Sure enough, she saw her clothes folded neatly on a chair on the other side of the room. He'd left her panties on top.

"Alex." He'd stopped in the doorway, looking back, one hand on the knob. They exchanged a long serious look. "Are you sorry?"

"No," she answered. "You're not, either."

She saw his lips twitch in that controlled smile as the door clicked shut behind him. She lay back, luxuriating in warmth, in the soft drag of sheets over her hypersensitive skin.

Rolly, she thought suddenly, and felt sick. *Less than a week ago.*

She couldn't deny the hurt inside, the vision of him burning and screaming. But Rolly had been a long, painful game of Russian roulette, and it hadn't just been Rolly, after all. She'd been performing for Susan Eastfield too, posing for ugly little pictures, faking orgasms for them both.

If she was sorry for anything, it was that.

Long minutes, dragging. The voices buzzed and faded. She heard the front door slam.

He didn't come back. She felt something chill her and decided to get up. There weren't any more bathrobes handy, so she pulled on another of his thin white t-shirts. The door didn't make a sound as she opened it, the carpet felt thick and springy under her bare feet. The stairway was dark, but sunrise spilled a garish pink through the downstairs windows, lit up the carpet with blush-colored splashes. Alex paused on the first step to look over, and saw Lipasky sitting alone at the table with the phone at his ear

"No," he said. His voice sounded hollow. "Listen to me. They were here, they found it. Somebody tapped into the line. We don't know how long it's been active, but it looks old."

She went down another step. His head was bowed, his shoulders bent under a heavy weight.

"It's my fault," he said. The voice at the other end buzzed like a trapped insect. "Damn it, it is. I should have guessed something like this earlier, and I didn't.

How the hell else did she know where you were? Where you lived?"

The silence stretched. Lipasky's shoulders straightened.

"She's still here. I kept her here."

Alex felt something slice deep, looking for her heart. She pressed a hand under her breasts to stop the pain.

"Yes, I can do that. Listen, you were right. It's definitely her."

The pain burrowed in, screaming.

"Yes," Lipasky said, very quietly. His voice dropped lower. "Tell me."

Tell me, he'd said, leaning across the table toward her. *Tell me.* The pain finished digging, found what it wanted. Killed it. Alex shut her eyes and watched shadows drift over her lids. Not shadows. Snow, cold and soft and fatal.

Lipasky didn't say anything else. He could have been dead, except for his breathing. She stopped short of wishing he was.

Masochism dictated that she wait, so she did, sinking down on the steps. She rested her forehead on her palms, her elbows on her knees. Below, she heard Lipasky shift positions.

"Be careful," Lipasky whispered. It sounded raw and painful, like abraded skin. "God, be careful. I'll be there soon, Gabriel."

Alex bit the heel of her hand to keep the pain in her throat, away from his ears. Lipasky hung up the phone in a rattle of plastic.

He didn't move. After a while, she stood up and braced herself with one hand on the wall, smooth almond-white paint cool under her fingers. She went back to the bedroom and put her clothes on.

He pushed the door open as she zipped up her pants, and she thought she saw alarm flare on his face before it shut down. He was still wearing the bathrobe, tightly belted.

"Going somewhere?" he asked. There was nothing in his voice, no anger, no accusation. She found her shoes and put them on. "It's Marjorie Cassetti."

It was enough of a non sequitur to make her pause in groping for her purse. He left the doorway and came a couple of steps closer, but not too close. Blocking her way out.

"You shouldn't listen to half of a conversation and jump to conclusions, Hobbs, it's unprofessional. Let's see, I told Davies that you were still here, that I kept you here. Sorry, but I didn't particularly want to give him a play-by-play about that. Then we talked about the woman in the van. That's all."

Alex opened her mouth and felt her questions float away, sour and lost. Lipasky's gray eyes weren't luminous now, or trusting. They reflected her back at herself, and concealed anything he might have felt.

"I don't believe you," she said. He shrugged.

"Believe what you want, Hobbs. We talked about the letters he's been getting. I got a letter, too." He cocked his head at her, raised his eyebrows. "You're not the only one who thinks I've been fucking Gabriel."

He reached into a drawer by the bed and tossed the letter to her. She looked it over—cheap notebook paper, plain block printing, painfully clear.

203

Detective Anthony Lipasky, it said. *Stop or die with your lover Gabriel.*

It wasn't signed. Alex handed it back and saw him glance over it again, no sign of anger on his face. It was just a piece of evidence, that was all.

Jesus, he was calm.

"When did it show up?"

"Yesterday. Before I met you, as a matter of fact. I had a few bad moments wondering if you'd delivered it." He paused, and his gaze roamed over her face, hungry and oddly vulnerable. "But I know you didn't."

"Would have been hypocritical of me to accuse you of being gay and then sleep with you."

"There is that."

"So how much danger are you in?"

"Oh, about as much as you, I guess. Which was one reason I thought you'd be better off at a hotel." He came closer, finally, put his hands on her shoulders. "There was a tap on the phone. I've been telling this bitch everything she needed to know for years, Alex. I've been betraying him all this time."

"Not you," she said, and put her arms around his waist. It seemed such a natural thing to do, and to let her head lean against his chest. "But now you're expendable. She'll know that as soon as she finds out her tap is dead."

"I've booked us a flight out, early afternoon, under the name of Fred and Freida Pollard," he said. She buried her laugh in the thick white fabric of his robe.

"Freida?"

"Don't complain. My fourth-grade teacher's name was Freida. She was beautiful." Under the cover of conversation, his hands slid over her ribs and found the buttons on her shirt. The clasp of her bra. She unzipped her pants and stepped out of them and left it to him to peel the panties down, silky over her thighs, drifting down to the floor.

The tie on his robe was ridiculously easy, a single pull and it was open. His skin tasted of the dawn light flickering over them from between the blinds.

As her mouth traveled down, the taste was hotter, sweeter.

No one had ever said her name the way he whispered it.

Chapter Twenty-Four
Davies

From the diaries of Gabriel Davies, found in Haley Landrum's effects.

Unpublished.

September 14, 1988

There is nowhere to be free of the dream, noplace safe from the sight of red angel wings and the sounds I wish I had never remembered. I sit here again beside Viva's bed. The television is on, preaching to me to wash my sins away in the blood of the lamb. I wonder if Viva understands any of that, or finds it horrifying, as I do.

So many sins. I have bought a candy bar but it tastes like nothing to me, and leaves thick chocolate smears on my fingers. A nurse looks in on me at the door and smiles. She likes me. She has given me her phone number, but I have dropped it somewhere, and I don't remember her name.

She has given me a cup of coffee from the machine. I drink and let it burn the roof of my mouth.

I have remembered more, of course. I remember the boy, staring out a red-spattered window. He pulls down his blinds and gets back in bed.

After a few moments his door opens. Father stands there. Behind him Mother screams and weeps. Her voice is choked and unrecognizable. She cradles something in her arms, some wet red bundle of clothes, and the boy's eyes widen and fix in something like terror.

And Father stares at the boy. Promising.

The police come, take Viva's still-breathing body away. They ask the boy questions, but he is quiet. They leave him alone. The doctor comes and gives him a shot, and the boy sleeps.

In the morning Father washes the blood from the house, and Maxi's body disappears.

Two nights later Father comes to the boy.

And the boy, remembering red angel wings, chokes on his tears and screams.

It is a terrible thing, memory. The television still plays, annoying me, annoying Viva, whose eyes roam randomly to avoid looking at it. I turn it off. In the last flicker of light I see Father's face.

Father is out shopping. He doesn't visit Viva, hasn't since Mother died six years ago. He avoids any mention of her. In fact, he avoids me, as well.

I wonder what he is buying at those stores.

Viva is quiet, always quiet. I kiss her on the scarred forehead and go away, into the dreamworld.

I have been in the shower. The water was cold, though the faucet was turned over to HOT. My skin is wrinkled in on itself, huddling against the cold now, and I wonder how long I have been standing under the spray.

There is a garbage bag in the bathroom, tied shut. I don't remember filling it. I lift it, and it's light. I start to open it but my fingers shake and I can't make myself do it.

I will take the bag out to the dumpster. It will disappear with a hundred other bags like it, gone. I try not to think of what is in it, because I know I don't want to know.

The clothes I wore to visit Viva are gone, even the shoes.

Anthony has called me to tell me my father is dead. He tells me it was quick, and I don't ask how.

I remember a sound, as I hang up the phone.

A thick, wet sound.

It sounds so familiar.

Chapter Twenty-five

Someone was calling her Freida. Alex jerked awake, slammed the back of her head against a cushion placed there for that purpose. Sunlight glared brutally in her eyes.

The airplane atmosphere tasted dry and metallic. Through the soles of her feet she felt a numbing vibration of metal and noise. The sound of air whistling was either the air conditioning or her own imagination.

She looked over at Anthony Lipasky, who had touched her on the arm and called her Freida. He didn't smile.

"Freida, it's dinnertime."

She glanced right and saw the stewardess there, waiting with two things that steamed, a fake smile and a tray. Alex shook cobwebs out of her head and fumbled her built-in table down in time to catch the tray as it descended.

She almost ordered a vodka to kill the taste, changed her mind, and got a Diet Coke instead. The stewardess thumped the minicup down on her tray and wheeled down the aisle. Alex freed her utensils from their condomlike packaging.

"Don't call me Freida, Fred," she said, and yawned. Lipasky's eyebrows quirked. "What is it?"

"Cardboard with gray, limp vegetables, and a roll hard enough to show up on a metal detector. Enjoy." Lipasky, she noticed, had skipped the meal and was using his fold-down table as a workspace. The centerpiece was a cute little computer about the size of a notebook. He hit a button to start it up, and as it chimed happily, dug a pair of glasses out of his coat pocket. "If the food doesn't kill your appetite, I've got some stuff that will."

"Like?" Alex shoved in a defiantly big mouthful of cardboard-textured meat. The gravy tasted like cornstarch.

"Like the Barnes Broward file on disk. Complete with photos. Ready?"

"Sure." She swallowed and took a swig of soda to wash out her mouth. Lipasky swiveled the screen around so that she could see it.

"Okay, here's the first victim, Caroline Pitney. Six years old. This is her school picture." He hit a key. "Here's the after-school."

The bite of food she'd taken balled up in her stomach. Alex cleared her throat and stared at the digitized image, wished he'd picked up a laptop with a black-and-white screen instead of a full-color one.

"Typical Broward dumping, all the limbs severed at flexible joints, a clear plastic bag for disposal. The knot he tied in the top wasn't too distinctive, unfortunately, not a fancy one or anything. The plastic bags are common lawn and leaf bags." A click as he tapped the key again. Another picture, this one obviously an autopsy photo focusing on long pink grooves near the bulbous end of a bone. "These are trial cuts. He was experimenting, finding the right way to dismember the body. These don't appear on later victims."

"She's the one Broward took out in public after he'd chopped off her arm," Alex murmured. "I remember there were semen traces—"

Alex had instinctively lowered her voice, and leaned closer. Lipasky nodded.

"We figured he masturbated over the remains. Found that in all but three victims."

Click. Another picture, this one of a boy. Bryan Dortmund. School photo. After-school photos. Alex snuck a look at Lipasky and saw that his face was pinched in the vise of memory. He hit another key.

"Jesus, I hated this case," he breathed. "This is Regina Montoya. Here's the disposal."

Clear plastic bag, cloudy from within, spotted with mildew. A child's pallid cheek, pressed against the side. A milky eye, staring.

"Jesus," Alex whispered.

"We wasted some time chasing ghosts here. David Pitney had a 1983 convinction on child endangerment —left the kid alone for twelve hours in the house while he went off to score and get high—but he checked out okay, and in the meantime we got number four, Paul Parks. Here's where things go strange. Paul Parks was the first victim to show evidence of antemortem sexual abuse, also the oldest victim, twelve. Also, he's the first to be dumped in a black plastic bag."

The after shot was mercifully nondescriptive, just a lumpy dark bag, half-hidden by a fall of leaves.

"The cuts were clean, but there was no evidence of semen in the wounds. He went for the mouth on this one."

"Don't show me a picture," Alex said faintly. Lipasky hit a key, hit again. The image was just a flash, and more than she wanted to see.

"Okay. At this point we were way, way off base. Parks and Pitney both attended the same church, so we checked out the workers, the pastor, the other members. We came up with a couple of small-time molesters, nothing like what we were looking for. Meanwhile, Gabriel had linked in to the mall."

"The mall? The kids didn't disappear at the mall, did they?" Alex asked.

"Nope. But they all lived pretty close to it, and it was a good bet that they'd all been to the mall, to the movies, something. Davies had a hunch that the killer followed them home from the mall, followed the kids around for a while before taking them. He never took them where he tagged them, and that was what kept throwing us."

"Barnes Broward worked in the mall."

"Yep. And he typically left work about six o'clock, when families would be taking kids home to dinner."

"Davies followed Broward. How did he know he had the right guy?" Alex asked. Lipasky shrugged.

"Don't have a clue, and he can't explain it. Here are the two ten-year-olds who disappeared together, Jason Gardner and Charlie Cassetti. They were best friends, always together. If Broward wanted one, he'd have had to take both."

The after picture, inevitably. Two black plastic bags, stuffed with death.

"If Parks was different, these were off the god-damn map. No semen traces anywhere, for one thing. Very sloppy cuts, angry cuts, not like the others. In these two, unlike with the other boys, he severed their genitals. Lipasky hesitated over the key, pressed it, pressed it again. She was grateful that the closeups were so brief. "It's hard to explain, but the other murders were calm, meticulous. Not these two. Very angry."

"And then Shalanna North," Alex said. Lipasky punched up her school photo, a beautiful little black girl, big brown eyes. "She's still alive."

"Shallow cut on the throat, that's all. And some real bad dreams."

Alex sat back, still staring at the screen. Such big, beautiful eyes. She wondered if they were still like that, or if they were dull and scared of life.

"Why are you showing me this?" she asked. Lipasky smiled and entered a string of commands on the computer. The pictures vanished.

"Because I want you to understand how we came to realize that we might have been wrong."

The stewardess came around to collect her tray, looked murderously at the congealing remains of the uneaten meat patty. She obliged Alex with another Diet Coke.

"You weren't wrong," Alex said slowly. "Davies found Shalanna North with him, ready to be killed. How could you have been wrong?"

"Sorry, I wasn't clear. Sure, Barnes Broward was a killer. I'm saying we're no longer sure that he was the *only* killer. See, I think somebody got lucky. Somebody copycatted and dumped bodies and got away with it, because of Paul Parks. Because Broward altered his own pattern, and we fucked up by thinking that explained the bodies of Gardner and Cassetti," Lipasky said, and took his glasses off. His eyes looked tired and swollen. "Gabriel even fucked up. Hard to believe."

"I don't follow you."

"Okay, let me run this one by you. Marjorie Cassetti had no criminal record, but her next-door neighbor didn't much like the way she treated the kid, Charlie. She was obsessive about him, always touching him, hanging on him. Dianne Gardner, on the other hand, was described as a good mother. And Dianne was not friends with Marjorie Cassetti. In fact, she'd told her son Jason not to go over to the Cassetti house anymore."

"She tell you why?" Alex asked.

"No." Lipasky rubbed at his eyes, but they weariness didn't wipe away. "She didn't really have a reason, just free-floating anxiety."

"Enter Barnes Broward."

"In a manner of speaking. Actually, enter Jason and Charlie, ten years old, playing doctor in the woods in back of Charlie's house. That's what I figure, anyway, from what I heard from a couple of kids from their gym class. Enter Marjorie Cassetti, who as we know had an obsessive fascination with her son. I don't know what kind of button got pushed, but I think Marjorie Cassetti killed those kids and tried to conceal it by disposing of them like Barnes Broward.

And because we were too tired, too fucking sick of it all, we bought it."

Alex opened her mouth, closed it. She watched his face for a second as the anger rippled over it. The beautiful gray eyes were hooded again, secret.

"You've got it," she said. "That's why she called you his lover in the note. Because she's hung up on homosexuals."

"Because her son might have turned out to be one. Because the two of us didn't punish her for what she'd done. Yeah, that's what I figure. And now I figure Dianne Gardner's dead because she expressed doubts about Marjorie—and Harry Verdun is dead because he was homosexual, and a friend of Gabriel's." Lipasky smiled, a thin stretch of lips. "Marjorie used to work for the phone company as a repair tech. No wonder she was able to tap my lines."

"When did you start putting this together?"

"I didn't." Lipasky stared down at his computer. "Gabriel did. He called me about six months ago, out the clear blue, and asked me what I thought about the theory."

Alex sat quietly for a couple of minutes, watching the clouds float by behind him. The plane dipped forward, the vibration changed. They were going down.

There was something about phones she wasn't remembering.

"That's why she waited all this time to kill Gardner. He must have gotten new information from her, recently."

"Yeah. And once she started, she just couldn't stop. It's fun now. She likes it." Lipasky met her eyes and gave her a grim, tired smile.

215

"You're not telling me everything," she said. "Davies said there had been other murders, other bodies dumped near him. That was before Dianne Gardner. What was he talking about?"

Lipasky started to say something, then stopped and concentrated on folding up his computer. She put a hand on his arm, felt his muscles tense up under the rough fabric of his sleeve.

"It isn't related. It wasn't near him, really." Lipasky avoided meeting her eyes. "His father was killed in a mugging. Head beaten in with a lead pipe."

"How close was it?" Alex whispered. He pretended not to hear. "Lipasky! How close?"

"About a mile from his apartment in Chicago. His dad was visiting him from out of town, went shopping, got killed. That's all there was to it."

Alex sank back in the soft cushion of her sat, watched her Diet Coke jitter nervously on her tray table. She closed her fingers around it and steadied it, anchored herself.

"I don't think that's all there is to it," she murmured, and felt Lipasky's body tense next to her.

He didn't think so, either.

Chapter Twenty-six
Davies

From Gabriel Davies' diaries, found in Haley Landrum's effects.

Unpublished.

September 30, 1988

Pieces. Pieces of him everywhere, now. On the floor. In the sink. In the bedroom.

I can't go near them. When I do I see him looking back at me, not gone, no, broken into a thousand pieces, waiting for me to get close enough to grab. I have turned out all the lights except for this one on the desk, and I try not to look toward the bathroom, toward the bedroom, where pieces of him lie.

I cannot get my breath. Maybe I will die.

There are cuts on my hands, thin cuts. I must have rinsed them off because they sting but have stopped bleeding. I wonder how I did that.

Oh, of course. He did it. Defending himself.

Each one of the cuts is another innoculation of his disease. I am a terminal case, now.

Someone is ringing the doorbell, concerned about the noise. I hope they will go away; I don't think I can talk to anyone right now. My voice would be too deep, too much like Barnes'.

My eyes feel lighter. I think they are blue again. They will never be brown again, not after this—too much infection.

I can hear his pieces laughing, in the bathroom, but I don't dare go in. I will only be cut again, and infected again, over and over.

There isn't anyplace I can go to be free now, except here, where there is no mirror to show me the changes. I have photographs. They remind me of how I used to look.

I wonder if anyone would recognize me, now. Anthony might. Or he might recognize Barnes, and have no choice but to kill me.

Perhaps I will invite him over.

Anthony came, was appalled at what I'd done in the bathroom. He stayed in there for an hour, sweeping up the pieces. Broward's face was hiding from him, but I know it would have been there if I'd gone to look. He cleaned him from the bedroom, too.

Anthony has begun to seriously doubt me, I can sense it in the way he hangs back now. But he still listens, and when I need him, he's there.

When he isn't there anymore, I will be alone with the pieces of Barnes, hiding under my skin, waiting for the chance to break out.

God help me.

Chapter Twenty-seven

"Fred. Hey, Fred."

Alex nudged Lipasky with a not-too-gentle elbow. His head bumped against her shoulder and rebounded straight up, eyelids flipping up like windowshades.

"We're landing," she said, unnecessarily. They jerked as wheels skidded and caught on tarmac. "Fun's over."

Lipasky ignored the physical laws of inertia enough to lean over and kiss her, long and slow. The heat trickled down her throat and dripped down someplace below her stomach to take up residence.

"*Now* the fun's over," Lipasky corrected, and clicked his seatbelt off before the aircraft came to a complete and final stop. He, like businessmen all around them, stood up to open up the overhead bin and grab his briefcase. The protests of the stewardesses fell on deaf ears. Alex scooted out of the way as the plane lurched to a halt at the gate and managed to insinuate herself in line ahead of an elderly woman with three large shopping bags. "Freida!"

Alex looked back, saw Lipasky was now separated

from her by four frowning, shuffling passengers. She was propelled along like a lemming. She waved helplessly and let the tide carry her to the jumping-off point of the door.

She was able to press to the side in the narrow walkway and wait. Lipasky came off looking ruffled and leonine, and she linked her arm with his.

"I wouldn't leave without you, Fred," she smiled. Lipasky gently disengaged his arm from hers.

"Fun's over, Hobbs. Don't get in the way."

He couldn't have hit more accurately with a heat-seeking missile. She felt the shredding pain, and that was all the other half of her head needed to jump into the command chair. *See?* it said. *Let 'em fuck you and they'll fuck you forever, Hobbs. How could you be so stupid?*

She felt her face freeze over. She shouldered her purse more squarely and, without a word, walked on ahead. Lipasky didn't offer a word of apology. She heard his heavy footsteps booming behind her like bad news.

Fun's over, she thought. *When he says it's over, of course. Not when I do.*

It was Rolly Eastfield all over again.

As she turned, she saw Lipasky standing behind her, surveying the passing swarms of people. No one was paying the slightest attention to them, as far as Alex could tell, but Lipasky was tense.

"Quarter," she said. He dug one out of his pocket and handed it over. "Tony, it's okay. There's no way she could know we're here."

"I'm not looking for Cassetti," Lipasky said in a tight, quiet voice. "I'm looking for Gabriel."

She stood there, quarter clutched in her fist, and felt her heart sink.

"You called him from the Chicago airport," she whispered. He didn't acknowledge the guess, but she knew it was right. "You told him we were coming here."

"The quicker I'm with him, the faster we can get this thing done, Alex. Use the quarter, call a cab. Go home. Lock the door."

He was cold as a Chicago winter now, solid as a block of ice. He didn't let himself look at her for long, but even then the gray eyes looked through her, cop's eyes. She swallowed hard and felt the cool quarter warming between her fingers.

"You're going to get killed," she said reasonably. He wasn't listening to her anymore. He resumed his scan of the crowd. "Listen to me, goddamn it! You're going to get killed, and I—"

"What?" Lipasky cut her off. His voice was ruthlessly bland. "Hobbs, you don't even know me. Call a friend and go home."

She wanted to scream at him, but that wouldn't have done a damned thing except attract a lot of unnecessary attention. She settled for grabbing his shoulders and pulling on them with all her might. She might have been wrestling a steam engine, for all the difference it made.

Once he'd made the point, though, he bent down. She kissed him one more time, just for fun. His lips weren't as cold as his expression.

"Be careful," she whispered, and let him go. Before she could look at his eyes and know how bitterly wrong she was, she turned back to the phone and fed the quarter in the slot with trembling fingers.

She turned around with the receiver held to her ear as she waited for the number to ring. The phone swallowed her quarter with a meaty grinding sound.

Gabriel Davies sat across the aisle from her, staring. It hit her like a physical surge of electricity, snapping along her spine and out her fingertips with a painful jerk. Adrenaline pounded her heart for her. Davies didn't move, just sat, cross-legged, staring. No smile. No frown. Nothing.

Wheaton Sinclair's answering machine was surly to her. She hung up on it without speaking.

God, he looked dead.

"Lipasky," Alex said, and shot a glance at him. "Tony!"

Lipasky put a hand on her shoulder, gentle in spite of everything he'd said. He never took his eyes off of Davies, as if he were a wild animal likely to charge.

"Go home, Alex," he whispered, and she thought she felt his lips brush her ear. "Be careful."

She nodded, shaky. Lipasky walked past her, heading for Davies. A fat woman waddled across Alex's field of vision; she craned around the yards of spandex and caught a glimpse of Davies' face as Lipasky reached out a hand to him.

She had never seen a look like that on any human face, but she thought it was probably what, in Gabriel Davies, passed for love.

She wished she could see Lipasky's face—and then was glad she couldn't.

"Hey, lady, we gonna go or what?" her cab driver, a very nice Nicaraguan by the way of Emmanuel, asked. She handed him a folded twenty. "Oh. Okay."

He sat back and flipped open a *Fortune* magazine. Alex waited, tense and sick, crouched low in the back. They were out of the cab stand, but pulled over to the side by the exit. If Lipasky and Davies were taking a cab or renting a car, they'd pull out this way. If not, well, she was out a lot of money.

"Hey, we doing some spy thing?" Emmanuel asked. She took a peek out the back window, didn't see anybody that looked familiar. "Nothing dangerous, okay? I don't get into that stuff."

"Okay, okay, just shut up!" she snarled, and he shrugged and went back to the restructuring of IBM. A limousine glided by, all smoke-gray sheen and black tinting. She remembered Harry Verdun's Jaguar, whose tinting was a little more extravagant. "How about some music?"

He obliged. The radio spat out something that sounded like reggae hip-hop electronically synthesized disco, with rap lyrics. She was sorry she'd asked.

A man in a cap passed close by the taxi. She whirled to focus on him, but he was short, too dark, too muscular. Lipasky would be easier to spot. He stood out in a crowd.

"Lady?" Emmanuel said. She hissed in frustration. "What?"

"Lady, we gonna sit here all day?"

Alex shut her eyes in frustration, popped them open again, just as Anthony Lipasky came out of the airport and ducked into a cab. Behind him came Gabriel Davies. She slouched farther down as his eyes raked the area.

"Hey, lady!" Emmanuel had a short attention span. She stayed low as the cab pulled away from the curb and glided by. Davies and Lipasky were deep in conversation.

They didn't even glance her way. Alex sat straight up and flung herself half over Emmanuel's seat. He recoiled in surprise and muttered something that sounded unflattering.

"Don't lose that cab," she snapped, and pointed. Emmanuel jammed so hard on the accelerator that she flew backward and bounced against the worn upholstery. Ahead, the white cab dodged around a van and disappeared.

"Ooops," Emmanuel muttered. They screeched forward, cut in ahead of the van, just in time to see the other cab turn left.

"Don't attract attention," Alex warned him nervously. He gave her an irritated look.

"Do you want to follow or not?"

"Do you want to get paid or not?"

Emmanuel shrugged and eased off the accelerator. Alex relaxed a little and saw the white cab ahead in traffic, going at a smooth, even speed. Emmanuel turned the music up louder, drumming on the steering wheel with the beat.

It occurred to Alex, as her heartbeat stepped back down to normal, that the van they'd gone around was white. Fresh paint job. She twisted to look behind her, but there was no sign of a van in traffic, nothing like the one she remembered.

It was a long road. She kept watching out the back,

and the miles clicked by on the meter in the front seat, sucking off her money like an overdriven Hoover. Emmanuel hummed happily, more cheerful with every passing dollar.

She could only keep her back to the bad news for so long. Alex turned to look at the total on the meter; ahead, the other cab slashed across three lanes of traffic and took a screeching right turn.

Emmanuel sped serenely on, oblivious, in the far lane.

"Hey!" Alex yelled, and pointed inarticulately. The white cab disappeared in the distance. Emmanuel kept humming to his song. "Hey, they turned!"

"I know," he said, and gave her a bright, gap-toothed grin. He picked up his radio and waved it at her. "Same cab company. I call and find out where he's going."

Alex, after a long second of gaping, closed her mouth and shut up.

Emmanuel let the cab glide to a smooth stop at the curb. The meter kept running.

"Well?" he asked. He was more disgustingly cheerful than before; that wasn't surprising, considering the total on the meter. "We wait?"

The street was deserted. No cab, no Davies, no Lipasky. And, luckily, no van.

Alex glanced around with a frown, waiting for inspiration. Nothing came. The meter ticked like a terrorist alarm clock. Four men clustered at the far corner, drinking malt liquor out of oversized bottles.

"Did you find out what the destination was?"

"Here, lady. Right here."

She scanned the buildings. A you-store-it ware-house, with rusty gates sagging open enough to allow anything smaller than a grand piano to be slipped out between them. A liquor store, conveniently close to the men on the far corner. A hardware store, hiding under a thick layer of oily dirt.

A telephone company substation.

A dingy-looking bakery, with a crooked CLOSED sign hanging inside the window. A check-cashing, money-lending place that looked like the most prosperous thing on the block.

Alex's eyes wandered back to the telephone company substation. It was a maintenance substation, not a customer service center. It didn't even have a street entrance, just the logo on the building and a pair of electronic-entry gates to the side.

"The phone lady," Alex murmured, and she remembered the too-curious shine of the phone lady's eyes, the long tied-back blond hair.

The bizarre conversation about husbands and children.

The phone lady was Marjorie Cassetti. She'd been in her home, touched her things, asked her questions.

Alex couldn't take the time to feel sick. She leaned forward and tapped Emmanuel on the shoulder.

"If you wanted to get in there, how would you do it?" she asked him. Emmanuel took a long look at the substation.

"Why would I want to get in there?"

"Say you were looking for somebody."

Emmanuel stared at the fortresslike bulk of the

building, then glanced mistrustfully in the rearview mirror at her. His eyes widened.

"Who you looking for?" he asked. She sighed.

"The two men in the cab, the one we followed here."

"The ones behind us?"

She spun, sinking down as she did so. It didn't conceal her.

Lipasky. Davies. Staring into the cab, right at her.

Alex felt a deep stirring, something that was either cell-deep revulsion or cell-deep attraction, and didn't want to guess which it was. She slowly rolled down the window. Lipasky leaned over and braced himself on the cab frame.

"Hobbs, you're a regular Girl Scout. Move over."

She hesitated, watching him. His gray eyes opened a little, showing her a little glimpse of sincerity.

"You're safer with us," he said quietly. Alex blew out a shaky breath.

"Then I'm completely fucking worried."

"You ought to be," Davies murmured from behind him. She flipped the handle and opened the door, and Lipasky got in next to her. She slid across until the door stopped her on the other side. Davies pressed in after Lipasky.

Emmanuel looked worried. Alex smiled at him, hoped it looked reassuring.

"You know the Alysium Apartments?" she asked. Emmanuel nodded, still checking out Davies.

"No," Davies interrupted. "Too easy for her to pick us up there. Take us to the Continental Hotel on Grand."

Lipasky looked doubtful, but didn't contradict him.

Alex shut her eyes for a minute, glad that she felt Lipasky's warmth next to her but knowing it couldn't last. They were like a pair of hunting wolves, and she was just a big-eared clumsy puppy. Something to be nosed out of the way, gently if possible, harshly if not.

And, sometimes, snapped at until it went away.

Chapter Twenty-eight

The Continental Hotel was a four-star hotel, which surprised Alex no end. She had pictured a seedy, hole-in-the-wall no-tell motel where nobody ever showed ID. But Gabriel Davies' posture altered the minute they crossed the elegant brass-and-glass threshold; he moved more slowly, more gracefully, and instead of the strange, lost man she'd known before, became something elegant and confident. He smiled—a full, charming smile—at the reservations clerk, a model tricked out in a dark blue vest with a silver name tag that said PAULA. She smiled back, as if she'd seen Davies before.

"Messages for 1017?" he asked her. His voice held new undertones—boredom, amusement, a hint of flirtation. Paula checked her computer and shook her head. "Lovely. I'll check back later."

"Certainly, Mr. Grant."

Alex had felt out of place at the Alysium, but the Continental Hotel's magnificence dwarfed anything she'd seen outside of Park Avenue, New York. She fell into step behind Davies and Lipasky, feeling again like the puppy on a leash. A passing bellman gave her a quick, mistrustful look. She supposed even the pickpockets in a place like this were better dressed.

The elevator talked. It soothingly mentioned floor numbers and, in between, sang the praises of the rooftop restaurant and the exercise facilities. Since the three of them were sandwiched in with four other expensive-looking guests, nobody said a word. Alex contented herself with adding up the cost of the other women's wardrobes. Score: them, three thousand dollars, conservatively estimated. Alex, twenty-four.

Everybody else got out by the ninth floor. Alex leaned against her own shoulder, mirrored on the wall, and waited for Lipasky to say something.

"How do you know she doesn't know this place?" Lipasky asked. Davies turned slightly, raised an eyebrow. He looked more self-possessed now than Alex had ever seen—his turf, his rules.

He didn't answer. The elevator door opened onto a rich maroon-carpeted hallway. He led the way to a thick door embossed with brass, and slid a card-key into the slot. The lock clicked open.

The room was meticulously clean and opulent, but there were enough personal touches in it to make Alex think that it wasn't a recently-rented room. She checked the rates posted discreetly on the back of the door and blanched. He paid as much in three days for this room as he did for a month at the Alysium.

"Make yourselves comfortable," Davies said. He went to the bar and poured out a glass of Scotch for Lipasky, who downed it without a word. Davies set

230

out another Scotch for himself and waited for Alex to indicate a preference. *Vodka* was on her tongue, or *bourbon,* but she swallowed it and pointed to an Evian. He handed it to her. Clean, clear, completely tasteless water.

She sucked most of it greedily down in one long gulp.

Lipasky took his drink over to the window and stared out at the skyline around them. He swirled his liquor and took small, meditative sips.

"I'm sorry for the change in plans," Davies said into the silence. "Perhaps you two had things to do. Together."

There was nothing in his voice, but Alex avoided his eyes just the same. Lipasky continued to look out the window.

"Don't be stupid. What's our plan?"

"You mean, other than to wait for her to kill one of us? Alex thinks we should throw ourselves on the mercy of the local police." Davies' voice had taken on a sinister edge of amusement.

"You should have done it a week ago," Lipasky rumbled. Davies cocked his head and shrugged. When Lipasky took a sip of Scotch, so did he. "Too fucking late now. They're probably already looking for you—and Hobbs. Bad move, Alex, running out of town after your friend got smoked. They'll fry you for that one."

"Better them than—her," Alex said, and swallowed more Evian to wash the taste of bile out of her mouth. The phone lady. "She was at my apartment, when all this started. I didn't make the connection until today."

Lipasky whirled toward her, and so did Davies. She took an involuntary step back and nearly knocked over an expensive antique vase languishing in the corner.

"You can identify her," Lipasky said. She shrugged.

"Sure." A thought occurred to her, a nasty one that made her stomach lurch. "She—she came just after Rolly Eastfield left that day. She could have seen him. Do you think she—"

Neither man answered her, which was answer enough. Alex sank down in a velvet wingback chair and rolled her cool glass of Evian across her forehead. It didn't help the pressure in her head.

"Jesus."

The silence stretched long and thick. Lipasky sipped Scotch. So did Davies. Alex felt alone and forgotten; Davies' eyes never left Lipasky, drinking him in, devouring him. She set her glass aside and escaped into the bathroom, where discreet indirect lighting made her look less haggard then she was. She slopped cold water over her face and looked at her reflection, the tired bloodshot eyes, the tight lines around her mouth. The gray in her hair.

"Stupid bitch," she murmured. There was a telephone in the bathroom. She sat down on the toilet and picked up the receiver; the dial tone sounded soothing and homey, the same in her own humble apartment as here in this overpriced whorehouse. She read the instructions and dialed for an outside line.

"*National Light.*" She felt a rush of gladness for the sound of Wheaton Sinclair's growl, didn't even mind that she'd probably been fired and would remain so. She clutched the phone tighter in an unconscious effort to muffle it. She turned on the bath water to cover up her voice for any listeners.

"Wheaton, it's Hobbs. I'm in bad trouble, don't say anything, just listen. I need a gun. I know you keep one in the office. Just bring it down here for me. I'll be your buddy for life, promise."

There wasn't the explosion she'd expected. In fact, the silence was long and strange. He hadn't forgotten her, surely.

"Yeah. Go on. Where would I meet you?"

She'd had a long couple of days, but her brain was still clicking. Wheaton sounded totally different.

"Somebody's there with you," she guessed.

"Uh-huh."

"Cops?"

"Yep."

"Shit. They're looking for me because of Rangel's murder?"

"Sure thing. How much you want for this?"

"Continental Hotel, Wheat. Room 1017. For God's sake, lose the cops before you come, okay? Or send somebody else. I can't explain, but you'll have to trust me. I'm gonna make you a rich asshole," she said, and heard a dry chuckle on the other end.

"Well, lady, it sounds promising, but I'm not sure that's exactly what we're looking for in the *National Light*. We're a classy publication, you know. Maybe you should call the *Weekly World News*."

"God bless you," Alex whispered, and hung up. She shut the bath water off and watched the remaining backwash swirl down the gleaming brass drain.

A bath sounded like a damned fine idea, suddenly. She locked the door and turned the taps on HOT. Her clothes made an untidy, tired pile on the expensive floor.

"Alex."

"Go away," she yelled through the door. The knob rattled.

"Alex, we have to talk."

"Men. How come it's always when *you* want to talk?"

There was a scratch at the door.

"Better put a towel on," Lipasky warned. She snatched for the thick white robe hanging on a hook, compliments of the Continental. She had just enough time to belt it closed before the door swung open and Lipasky walked in. He cocked an eyebrow at her.

"Hell of a time for a bath."

"I thought you two wanted to be alone," she snapped back, and Lipasky's eyes flared briefly, not angry, just amused.

"Jealous?" he asked. She glared at him. "We're going out to do some cruising. You stay here, order room service, whatever you want. And don't open the door. To anybody."

Well, except to Wheaton, who was today's version of the cavalry. She shrugged and dipped her fingers in the bath water to test it.

"Listen," he said, very quietly. "Don't go back to your apartment. If Cassetti knows you, she'll know where you live. Don't make yourself a target. I'll be back soon, and I'll take you someplace safer."

"I want to go home," she said, and realized that she no longer knew where home was. Was home a slick-looking little apartment at the Alysium? Or was it in Anthony Lipasky's house?

"Soon," he promised. "She's crazy, not smart. We'll find her."

He closed the bathroom door behind him. Alex took the fluffy white robe off and slipped into the tub, into a blessed quiet minute of rest. And wondered why he didn't think Marjorie Cassetti was smart, considering she'd fooled him and Gabriel Davies pretty thoroughly for more than five years.

She nodded off in the tub; when she woke up the water was cool, and she had the beautiful skin complexion of a day-old drowning victim. She hauled herself wearily out and put the robe back on. It hung heavy around her, like velvet, and she opened the door and peeked out. The room was dark. It smelled of men, booze, and cigarettes.

A nice smell, sometimes. Both Lipasky and Davies were gone. She stretched out on one of the king-sized beds and flipped on the console TV; Gilligan and the professor were still having trouble figuring out how to build a boat, even though they'd managed to build everything else. Soap operas wrestled with incest, rape, murder, and extramarital affairs. Tabloid talk shows discussed the serious problems of women who stole their daughters' boyfriends, or the social merits of tattooing as an art form.

She wondered where the hell they'd gone. The

robe's warmth and the general vacuousness of television lulled her back to sleep.

She hit the floor with both feet, ready to run, not sure what had shaken her out of her coma.

A knock. At least the Continental Hotel had their security peepholes set at a decent eye level.

Wheaton Sinclair. Thank God.

"Al—" She grabbed his arm and propelled him inside before her name could wiggle off his tongue; he glared at her and straightened his sleeve as she closed the door, then took a good look around the room. "Nice digs. Ben Hughes putting you up?"

"Very funny. Did you bring it?"

"Of course I brought it. You think you can't trust me?"

"The cops didn't follow you?"

"Nah, they left. That cop Markovsky's pretty pissed at you, you know." Wheaton felt around in his pocket and pulled out a folded handkerchief. He unfolded it to show her a blue steel snub-nosed .38. She took it and tested the weight.

"I don't know. It looks like something out of *Casablanca*. You couldn't have gotten a bigger one, maybe an automatic?"

"Automatics jam, Hobbs. You want your basic reliability, this is it. It'll knock him down and sit on him." Wheaton eyed the way she held the pistol. "Uh, you do know how to shoot, don't you?"

"I'll wing it," she answered grimly. "Nobody's showed up to work on the phones lately, have they?"

"The phones?" Wheaton stared uncomprehendingly, then brightened. "Yeah. We had a problem with line three, and they sent somebody out."

"Wasn't a woman, was it?"

"Yeah, I think so. What? What did I do?"

She just shook her head and sighed. The revolver felt like a lead ball in her hand, no comfort there. She was as likely to shoot herself in the foot as to hurt anybody she aimed at, but still—

"Have the phone company come out and check it for bugs," she said. Wheaton's eyes widened. He fumbled in his pocket for his breather and took a long gasping hit off of it.

"Bugs? Listening devices? Christ, Hobbs, who are you working for, the C.I. fucking A.? Now I got *bugs?*"

"Just shut up and do it. And *don't* let them send a blond woman out to do it. Ask for a man."

"Isn't that politically incorrect?" Wheaton wheezed. "Okay. Okay, I'll do it, but you *owe* me, understand? Big. Whatever this is, I get the story. First."

"Absolutely." Alex flipped the cylinder out of the .38 and checked the rounds, then flipped it back in again. She had no idea of what she was looking for, but in all the detective movies it seemed to be the thing to do. "Better get out of here, Wheat. Could be real dangerous around here."

Wheaton's eyes lit up.

"You promise I got the exclusive?"

"Honey, if I survive this, I'll publish the whole thing in the *National Light,* scout's honor. Now get out of here, and don't forget about the phone company."

Wheaton gabbled his thanks all the way to the

door, and she could hear him still mumbling as he walked away.

The .38 stayed cold and hard in her hand. She put it in the pocket of her robe and stretched out on the bed again, waiting.

Chapter Twenty-nine
Davies

An excerpt from Gabriel Davies' private diaries, found in his apartment.

Unpublished.

August 2, 1993.

I saw Rachel and Jeremy today, from a distance. She took him to the lake, and he sailed a remote-controlled boat. He was wearing blue jeans and a gray sweater, and Rachel wore a full skirt, an unwise choice in the high wind. I caught a glimpse of her thighs as it swirled up, and as she grabbed it and held it down she looked around to see who'd noticed. Her gaze skipped over me without any recognition.

I should not watch them. It's dangerous. I will not do it again.

I keep her address memorized, and I keep Jeremy's picture in my wallet. It looks so lonely there, next to those empty plastic pages. I had to give someone my address on the telephone today, and I gave them hers instead.

It frightens me when I do that. It means, I suppose, that I still think of them.

I wonder what she would say if I called. Would she say she'd missed me? Would I just hear a click as she hung up? Would she scream?

Does it matter at all? They're still part of me, will always be. As I was a part of Father, and Viva, and all of the horror of that house.

I will not allow myself to hurt Jeremy. Ever.

Sometimes, when I imagine what it would be like with a child, I see his face. The fantasy makes me feel sick and weak, but at least it is a fantasy, and still under my control. Harmless.

I am watching a television special about Jeffrey Dahmer and his crimes. It sounds as if they're talking about me instead of some flesh-eating monster: I recognize the look in his eyes, because I see it in my own when I forget and glance in a mirror. Barnes had that stare. Dahmer has it. I have it.

Dahmer lasted years after his first murder, drowning himself with alcohol and fantasies and, at the last, religion. I have lasted so long, and I am so tired of the fight. So very tired.

Perhaps I shall write him a letter. Anonymously.

Chapter Thirty

Alex woke in the gray light of morning, still wrapped in the white fleece robe, still weighed down with the .38 in her pocket.

Lipasky and Davies were no-shows. She shuffled into the bathroom, winced at the bright light, and tried to drag the complimentary hotel comb through her tangled hair. Her mouth felt fuzzy and slick with bacteria, and the Continental Hotel hadn't provided a complimentary toothbrush. She made do with rubbing toothpaste on her teeth and swishing a little complimentary mouthwash around.

Coffee. She needed coffee.

As she straightened up, she felt a muscle flutter deep around her pelvis, stretching like a rubber band. Not painful, just—uncomfortable. Her lower abdomen had taken on a dull ache, as if she'd received a punch there.

"Shit," she murmured, and opened her robe. A bright bead of red trailed lazily down the inside of her thigh. "Wouldn't you know?"

The hotel fell down on the job. No complimentary

feminine products. She made a pad out of toilet paper and jammed it in her panties—now there was another problem, a dire need for underwear. And, she realized as she sniffed her shirt cautiously, a complete new wardrobe.

She could, she figured, send all her clothes with room service to the hotel laundry, and she could probably get some tampons the same way. But the idea of cowering in this luxurious little prison cell made her crazy, and besides, she had *work* to do.

She yanked open another drawer in the bathroom, just for fun. No feminine products.

But there was, pushed all the way to the back, a girl's bright pink barrette with purple flowers on it. Alex picked it up and turned it over and over in her fingers. *A previous guest had left it,* she told herself. *The maids would have found it.*

The plastic felt cool in her fingers, gradually warming to blood temperature.

It was Gabriel's. Had he found it on the ground, or had it been in the hair of a little girl?

Alex realized that her hands were shaking, and let the barrette drop back into the drawer. She pulled open other drawers. Under the neat squared piles of Gabriel's underwear she found a small pair of horn-rimmed glasses. Too small to fit on an adult face.

Alex's breath didn't seem to want to come out of her lungs. She felt dizzy, on the verge of blackout.

She shoved the glasses back under the shorts, slammed the drawer, and grabbed her shirt and pants from the bed. She dressed with frantic haste, mismatching buttons, undoing them, trying again. She jammed her feet into tennis shoes so forcefully that she felt a blister on her heel break open.

She paused in the doorway, gasping for breath. If she left, there was no getting back in. No key for her.

The gun. Jesus. She darted to the fallen white drift of robe and yanked the .38 out of the pocket. Noplace to hide it on her person; she jammed it into her overcrowded purse and hoped it wouldn't fall out when she opened it again.

The sound of the door clicking shut behind her brought a sweet feeling of escape. She forced herself to walk normally down the plush carpeted hall, to the elevators.

One of them rang before she reached it. She felt a cold surge of knowledge that it would be Lipasky and Davies, and she'd be trapped again.

The ice and soft-drink vending machines were discreetly hidden in a little alcove. She jammed herself into the corner next to a warmly humming Pepsi machine and waited while the elevator doors rumbled open and footsteps marched past her hiding place.

She peeked around the corner. It was a tall man with a blond woman, both in business suits and carrying attache cases. She breathed a sigh of relief and, remembering her dry throat, jammed a ridiculous four quarters into the Pepsi machine's gaping slot.

She didn't even taste the first three long gulps, but the sweetness lingered in her mouth as she pushed the DOWN button and heard the elevator respond somewhere floors away.

No sign of Lipasky and Davies. She got more disapproving looks from the lobby staff as she passed the desk, but no one stopped her. She pushed open the heavy glass door onto dazzling morning, and smelled rain in the wind.

She had just enough money left to take the cab that waited out front.

The Alysium was, she knew, the most dangerous place for her to go, but there were three overriding reasons to go there: clean clothes, tampons, and four thousand dollars stashed in plastic at the bottom of her flour canister. She paid off the cab at the curb and keyed in her entry code; the gates glided aside for her, and she half-jogged, half-ran through the pool area and up a flight of stairs to her apartment.

No sign of anyone watching. She fumbled open the locks and got safely inside, locked in, alone. She rested her head briefly on the cool metal door, set the half-drunk Pepsi on the counter, then walked back to the bedroom, unbuttoning her shirt as she went.

There were only two tampons left after all that. Alex muttered a curse and kicked the empty box across the room. It missed the trash can. She wished she'd bought the completely flushable applicator kind, now that she knew cops would be going through her trash. Oh, well. She wrapped the plastic in toilet paper and put it far down in the trash, under old magazines and junk mail. The other one went in her purse, next to the gun.

The money was still there. She dusted flour off the plastic and unwrapped the bills; she emptied out her purse on the counter, and put the gun aside for the moment as she sorted through the detritus: an old electric bill, already paid; scraps of paper with phone numbers she didn't recognize; a couple of computer disks, unlabeled. A dog-eared paperback, pushed way down in the bottom. She left it there, put the gun on top of it, then piled some cash and her ID in. Nothing else. She scanned the apartment, feeling a stab of loneliness, but there wasn't anything else she could carry with her. Her pictures would have to stay. Her files. Her notebooks.

One of the two computer disks would be her Davies story. She grabbed both and shoved them in her purse, somewhere among the rubber-banded twenties.

As she reached for the door, someone knocked. She backed up a step, watching the metal gently vibrate. If she looked through the peephole, they'd know she was home. She pressed her ear to the door and listened.

The knock came again, almost deafening her. She mouthed a curse and waited.

"Nothing," Markovsky rumbled on the other side. "Go get the manager."

Shit, he had a warrant. She glanced wildly around the place. No other exits, except the balcony, which overlooked the pool and, consequently, the office. She eased over to the vertical blinds and looked outside. Markovsky's female Doberman walked out onto the concrete, circled the pool, and disappeared into the office. Alex unlocked the screen door and eased it open. It squealed.

No time for subtlety. She eased out, shoved it closed, slung her purse around her neck. Her menstrual cramps didn't like the exertion of climbing over the rail, and her fingers didn't enjoy the strain of lowering her down to arm's length for a safe, non-bone-breaking drop.

She kicked a little as she dropped, and landed in a crouch inside the ground floor apartment's patio. Just in time. Markovsky's assistant—what was her name? Shonberg?—reappeared with a dyspeptic-looking Lisa in tow. Lisa had a bundle of keys in her hand.

Alex turned her back to them and puttered around a little boxed arrangement of potted plants. If anybody was home in the ground floor apartment to wonder what she was doing on their patio, they had the good sense not to open the door and ask; she waited until Shonberg and Lisa had passed, then vaulted over the rail and jogged around the pool, into the shadows by the laundry room. Perfect.

Except for the vertical blinds on the second floor, still swinging where she'd disturbed them. Alex bit her lip and headed for the gate.

One minor problem. She couldn't trip it from this side. It reacted to a car's weight.

She'd have to climb it. The idea did not appeal to her cramping lower body, or her strained shoulder muscles.

A car pulled into the driveway on the other side, and the driver punched in an access code. The gates rumbled.

Alex hit the street at a flat-out run, ignoring the driver's amazed look, and took her inventory while moving. Nothing much in running distance for hiding, except for more apartments and a convenience store on the corner. No, wait. Grocery store. Three blocks away.

The regular thump of her feet soothed the panic in

her heart a little, and she began to breathe again, deep, clean lungfuls of air. Two blocks. She risked a glance back, didn't see any cars coming after her. She attained the grocery store parking lot.

She lingered in the coolness of the produce section, squeezing melons, poking tomatoes. She picked out an orange, found the deli, and had them make her a sandwich. She picked up a cold Pepsi from the refrigerated case.

I left the Pepsi on the counter, she remembered. A cold Pepsi, sweat beading on its sides.

No way they'd miss that clue, even if the vertical blinds stopped swinging in time.

The sandwich tasted like corned beef ambrosia, melting in her mouth and giving her the strength, if not of ten, at least of ten of what she'd been before. The orange was tart and juicy and sensuously pulpy. She ate sitting in the little restaurant area by the door, and scanned the parking lot outside for cruising cop cars.

She still wasn't clear what to do after she'd finished, but at least she had clean underwear, and a tampon, and four thousand dollars.

That was worth the risks.

She needed to talk to Lipasky, privately, without Davies around. To tell him about the barrette, the glasses. Her fears. *Not that he'll believe me,* she thought, and took a long, meditative bite of an orange slice. The juice coated her fingers, sticky and warm like blood. *I have to make him believe me.*

Of course, she could be wrong. It could be something completely innocent. It could be bad housekeeping (at a four-star hotel?). Just because Davies was collecting children's things didn't mean—

She didn't want to think of what it might mean. She crumpled her trash together and dumped it, hefted the weight of her purse. The gun made her paranoid, the money even more so. She couldn't carry all of it with her, not unless she wanted to be the target of every mugger with a halfway decent grasp of body language.

Friends. She must have friends, she couldn't have gotten to be thirty without—

The sad, deflating truth of it was that she had no friends, not anymore. Rob Rangel had been the nearest thing—she forced the picture out of her mind, with an effort that made her hands shake. Her stomach started to turn the food in it over and over, a lunch lottery that she couldn't help but lose. Her sister, then. No, too far, too easy to guess. She'd already pushed Wheaton for every favor she could call in.

The terrifying truth was that Gabriel Davies might be the nearest thing to an old friend she had left.

The grocery store was full of strangers, scurrying like hungry ants. She clutched her purse closer and walked out into the sunshine, alone, hanging all alone again.

She hadn't warmed up before her three-block jog. Her calf muscles hummed with tension, and her back felt on fire, and the purse hung on her shoulder like a brick in a briefcase. She shifted it slightly and let it start a new groove on her shoulder, but it crept back to rub right along her bra strap, an old and definite fault line. The afternoon was getting warm, and heat whispered up through her shoes and fanned her face

248

in the humid air. Bus stop, she thought as she walked. Not too far. Just a half mile or so. People ran that distance in under two minutes, didn't they?

However fast *they* might have run it, she wasn't in shape to try it. She wished she'd bought another Pepsi, or, better, something with more kick. A car cruised by, slowly. She eyed it nervously. The man eyed her back.

"Hey!" he yelled. "Need a ride?"

Great, she thought. I've got one potential serial killer on my mind, and now some other one crawls out of the woodwork. She gave him a look that made him step on the gas and speed away, but as he did, she started smiling a little. He was a punk. She had better things to be afraid of, now.

A car turned into a driveway ahead of her, idled there, not quite blocking her path. It wasn't the punk. She couldn't see the driver clearly, but it looked like a woman.

The thought occurred to her that she might be exceptionally paranoid, but she couldn't afford to trust anybody right now except children under twelve and old people confined to their beds. The best she could do was give the car a wide berth. She went all the way to the curb, stepping over thick, glittering shards of bottles, and took two steps downslope to the middle of the driveway.

The sound of the engine changed, growled into reverse. *Shit*, Alex had time to think, and flung herself forward. The car came toward her with blurring speed. She hardly felt the impact as it hit her leg, but at least she was knocked aside and didn't go under the wheel. She landed and rolled, catching more broken glass in her outstretched hands. A knife-edged bottle rim caressed her cheek and drew a hot line across it.

A hand reached down and grabbed her hair. She fought blindly, hands curled into claws, purse dragging like gravity at her left arm.

The woman who had hold of her was dark-haired, not blond. Not the phone lady at all.

But Alex had seen her before.

Mrs. Susan Eastfield didn't look so bad, for being a crispy corpse.

Chapter Thirty-one

Her leg felt like she'd dipped it in acid, but it wasn't broken. A long bloody scrape ran down the side, souvenir of the chrome bumper, but Alex figured she was lucky, all things considered.

So far.

Susan Eastfield drove well, keeping most of her attention on the road while the remainder looked her captive over. Alex didn't have to wonder what Susan thought. It was written all over her face: contempt, anger, hatred.

Alex's purse lay on the floor by her feet. Alex nudged it with her uninjured foot; it still seemed heavy enough to contain the .38. She hadn't seen Susan search it.

The car was littered with the detritus of Susan's life—junk mail tossed carelessly on the back seat, a fast food bag going to seed stuffed under the seat. A few half-chewed children's toys were scattered around, partly concealed by drifts of paper. An empty can rolled around somewhere under Alex's seat, clinked against something made of glass.

"I thought you were dead," Alex murmured. Susan fixed her with a brief black stare.

"No, dear. Rolly was with one of his tarts in the van. Excuse me. One of his *other* tarts. He never even saw me coming." Susan was, startlingly, English, or at least, she'd cultivated a decent upper-class English accent. Her smile was frightening, because it was so natural, so warmly satisfied. "I thought at the time that it was you. Must have been his Wednesday night tramp."

Alex broke the stare and looked out at the road. Her cheek felt numb. She wiped at it, found blood on her fingers. Susan fumbled under some old bills for a box of sun-aged tissues and handed her one. Alex took it and patted at her cheek, hissing a little when the nerves woke up.

"How long did you know?" she asked. Susan went back to watching the road; the question was, apparently, too pedestrian to hold her interest.

"About you? For around two years. About the others, well, they come and go. I really have no idea which one was incinerated with him. Do you know anything about the Indian custom of suttee? A wife shows her devotion by leaping on the pyre with her dead husband. Never had much appeal for me, dear, but I'm sure she didn't mind taking my place." Susan's voice took on a rich crimson shade of malice. "You all *love* him so much."

Alex looked away again, at the people in passing cars. So many people. What a busy, busy world.

"He was a bastard," she heard herself say. "And I was a fool."

"Yes, you were, dear. Did you expect him to leave

me for you? Or was the sex good enough to keep you in his thrall?"

Alex didn't answer. Susan's slap came out of nowhere, hitting her right along the cut in her cheek, bouncing her head off the cold glass of the window.

"Don't ignore me," she said. Alex wiped at her cheek with the rough, dusty tissue again. It came away with spreading red blotches.

"You put up with it for years. Why kill him now? Why kill me?" Alex's voice was extraordinarily calm. How stupid, to be dying for Rolly Eastfield, after everything else. No mysterious gunwoman killing her for befriending Gabriel Davies. No Davies foaming at the mouth like a rabid dog. Not even a goddamn crosstown bus.

She wanted to throw up.

Susan Eastfield had acquired some of Alex's blood during the slap. She wiped her fingers fastidiously on another tissue, never taking her eyes off the road.

"Tell me something. Did he use a condom with you?"

"Yes."

"Always?"

"Yes," Alex answered quietly. "I—I made him. He didn't want to."

"Bought your own, I suppose."

"Yes." All those nights in the grocery store, comparison shopping with young teenage boys who shot her sidelong glances and checked her finger for a wedding ring. Knowing looks from checkout boys. "Yes, I did."

"Lucky you." Susan fumbled in the seat beside her, dug a cigarette out of a half-empty pack. She

253

popped the car's lighter in and tapped her fingers impatiently on the steering wheel until it popped out again. "Some of us were considerably stupider."

Alex already knew. She could feel it coming, knowledge welling up like blood from somewhere around her stomach. Another slice, this one nice and deep and mortal.

"Might want to get tested, dear," Susan said, and grinned. She was thinner than the picture Davies had thrown in her face, harsher. Alex could see the bones beneath the skin on her hands, bird-thin, the hands of a woman twenty years older than Susan's age. "Dear Rolly never bothered, until I got sick. Seemed like the flu, at first. But it just—kept on. And on."

Alex tried to speak, couldn't get the words past the internal bleeding inside. Jesus, oh Jesus.

"The docs say I have at least another year. Probably on life support in the next three months. I've already stopped eating, but they'll keep me alive, through all of it. All the pain. You know what it is, Alex? It's decomposition. Your body just rots around you." Susan lost her grin, looked deathly even in the midafternoon sun's glare.

"You—you tested HIV positive," Alex whispered, just to be sure. Susan laughed. It gave the appearance of being carefree, mad, except for the tight little panic lines around her eyes.

"No, no, of course not. I tested positive for AIDS. Full-blown, full-steam. It's Rolly who was only HIV positive. A carrier, probably. Never even got a sniffle," she said. She took a deep drag on the cigarette, enjoying it to the fullest now that she had nothing to lose. "Karen wasn't so lucky."

"Karen?" Alex knew her voice was faint, timid, and she didn't care. She didn't want to know any more. She was too sick.

"Our baby. Only a year old, unfortunately. She didn't last long, once it hit her. Thank God."

Alex looked down at her hands. They were death-white, gripping the tissue. Her bloodstains looked virulent on them. *Anthony,* she thought suddenly, in a white panic. Oh, no, please. No.

"You were sterilizing him," she said. She felt Susan shift to look at her. "With fire."

"However did you guess? I wanted to be sure he didn't live through the crash, didn't contaminate anybody else. I called the hospital and warned them to take all precautions. I hope they did." Susan took another puff, eyes slitted against the smoke. "If you used a condom, you're probably all right. Get yourself tested, dear. It's the only way to be sure."

She was seized with a racking cough, doubled over the steering wheel. Alex grabbed for her shoulder and steadied her, feeling the sharp bones underneath, the terrible tension. She heard Susan's breath bubble liquidly, and reached out to stabilize the wheel until she felt the spasms ease.

Susan turned right at the next light. Turned into the parking lot of a convenience store. Shut the engine off.

Here it is, Alex thought. *What a stupid, stupid way to die.*

Susan leaned past her and flipped the door latch. A blast of air fanned Alex's face as her door slid open. She stared uncomprehendingly.

"Get out of here," Susan said. Her eyes were all

pupil, black now, huge with pain. "I never want to see you again."

Alex slid out, dragged her heavy purse with her. She shut the door and leaned over, spoke into the open window to the side of Susan's rock-hard face.

"I'm sorry," she said. Susan didn't spare her a glance, just put the car into reverse and drove away. Alex backed up unsteadily to lean against the concrete wall. Her cheek was bleeding again; she fumbled with the tissue to mop it up.

There were other wet patches on the tissue, besides the red ones. Wet, salty ones.

The enormity of it sliced at her again, and she stumbled off to the alley, to throw up her lunch and kneel and weep, not for herself, but for the dying rage in Susan Eastfield's eyes.

Guilty, she thought. Guilty as charged.

What had she done to Anthony?

Chapter Thirty-two
Davies

Except from Gabriel Davies' diaries, found in his apartment.

Unpublished.

October 13, 1993.

Children are so careless with precious things. Pink barrette, purple flowers; I turn it over in my fingers, feel the plastic teeth bite as I grip it hard. A strand of blond hair, caught. Fine, straight hair. She had a fondness for the swings, small body straining against gravity, daring the swing to fly.

The glasses fell out of her pocket and were buried in the sand. I dug them out later. Her mother was a faded, worn woman, threadbare. Her eyes were lackluster, even when she saw me watching.

Barnes, help me. Please help me. I am not ready to feel these things, to think these things. You go too fast. Let me rest a while.

Just a while.

I am not sure if the pink barrette belonged to the

one with the glasses, or—no, no, I will not think. I will not. Go away, Barnes. I have broken all the mirrors now, and you have no way to eat your way into my head.

I called Anthony this morning and told him I went to the playground. I didn't tell him about the barrette, the glasses, the threadbare woman. These things are secret, mine only. Only you know, and understand.

The reporter wants me to trust her. I shall, this time. I will be a willing partner in my own destruction. As Barnes was a willing victim, at the end, and I his executioner.

She does not suspect, I think, that I have picked her for this. She'll think, to the end, that it was her own idea.

I love her for her greed.

Chapter Thirty-Three

As Alex drank her orange juice in the hotel bar, she toted up all of the strikes against her. Gabriel Davies, that was a big one. The mysterious Marjorie Cassetti. Susan Eastfield, who at least didn't seem to be interested in killing her any more. Markovsky, after her for Rob Rangel's murder—and, probably, Rolly Eastfield's as well.

Four thousand dollars and change made a heavy weight in her purse, but it wasn't a lot to finance her flight from justice.

Of course, she could always get up to the roof and scream "Top of the world, Ma!" and fire randomly at the cops when they arrived. That scenario ended with her bullet-ridden corpse tumbling twenty stories, however, and therefore was not especially attractive.

She'd bought a pair of wraparound sunglasses and a shapeless coat at Goodwill, and sat in the shadows in the not-very-well-lit bar, the better to catch a glimpse of people coming through the hotel lobby. No Davies, yet. More important, no

Lipasky. She'd buzzed the room and gotten no answer.

The specter of Susan Eastfield rose up in front of her, those tired, rage-filled eyes, those thin hands. She shivered and took another drink. Tart-sweet and thick enough to gag her. She needed a shot of vodka.

Tomorrow she'd go get a test—

But she needed to leave an address, didn't she? Did she dare do that, now?

What if it was positive? Wasn't it better not to know? Anthony—

Oh, God. She drained the last of the orange juice and put the glass aside. The waiter swept it away and waited for her next request. She scanned the menu. She'd lost her appetite, even after having left her lunch next to the 7-Eleven.

"Water," she said. He went away and left her alone in the sweet dark.

A tall man passed through the lobby, a quick, impatient stride, shoulder-length gray hair wild from the wind. Alex felt her stomach clench and hardly noticed the waiter deliver her order.

She didn't see Davies following. She tossed a hasty five-dollar bill on the table and slipped out. Her tennis shoes made a squeaky sound on the marble floor, and an uneven one, since her leg still hurt like hell. She limped fast enough to meet him at the elevators and put her hand out to touch him.

"Where the hell have you been?" he asked roughly, before he turned. When he focused on her his eyes widened just a flicker, and then they went back to half-closed indifference.

"Having an adventure."

"I told you to stay put."

"Yeah, I know." She watched him in silence as the elevator pinged behind them. His lips twitched in a grimace.

"Well, don't get all sentimental, Hobbs." They stepped into the elevator, and the doors hissed closed. The floor trembled.

They were alone.

It took Alex three heartbeats to make the move into his arms, took another flash of a second for him to grab her and hold her close. He smelled of sweat and old aftershave and she drank it in, gratefully, so glad to have him again, even if it was only for an elevator ride.

"You okay?" his voice rumbled, close to her ear. She felt his lips press her hair.

"Yes." *I don't know,* she thought, but she couldn't have *that* discussion in an elevator, and not with Anthony, not yet. "Just my leg, nothing much, a little bandage and it'll be fine."

"Clumsy." There was fondness in the word that made her clench her eyes against tears, and hold him closer.

The elevator babbled pointlessly at them.

They were silent, but their fingers spoke for them, clinging tight against the pull of gravity. A bell rang, and the elevator had the last word.

They pulled apart, all but their intertwined fingers. Lipasky cleared his throat and dug in his pocket for the card key as the door rumbled open. The hallway was empty, dark, and plush.

"Tony, I have to tell you—"

261

"Wait," he said, and pushed the key into the slot. The lock clicked.

"But it's important—I found—"

She stopped talking as the door opened on its own, and Gabriel Davies' cool, quiet face loomed out of the dark at her. His eyes were slow in adjusting to the light, like an owl's surprised by the sun.

He held the pair of child's glasses in one hand. As her eyes fastened on them, he slid them into the pocket of his coat and stepped backward to allow them entry.

Lipasky turned toward her, but she shook her head, a silent "later" lingering between them. He'd dropped her hand, at the first sight of Davies. Now he turned away from her, followed Davies into the room where a single light glowed over the table in the corner. Lipasky's laptop computer sat under it, suspiciously silent.

Alex knew that Davies had been looking at the Broward pictures, fondling the glasses in his hand. She felt the orange juice slosh unpleasantly in her stomach, and sank down on the farthest corner of the bed as Davies and Lipasky walked over to the table.

"So what do you have?" Lipasky asked. Davies picked up a pad of paper from the table and held it out. "212 North Clarence."

"That's the latest address I could find on her, but she's not there now. You can probably get more out of the GTE personnel office, if she's changed anything with them. If she was driving a van, it isn't listed under her name. There are about ten stolen vans of the same description listed as of today."

"Friends? Anybody she was close to at work?"

"Rosarian Chavez, lives in an apartment at 4219 Dover."

"I'll take that one. Alex." Lipasky's voice brought her upright again, uncertain of whether to come closer or stay close to the door, the better to make a run for it.

"Yeah?"

"While you were out wandering, did you go to your apartment at the Alysium?"

She cleared her throat and nodded. Lipasky's face tightened with exasperation.

"Cops were there," Alex volunteered. "If she had been there, I don't think she'd stick around while they were going through my apartment."

"You're sure you weren't followed."

"I'm sure," she lied. Well, Susan Eastfield didn't count, as far as they were concerned. "Look, aren't you guys overreacting a little? I mean, she's not the Terminator or anything."

Gabriel Davies turned to look at her, eyes wide, face blank. His smile was wholly inappropriate in contrast.

"She has chosen to devote her life to destroying me, punishing me. And herself. Fanatics are *very* dangerous, Miss Hobbs, as you should know. She knows where I lived. She knows where you lived. She knew Anthony's whereabouts intimately enough to slip a letter in his door. She has killed, to my personal knowledge, three people with connections to the Broward case, me, or you. I think we should give her the benefit of the doubt, don't you?"

"Wait a minute," Lipasky broke in, frowning. "We

tipped her off to Gardner with the recent questions. Harry Verdun was murdered in retaliation against you, or because she wanted something from him. The reporter—"

"Rob," Alex said softly.

"Rob, was killed because he got too close to her trail. She's not exactly blasting away at everything in her path. She hasn't made a move on Alex, or even on you, yet. And all I got was a nasty note."

"She'll try to kill us all," Davies said woodenly. Lipasky stared at him, face bunching into a frown.

"How do you know?"

"Because it's what I would do."

"You're a fucking fruitcake, Gabriel," Lipasky smiled. There was no humor in it. Davies looked back at him, unsmiling, and shrugged. "Okay. You think she's waiting for—what?"

"She's been quite careless so far. I don't think she intended to kill Gardner, but things got out of hand for her, and then she thought she'd make a messy example of it. Stupid, careless. She could easily have been caught for that. Then Harry Verdun, which she did with a little more finesse, but still more desperation." Davies paused. "I think she was trying to find something out from Harry. The first few bullets weren't in the head. They were nonfatal."

"What would she need to know? Where you were?"

"She knew that." Davies frowned, rubbed his forehead. "What did Harry know that she didn't?"

The silence stretched. Lipasky shrugged.

"Nothing. She had my phones tapped, probably Alex's, too, by that time." Lipasky flipped pages on the pad, reading scribbled notes. "She was stupid to kill Rangel. She knew you saw her."

"She knew she was safe." Davies' smile was brief, artificial, and bitter. "Who would I tell?"

"Me," Alex said. "You'd tell me. And you did."

She pulled a thick pillow from the pile at the head of the bed, put it in her lap. She wanted to wrap her arms around it but knew better, knew she had to look every bit as hard as the two men standing by the window. Lipasky's face was rough and furrowed, made harsh by approaching sunset. Davies just looked— smooth. She saw the outline of the small glasses in his pocket.

"So what do we do?" she asked bluntly. "Hole up here, or go out and look for her?"

"You hole up here, Hobbs. *We* go out and look for her—and she'll be looking for us, too, so that's convenient. This isn't a goddamn investigation. It's the showdown at the O.K. Corral," Lipasky said, and sat down heavily in a padded chair. "We've just got to shoot first."

Alex thought of the gun lying heavy in her purse.

"Why can't I help?" she asked. Lipasky gave her a weary look.

"Because you can't. This isn't some pissed-off housewife, Hobbs. This is a woman who probably systematically sexually abused her own son, then stabbed him to death when she caught him with another boy, and chopped them both up like a couple of sides of beef. And *then* carried it all off well enough to get it by the two of us. She's smart, she's organized, and above all, she's goddamn gutsy. You wouldn't have a chance in hell of spotting her, or of getting her if you did."

"You don't know the first thing about me!" Alex exploded. She came up off the bed. The pillow slid forgotten to the floor. "What makes you think you have the corner on guts, Tony? A badge? I'm in this thing up to my goddamn eyebrows, and we know she's not going to overlook me because I'm female! I'm *in,* whether you like it or not! And I'm not staying in here like some geisha girl!"

Davies pursed his lips and looked away, out the window. The sun was sinking behind a sawtooth of buildings, washing orange over the sky.

"We cannot afford to watch you, Miss Hobbs. Stay here, or I'll call the police and have you taken into custody."

Blunt and perfect. Alex stared at him, taken aback, and saw Lipasky was surprised, too.

"You want to show the cops the glasses in your pocket?" she asked, very softly.

His eyes didn't blink. He slowly moved them away from the sunset, over the sweep of carpet and bed and pillows, up to her face. Evil eyes, she thought. Evil, blank, empty eyes, and she was afraid again.

"Be careful," he said. That was all. She sat down on the bed, knees trembling, leg burning along the scrape. Davies turned to Lipasky. "I leave it to you. What do we do with her?"

Lipasky leaned back in his chair, as expressionless as Davies. He had to be, Alex sensed. There was some tension between them, something not quite unpleasant but growing that way, the longer she was present.

266

"I'll take care of her, Gabriel. Can you get us a second room?"

It was the first reference, however oblique, to the relationship. Alex watched Davies' face, and saw the implication filter through. It struck in his eyes, spread outward in a ripple of muscle through his face. Subtle, but definite.

"I will need you here," Davies said flatly. Lipasky held his gaze with no sign of uneasiness.

"No."

"You must."

Lipasky's head tilted slightly, but the eyes didn't waver. She could feel the strain, remembered how that pressure felt when Davies had done it to her. Those eyes, boring in like power drills, willing her to give in.

Lipasky didn't blink.

"Gabriel, I'm your friend. But I'm not anything else," he said. It was like a whisper, barely rustling the air. Sunset bathed Davies' face in gold and orange, and his eyes flared like a cat's. He looked feral.

"Because of her?"

"No. Because of me." Lipasky looked away, finally, and his eyes met Alex's. "I can't stay here."

Davies' face, for one brief second, looked ashen, and then it was demonic, a shift of muscle that made Alex's stomach surge up to her throat. This was what he looked like, when—when—

And then it was gone. Locked away again. Quiet.

"Very well," Davies said indifferently, and his eyes skipped quickly to Alex. They burned coldly, fury drowning somewhere under their shine. "You both stay here. No second room. Miss Hobbs, you might as well call room service for some dinner."

"How the hell are we going to pay for this?" Alex asked. Davies turned his back on her. Lipasky raised his eyebrows and shrugged. "Great. Well, order away."

Davies paced around the room, staying well away from where she sat beside the phone as she ordered their food. He moved like a cat, in quick, smooth moves, jerky sometimes, as if he'd half-decided to attack and then decided not to. He finally stalked into the bathroom and closed the door. She heard water running in the bathtub.

"Did I understand that correctly?" she asked Lipasky. He sat down on the bed next to her, took the menu from her.

"What?"

"You know what. Was he asking you to sleep with him?"

"Not—not exactly. Alex—"

"I think I'd better hear this, damn it." She was trembling, cold with her own anxiety. Lipasky put the menu aside and leaned forward to look directly at her.

"We never had sex, Alex. But sometimes he just needs somebody to—to hold him. A warm body."

"A warm male body."

Lipasky held his hand out, pleading no contest.

"It wasn't sexual."

"It was to him. It still is." She bit her lip. Davies was running the shower now, probably standing in the spray in his trance state, gaping. She'd been right about the glasses. The fury in his eyes had been hot

268

enough to scorch. "Damn it, you don't understand him, even after all this. He *loves* you, Tony. As much as he can love anybody, or anything. He thinks it's some contest between him and me, now."

"Well, it isn't."

She almost said, "You're sure," but held it back. No point in muddying the waters any more. He held out a hand to her. His fingers felt warm when her cold ones wrapped around them, and he came over to her and held her for comfort, the way he held Davies.

She tried not to feel the comparison.

He coaxed her gradually back to the bed, held her while her muscles slowly relaxed in his warmth. She told him, haltingly, about Susan Eastfield. And Rolly. And the fear in her heart, the fear Susan had left her instead of a bullet.

He listened in silence, eyes never moving from her face. Wide, gray eyes, beautiful, sensuous eyes, old with pain.

"So you're scared," Lipasky said. She nodded jerkily. "We'll handle it, Alex."

"Yes," she whispered, and gasped back a flood of tears that threatened to break over the barriers she'd placed. "But I guess if Marjorie Cassetti gets us, it won't really matter."

"Everything matters. Especially you."

The shower stopped. They exchanged a knowing look, and Lipasky sat up, moved to the other bed. He stretched out with his hands behind his head. She clung to the warmth of him, already fading from her skin.

Davies took a long time, even after the water had stopped. When he came out, he showed no signs of having been in the shower, except for a slight dampness in his hair. He avoided the two beds and sat down in one of the armchairs by the table. The sunset was gone, fading into a thick lapis twilight. The moon was gibbous on the horizon, chopped unevenly by one of the buildings.

It was, Alex thought, going to be a very long night.

Chapter Thirty-four

The compromise had been arrived at between Lipasky and Davies, without Alex's input. She slept in one bed. Davies slept in the other. Lipasky professed sleeplessness, and sat up in one of the armchairs, staring into the moonlight. She lay awake most of the night watching him, wishing he'd come lie beside her, knowing he felt he couldn't. Somewhere between four and five in the morning she slid into darkness, and didn't wake until she felt something touch her cheek.

She opened her eyes, expecting to see Lipasky. It was still dark, but the clock said 6:30.

Gabriel Davies' face was only inches away, ghost-white, eyes like black holes. She pulled in a breath to scream, and his hand clamped over her mouth. Her eyes darted to the armchair. Lipasky was gone.

"I can't let you destroy him," Davies said. She bucked against his grip, and he pinched her nose shut. Her scream gargled in her throat, drowned, too soft to be heard even across the room. "You must go away, Miss Hobbs. Destroy me, if you like. Publish

271

your sorry little story. Make me the monster of the hour. Have your fifteen minutes of fame at my expense.

"But you *will not* take Anthony Lipasky with you."

She flailed helplessly in the covers, unable to get a grip on him, brain burning from terror and oxygen deprivation. Her fingernails caught him a glancing blow, and she felt skin rip.

He let her go. She rolled away and fell off the bed with a thump, crouched there and gasped in deep, convulsive breaths. He sat down on the edge of the bed and waited.

"You fucking psycho!" she managed. His smile was a suggestion in the shadows.

"Why, you sound surprised. Miss Hobbs, didn't you already know?"

"I'll tell him!" she nearly shrieked. "I'll tell him you tried to kill me!"

"And he'll know that if I tried to kill you, I'd succeed. This was communication, nothing more. And nothing to worry Anthony with, I think. Do we understand each other?" He cocked his head. She knew she must look like a wild animal, crouched in a corner, hair wild over her face. He, by contrast, looked cool and controlled. Fully dressed.

"I understand you," she said, and felt pain in her chest. She was too old for this shit. "I understand that you feel so alone and disconnected that you can't stand to lose what little love you've ever known, even if it isn't really love. Jesus, Gabriel. Is he all you have?"

Davies was quiet for a moment. She sensed no

272

danger from him now, no desire to hurt. He just watched her, and thought.

"He's all you have, too," he said.

She opened her mouth, closed it. After an eternity, he stood up and went back to his own bed, calmly crawled under the covers, and turned his face away. She stayed where she was, shaking.

Finally, cautiously, she crept out and into the bathroom. In the discreet, indirect lighting she found that he hadn't even left a bruise to prove her word.

Probably had lots of practice in not leaving bruises, she thought. She opened the drawer next to the sink and felt in the back.

The pink barrette was gone, vanished, as if she'd dreamed it. She wondered if he'd put it somewhere under his clothes, next to his skin.

With the exception of a necessary new tampon, her freshening-up would have to wait. She did the necessary deed, splashed water on her face, straightened her clothes, and went out the door. When she glanced back in the room, Davies was a silent black lump in his bed, as if he'd never moved.

She found Lipasky downstairs in the coffee shop, drinking his morning caffeine black and thick while he read the morning paper. She sank into the seat across from him, and his eyebrows raised at her expression.

"Why didn't you wake me up?" she demanded. He folded the paper and put it aside.

"Your newspapers suck in this town. All happy-talk stories, and the bad news swept under the carpet. No wonder you don't work for any of these rags."

"God damn you, don't ever leave me like that

again!" she said, and rubbed her eyes to stop the tears from coming. She heard the creak of wood as he leaned forward, felt the warmth of his hand on her cheek.

"I'm sorry. I figured you needed the rest."

She laughed, a bark that didn't have anything to do with humor. "Yeah, sure. Next time, don't be so goddamn chivalrous."

He didn't say anything, but his eyes were cop's eyes, probing, suspicious. She flagged down the waiter and ordered coffee with cream. Déjà vu, she thought, as she and Lipasky sipped. At least when she added things to her coffee Lipasky didn't follow suit.

"You—you told me he called you every morning. Told you what he was doing," Alex said. Lipasky nodded. "Has he told you about—collecting— children's things?"

"Such as?"

"Such as the glasses he was holding. Like the pink barrette I found yesterday in the room."

Lipasky didn't answer. He looked down into the black surface of his coffee and watched his own dim reflection.

"You saw how he reacted when I called him about the glasses."

"I saw." Lipasky's voice was dry, quiet, giving away nothing. Alex leaned forward, crumpling the paper folded between them, grabbing for his hand. His fingers felt warm but inert, the hand of a man but recently dead.

"Did he tell you about them?" she pressed. He looked up, gray eyes veiled and opaque.

"No."

"What else has he not told you?"

He pulled his hand free and reached for his coffee cup. She chewed on her lip and watched him, hoping for some sign of her own fear, her own anger. Nothing.

"Right now, I just want to save his life, Alex. Maybe he just found the glasses. Bought the barrette."

"I found a blond hair in the barrette."

Lipasky just shook his head.

"What if he's—"

"Don't say it. Just—don't. I'm not ignoring it, Alex, I can promise you that. But I can't go in two different directions just now. He's in trouble. I'm going to help him. And God help me, if I have to put him away after that, I will, and so will you. Deal?"

"Deal," Alex said, and he reached for her hand again, curled his fingers over hers. She watched his face intently, fascinated with the lines, the planes, the harshness balanced by the luminous eyes. "And what about us?"

"Us?" Lipasky's voice was carefully neutral. Her heart sank, not that she'd expected anything else. *Just temporary,* some little voice whispered to her. *Like Rolly Eastfield. Like your whole fucking life.*

She withdrew her hand and picked up the breakfast menu. Her fingers looked like they were trembling. She gripped the plastic tighter, tried to interpret the overly French names for things like bacon and eggs. A thick, blunt-fingered hand forced the menu down, and she looked up into his smile.

"We," Lipasky said in that wonderful, low-pitched

voice, "are going to be together, Hobbs. Whatever comes. What the hell did you think?"

She stared, lips parted, unable to speak. His lips curved into a wry, self-critical twitch.

"Sorry that I haven't said it. I love you, Alex."

"You what?"

"I love you." He let go of her menu, leaned back, sipped his coffee. "Try the eggs benedict. They're good."

She started to ask him to repeat it again, decided against it. She just sat and watched him, and the way his eyes devoured her face. This was frightening, as frightening as Gabriel Davies' face looming over her in the dark, as that spiky little ball of virus roaming in Susan Eastfield's blood and now, possibly, in her own. This one quiet moment of trust—

She had been so long alone.

"Okay," she said. It was all she could croak out, but it served the purpose. He nodded, understanding, and she felt a smile ease out over her lips. Unfamiliar, and scared, but willing to risk it.

The waiter came. She ordered eggs benedict.

There was a commotion in the lobby, white-faced uniformed employees, a plainclothes guy in a suit she figured meant he was either a manager or house security. She craned around Lipasky for a better view. Lots of running and scurrying. Someone was on the phone, looking scared.

"Something's wrong," she said. Lipasky turned and sized up the situation at a glance.

"Wait here." He slid out of his chair and collared one of the uniformed women, flashed his Chicago badge. She looked unreasonably relieved. It only took

276

one sentence for him to get the drift of whatever it was that had happened, and then he was moving back to the table. There was no change in his expression, but she could sense the shift somewhere deep inside.

"What's happening?"

"Shots fired. On the tenth fucking floor. No, God damn it, stay here and don't move! I have to go up and take a look. You keep out of sight and keep a waiter in sight at all times. If anybody grabs you, yell like hell and go limp. She won't be able to drag you all the way through the lobby."

"She could put a bullet through my head," Alex protested. He gave her a quick, hot glance.

"Not while I'm around."

But then he was gone, running for the elevators, amazingly agile for someone so tall and gangly. She had never suspected he had a gun under his coat, but it was out and at his side now, a good-sized automatic. She put her purse on her lap and felt the thick shape of the .38 through the plastic.

He disappeared into the elevator. The waiter came back, asked her if she wanted more coffee.

"No," she said, and grabbed his uniformed arm. He looked faintly shocked at the lapse in propriety. "Listen, stay close, okay? There's trouble, and if somebody comes in here for me, I'll need help."

"But Miss—" he protested. She could almost hear the train of thought derailing. *I don't get paid for this.* She reached into her purse and peeled off five hundred dollars, put it not so discreetly on the table between them. His eyes widened.

"Reconsider."

From Alex's point of view, nothing happened. The

277

waiter hovered. The employees behind the reservation desk buzzed and looked frightened. The hotel security didn't reappear.

Neither did Lipasky. Alex sat nervously tapping her blunt fingernails on the silverware, too scared to sip her coffee or taste her eggs. The waiter shot nervous glances at every person who came even close to the entrance to the coffee shop; she wondered what he'd do for five hundred. Even if it was only a helpless yell, that was better than nothing. Distraction.

Her eggs got cold. The police arrived, discreetly, and two uniformed men took elevators up. Two more took the stairs. Alex waited tensely, hands fisted in the tablecloth. The waiter had taken a couple of cautious steps back, to see if she'd notice.

Just a second or two after the police took two elevators up, a down elevator dinged its arrival. And a woman walked out, calm, self-assured. She didn't look like the phone lady anymore; she wore a well-cut blue jacket and jeans, and her makeup was skillful enough that she looked thirty, not forty-something. Her hair was a shade too brassy to be natural, but in this world of liposuction and breast enlargement, who noticed dyed hair? Alex watched her with a kind of terrified fascination. There had to be a gun in her purse, recently fired. Had she killed Davies?

Jesus, had she killed Tony?

Alex rose from her table at the thought, and the woman's eyes skipped over the intervening busy lobby and the shadowy lighting and focused, completely, on her face.

Marjorie Cassetti smiled. There was something wrong with her eyes.

Alex waited, frozen, while she crossed the lobby and pushed out the thick glass doors. The waiter touched her on the shoulder anxiously.

"Lady—"

"Never mind," she told him, and took a deep breath. "Keep the money."

She didn't leave extra for the meal; it was only fair, she figured, that he pick up the tab for her. She went to the long glass window and took a look outside. No sign of Cassetti.

Somebody ran past the window, a tall blur, graying hair. Alex lunged blindly for the door, missed the brass push-bar, and hit her head against the glass. She shoved hard enough to send it flying back on its hinges; it hit with a musical thonging sound and she was out, out and running after Lipasky. Her purse banged painfully against her scabbed-over leg, but she kept going, falling behind. He turned the corner. She gasped for breath and reached for more effort.

Someone hit her from behind. She fell hard and rolled up against a rough brick wall; she blinked back stars and saw Davies glare at her once, venomously, as he ran on. *Was he trying to save my life,* she wondered, *or trying to kill me?*

He'd certainly almost accomplished the last. She sat up, moaning, and probed at the sore spot on her head. No blood, but she had enough bruises forming to make her look like a dalmatian. She caught her breath and levered herself up to a standing position. Took a step.

Her ankle barely held beneath her. She hobbled

279

around the corner and saw, in the distance, Davies turning another corner, running south.

The police would be coming any second. She wondered if she would be better off imitating a drunk in a doorway than trying to limp along in pursuit.

The sounds floated clearly over the noise of traffic, three quick popping sounds. Alex froze. Backfires, that's what they were—just backfires.

She forced her aching body to a shambling run.

No police passed her. No one else seemed to have noticed. She reached the far corner and clung to the rough brick. Please, she thought, don't let it be, don't let it happen—

Down the block, midway, a crowd was forming. Her leg hardly seemed to hurt at all now. She elbowed her way viciously past suited businessmen and expensively dressed executives.

Gabriel Davies' back was to her. He knelt on the pavement, holding someone in his lap. A wisp of graying hair blew back over his leg.

The last step was the hardest, but she made it. Lipasky's face was white, his eyes tightly closed. His shirt was covered with blood.

She knelt beside the two of them, and her eyes met Davies'. No more madness, not now. Just tears, shimmering in his eyes, confused tears of pain. He stroked Lipasky's hair with trembling, blood-smeared fingers. Lipasky's gun lay next to him.

Alex was too numb to cry. She looked down at Lipasky's face, saw his eyes flutter open. The gray looked washed out, pallid, like his face. She reached out and touched his face, and the eyes focused on her. His lips twitched, and he managed a smile.

"Hurts," he whispered huskily. She listened for bubbling in his lungs. Nothing. Surely that was a good sign. "Goddamn bitch. Never saw it coming."

"Be quiet. Somebody's called for an ambulance," Alex said, and looked around the circle of bystanders to see if it was true. A man who looked like an insurance salesman shook his head affirmatively. "Tony—"

His eyes drifted closed again, but his chest continued to rise and fall, and when she held his hand, his fingers tightened on hers. They felt cold, but then they would, from shock.

"Gabriel," Lipasky's voice said. She looked up and saw him staring up into Davies' upside-down face. "My mistake. I shouldn't have—followed so close."

"Quiet."

"No. Get out of here before they arrest your asses. Take Alex. Get her out of here. Promise me."

"No." Davies' flat denial left no room for compromise. "No."

Lipasky sank into silence again, exhausted. Alex heard sirens in the distance, crawling nearer. She looked up at the crowd, searched for the police she knew were coming.

Marjorie Cassetti stood at the outskirts of the crowd, staring over the shoulder of a short college boy. She had her hand down to her side, and Alex glimpsed something black and metallic.

Cassetti smiled. There were tears in her eyes, tears of triumph, of rage.

If she fired here, among so many people, she might kill five or six. Alex didn't dare scream. She just

281

stared back, and slowly shook her head. Cassetti's smile faded. She mouthed a word.

Later.

Then she was gone. Alex pulled in a deep, lung-hurting breath and looked over at Gabriel Davies.

He had not noticed. He was still staring down at Lipasky's linen-pale face, still absorbed in misery.

Alex was grateful for that.

Chapter Thirty-five
Davies

An excerpt from Gabriel Davies' diaries, found in his apartment.

Unpublished.

October 17, 1993

Nobody came to Viva's funeral. I am still in my suit, my tie, my raincoat. It was appropriate that it rained today.

I don't know who I expected. Who had she known, these thirty years? Who had cared, but me? Her nurses found her a nuisance, a drain. Her doctors never thought of her as anything but a vegetable and a source of fees.

Father loved her . . . in his way.

Right up until he killed her.

And I loved Father, didn't I? To the end.

It was quiet, they tell me. She contracted pneumonia, went very quickly. I wonder what they did to save her, or if they just sat outside at their stations and listened to her gasping for breath, dying again, dying horribly.

I listened to her die once.

I have listened to myself die, many times. The sound is the same.

Viva, I failed you. I am sorry.

Don't speak to me anymore.

I have to go now. Anthony's plane is landing, and I will have to meet him.

The reporter is with him. I wish . . .

I don't know what I wish.

Chapter Thirty-six

Another interrogation room. Funny how it looked like the last one, decorated by the same interior-design dropout. The floor was a slightly different color of linoleum. There was no drip stain on the ceiling.

Apart from that, Alex could have been in the same building in Chicago, waiting for Lipasky. She choked on the thought and rested her forehead on her crossed arms. Nap time at school. Cookie time later.

Nobody would tell her how Lipasky was doing, or where Davies was. She might as well have been in Chicago.

She'd asked to see Markovsky, had been roughly informed that he wasn't available. She'd enjoyed a morning in an antiseptic-smelling cell with three hookers, one of whom had been drunk enough to puke on the floor before lunch. Alex had stayed on the top bunk, inert, motionless, feeling her life bleed away into pavement miles away.

Why couldn't they tell her whether he was alive? Just give her that much?

The jail clock had read 2:45 when they'd pulled her out and brought her here, to the standard interrogation room. She'd been alone for what felt like thirty minutes or so.

She needed a tampon. She guessed the guards were used to those kinds of requests, but she wasn't. Maybe she could call—

Who?

They'd offered her one phone call. She'd told them she'd think about it.

The interrogation door creaked open, then closed. Alex straightened up and felt the morning's bruises complain.

Not Markovsky. His partner, what's-her-name, Shonberg. She slid comfortably into the chair opposite Alex, lit up a cigarette. Pushed the pack across to Alex, who shook her head.

"How are you doing?" Shonberg asked, and blew a polite stream of smoke at the ceiling. Her hair was bright gold, twisted back in a ponytail. She had a dusting of freckles, and looked about seventeen, but her eyes were cop eyes, hooded. "Holding up okay?"

"How's Anthony Lipasky?"

Shonberg didn't answer. She took another puff on her cigarette.

"Just tell me, goddamn it, is he alive?"

"Why don't you tell me what happened and we'll be able to find out, okay? You can do that for me. Just tell me what happened since the last time we saw you."

Rolly Eastfield, dead. With his Wednesday date. Susan Eastfield, smoking her unrelished cigarette, staring hollow-eyed at the future.

"I fell in love," Alex murmured. Shonberg blinked against the smoke.

"With Anthony Lipasky? How'd you drag a Chicago cop into this mess, Alex?"

"Doesn't matter now. Nothing matters." Alex felt so filthy, so weary. She propped her chin on her hand and stared at the distance behind Shonberg's head. A one-way mirror. Markovsky was probably behind it, cursing her. "You've got the other guy, I guess."

"Mr. Personality? Yeah. Want to give us his name?"

Did she? Alex stared at the other woman's opaque green eyes.

"Miss Shonberg?"

"Michelle."

"Blow me, Michelle."

Shonberg was unaffected. She took a long, comfortable drag and tilted her head back to stare at the ceiling. Blew a smoke ring.

"I got all day, Alex. And so do you."

"So take vacation. I got nothing to say to you. I want to talk to Markovsky."

"He doesn't want to talk to you. Confidentially, Alex, he's a little upset at you. He trusted you. You fucked him over." Shonberg grinned like a fourteen-year-old schoolgirl. "Reporters. Never know what they'll do next."

Alex looked down at the table. Said nothing.

"Come on, Alex, don't be so stupid. Who's the guy?"

"Is Lipasky going to be all right?"

Silence. Shonberg stubbed out her cigarette in a gray plastic ashtray.

Alex tilted her head back and studied the ceiling tiles through their thin veil of smoke. Shonberg didn't fidget, just waited. The irresistible force, Alex thought, meets the formerly immovable object.

She just felt tired now.

"His name is Gabriel Davies. I was in it for the story," she began, and imagined she heard a recorder whir up, somewhere out of sight.

Shonberg found the whole story unbelievable, or so she said, and Alex had to stop and request a bathroom break. She asked Shonberg who was at least female even if she was a cop, to buy her a tampon. Shonberg did, without expression. And waited outside the stall while Alex did her business.

I feel like the Snake-Man, Alex thought. *Lost in the jungles.*

She could have called Wheaton, decided to pass. He'd gone as far as she could reasonably expect him to go, and when it came to money he was notoriously tight. He'd probably count the three hundred he'd advanced her for the stripper story as going toward bail.

She froze in the act of zipping up her pants. Smiled.

She asked Shonberg if she could make a long-distance call. Shonberg held up one cautioning finger and took her outside to the squad room, to a desk piled with folders and crowned with a framed picture of a little girl, blond, like Shonberg, smiling out of a school picture.

"Your kid?" Alex asked as she dialed the number. Shonberg gave her one antiseptic nod, giving away nothing. "Cute."

Shonberg hadn't given her a yes or no about

whether they'd caught Marjorie Cassetti. Alex figured it was probably a no.

The line rang. Someone picked it up.

"Ben Hughes," Alex said. There was a short pause, then a voice. "Ben, this is Alex Hobbs. Yeah. Yeah, I know. Listen, you know the story I pitched you about? It's coming together, right now. Big time. Only I've hit a snag. Can you stake me some bail money, if I need it?"

Ben Hughes said something unprintable. Alex raised her eyebrows.

"Ben, honey, I'm not that kind of girl. Come on, you know it's a hot story. And nobody else can write it, I'm on the inside. It's legit. You know I wouldn't shaft you."

He probably didn't know anything of the kind, but he grudgingly agreed to wire money if she needed it. She hung up with a warm glow of satisfaction. Shonberg was waiting, a cigarette smoldering again in her fingers.

"Shall we?" Alex asked.

The interrogation room hadn't changed, except that someone had added coffee. It was traditionally bad, but Alex drank it anyway. They'd given her a cheese sandwich in the cell but she hadn't been able to touch a bite, and one of the other prostitutes had been happy to get rid of it for her. Coffee would keep her going a while longer.

Her jeans were starting to feel suspiciously loose.

Alex leaned back in her chair, sipped coffee, and told the whole story. Davies. Marjorie Cassetti. Anthony Lipasky. And then she told it again, pausing for questions as Shonberg picked at weak points.

All in all, it took about three hours. Shonberg had dinner brought in, ate it with her.

"That it?" Alex asked as Shonberg threw away the wrappers. Shonberg nodded. "So are you holding me?"

"If you want to wait here, I'll find out."

Alex grabbed her arm, felt Shonberg tense. The green eyes hardened, fixed on Alex's.

"Is he going to live?" Alex asked again, quietly. Shonberg's icy stare thawed a little.

"Yeah," she said, and pulled free. "Yeah, he'll be all right. Took a nasty one in the chest, but the surgery went okay, they say. The doctors say he'll make a full recovery."

Alex sank down in her chair and put her head down again. This time it had nothing to do with being tired. It had to do with tears.

Markovsky came back, not Shonberg. He looked as tired and drained as Alex felt, and his eyes were red. She figured his had less to do with tears than with forty-eight hours or so without sleep.

Alex stood up to greet him, a sign of respect that he acknowledged with a nod. They stood looking at each other for a while, and then Markovsky shook his head.

"Shonberg says you're limping, got something wrong with your leg. I'm gonna send you to the emergency clinic. You've got no problem with that, do you?"

"I've got no problem with anything, right now. Lipasky's going to be okay, did you hear?" She smiled. Markovsky didn't return it.

"He's a goddamn idiot. And so are you. Don't you

know who this guy is, Hobbs? Don't you know what he's like? Why the *hell* didn't you come to me before people got killed?"

She couldn't tell him the truth, *for the money,* so she said nothing. He sighed in disgust and opened the door behind him.

"Go with Shonberg. She'll take you to the doctor. After that, you're free to go."

Shonberg made a face at him, but didn't argue. She took Alex's elbow and guided her past Markovsky's desk, past the one with the little blond girl's picture. Out into the corridor.

"Are you charging Davies?" Alex asked. Shonberg shrugged. "Ah, come on, Michelle, give me something. Just a little bit."

"Can't give what I don't have. Markovsky's making the call on him, not me." Shonberg tugged Alex to a halt at the front desk, signed some forms, handed Alex her purse. It was a lot lighter. The cash was still intact, but there was no .38 loading down the bottom. Alex bit her tongue and didn't say anything. Shonberg guided her out the door, into the blasting sunshine.

"Hurts?" Shonberg asked neutrally, as Alex limped along. Alex grunted. "Got a place to go?"

No answer to that one. Home wasn't safe. She could find out where Lipasky was being treated, she supposed. That would be home for now.

"Just think, if you get crutches you can beat the shit out of me with them. Here." Shonberg stopped her at a beat-up gray Toyota, unlocked the door, and helped her in. The car was hot and smelled pleasantly of talcum powder and perfume. Shonberg probably did her toilette on the way to work, makeup at stop lights, antiperspirant in traffic jams. Alex let warmth soak into her sore bones and closed her eyes as Shonberg got in and started the engine.

It didn't seem possible to fall asleep, but when she opened her eyes again Shonberg had shut off the engine and they were in the parking lot of a minor emergency clinic. Shonberg gave her a wintry smile and reached past her to pop the passenger door.

"Don't worry, we called in an appointment. They know you're coming." Alex eased up and out of the car. "Hey. Hobbs."

Alex paused and looked back. Shonberg picked up a pair of sunglasses, slid them on. Her smile looked cool and professional.

"Dropped something."

Alex looked down. On the floorboard lay a .38.

She picked it up and put it in her purse without comment.

"Thanks," she murmured. Shonberg had already turned her head, had never seen it. Alex shut the door and watched her pull out.

The door seemed a hundred miles away. She limped toward it. A young Hispanic man with his arm bandaged saw her coming and held the door open for her; she managed a passable imitation of *gracias* and made her way up to the counter.

Thirty-five minutes in an examining room. Two minutes of cleaning and bandaging. The doctor looked bemused at her bruises, but she didn't enlighten him. As he was wrapping her ankle, she brought up the thing that had been digging at her all day.

"Do you do HIV testing?" she asked. His back stiffened only slightly.

"We can."

"Let's do it. Might as well do everything at once."

Forty-eight hours, and she'd know.

She was relieved of one hundred twenty-six dollars in cash, and spotted a bus stop across the way. She limped out again into the sunshine.

There was a van parked in the way. Primer gray. She hesitated, then decided to give it a wider berth. She'd gone about halfway around when the van door slid open.

Marjorie Cassetti's blue eyes looked white in the sun. She had a gun aimed directly at Alex's head.

"Get in," Marjorie said. "Or I'll leave you to cook on the pavement."

Alex had no chance of outrunning her, not even back to the safety of the clinic. Shonberg's car was nowhere in sight. Not even Gabriel Davies was around, however little comfort he'd be.

Alone. All alone.

She got in the van.

Chapter Thirty-seven

Alex lay on her back, feeling plastic crackle under her. *A plastic tarp. Like Gardner had been dumped from.*

Her hands had been taped together behind her, and her ankles. In a weird way, it felt good, like a stretching exercise. She lay as quietly as she could as the van swayed and bumped, and wondered where they were going. She didn't want to think about what would happen when they got there; she knew that part, and thinking about it wasn't going to help, one way or another.

The van smelled like old blood. Maybe that was all in her head. Maybe the old blood had been in Dianne Gardner's head.

"Comfortable?" Marjorie Cassetti called back. Alex, gagged, was not in a position to complain. "Sorry about the precautions. But you do get around, don't you? I could have had you there on the street, but you looked like you needed some time. So I gave you time."

Maybe Shonberg hadn't just dropped her off.

Maybe she'd seen the van, made the connection and pulled off to watch. Maybe, maybe, maybe.

"But your time is up, Alex. You know why, don't you? I need you now."

Lipasky. She couldn't die yet, she hadn't seen him, hadn't told him—

"I need you to be a messenger. Harry Verdun wouldn't, and he died. But I think you will."

A left turn. Alex slid a little on the plastic, tried not to think about dried blood and spatters of brain that she might be sliding over.

Cassetti was quiet for a while, and pulled the van to a stop. The engine sound changed to an idle, then stopped. Little clicks as it cooled.

Metal creaked as Cassetti stood up. She blocked out the light as she came back toward Alex.

Alex shut her eyes. Had the others shut their eyes? Not Rob. He'd taken it with both eyes open. Wide, staring, glazed eyes—

Cassetti's fingers touched her face, icy. Tore away the tape gag. Alex gasped for breath, for life, and opened her eyes as she felt the woman lean closer.

No gun. Not yet. Just that *smile*.

"You're going to be my messenger. You're going to tell Gabriel Davies that I don't forget what he did, what he does."

"What did he do to you?" Reporter to the end. Alex wanted to withdraw the question, as the smile flickered, but there wasn't time, and besides, she wanted to know.

"He let me go. After—he knew. He knew what I'd done, he and his pervert lover, and they let me *go*. To let me do it again, so they could catch me and be the big *heroes*. But I'm not *going* to do it again. I'm going to punish him for trying to *make* me." There was a rhythm to her voice, reinforced by a slight rocking motion as she crouched there next to Alex. "I didn't *want* Charlie to go away. It never would have *happened* if there hadn't been perverts like *them* for him to imitate."

Homosexuals. By God, Lipasky was right.

"I've got one of them. *You're* going to help me get the other one," the woman finished. Her hair was loose around her face again, and she brushed it self-consciously back as she leaned closer. She smiled. "Wouldn't you like that?"

"They didn't let you go," Alex gasped out. Marjorie sat back on her heels, pulled over a ratty-looking plastic bag. She dug in it. "They didn't know what you'd done until later. Jesus, please, don't—"

"Don't what?" She pulled out a picture of her son. "Here. Isn't he pretty?"

Alex nodded. She would have nodded to a picture of a shar-pei.

"I used to want a daughter." Marjorie cocked her head slightly and looked at the picture critically. "But sons can be fun. He was a good son."

A good son, doing what Momma said, and telling his friend about it in whispers, and sometimes clinging to him for comfort—and the good son, the good friend, just bloody, rancid pieces of meat stuffed into garbage bags, left for the dogs and rats. The smell of blood crawled over Alex's face like a moving wave, and she felt her stomach spasm. She swallowed frantically, breathed heavily through her mouth.

Marjorie Cassetti found another picture. She held it up for Alex to see.

"This is what happens when children get dirty," she said. It was poorly developed, too much flash echoing off white skin, pale faces, eyes staring panicked into the camera.

Just two boys. So frightened. Clinging together for comfort.

Another picture, produced with a magician's flourish.

"See?"

Underdeveloped. Too much red. Too much white. Too much blood, blood everywhere, a butcher shop's ten-gallon-drum spilled, was that a hand there on the floor, or—no—

Alex managed to turn her face to the side, press her cheek to the cool plastic, before she vomited. She heard herself crying miserably and forced herself to stop. *She doesn't understand tears,* she thought. No mother who did that could understand tears.

"That," Marjorie said, "was not my fault."

Alex wasn't sure if she referred to the picture, or Alex's vomit. Either way.

"What do you want?" Alex mumbled. The taste of bile in her mouth made her stomach heave again, and she grimly hung on, swallowed it, bit her tongue to help keep her steady. "I can't help you if you kill me."

"The others helped me. He started to panic, you know. I saw it in his eyes." Marjorie made a little it-doesn't-matter gesture and dropped her picture back into the plastic bag. "You're going to carry a little message back with you. I think he'll understand it perfectly."

Vomit was seeping into Alex's hair, clinging to the side of her face. She felt hysterical tears welling up again. *No.* Rob hadn't cried. Hadn't thrown up all over himself.

She had to live, for Tony.

Marjorie searched in her bag, found another photo. She turned it over and, with a felt-tip pen, wrote a short note. She grubbed a large safety pin out of her pocket and pinned the picture facedown to Alex's stained shirt.

"What is it?" Alex asked. Marjorie smiled.

"You don't really need to know."

She reached in the bag again.

Alex, in time-lapse photography, saw the cross-hatched walnut inserts on the grip, then the trigger, then the long, sleek barrel. She thought about her purse, lying an arm's length and a world away.

I will not . . .

Halfway out now, turning toward her . . .

I will not die like this . . .

Marjorie's smile, predatory, delighted . . .

Fuck this shit.

With a strength she didn't know she possessed, Alex brought her feet up from the floor, slammed them into Marjorie's head. The gun spun away into the shadows. Marjorie Cassetti went down, rolling. Alex squirmed up to her knees and went after her, sliding on plastic, out of control. She slammed into her with as much weight as she could throw into it and felt a rib, either hers or Marjorie's, snap in the collision.

She butted her head hard into Marjorie's face. Again. Again. There was blood all over her face, warm, soothing.

A hand slammed into the center of her chest with enough force to throw her back and halfway across the van. She landed on her bound hands, slid, rolled on plastic. Something wet underneath her, vomit or blood or someone else's fluids.

Marjorie's flailing hands banged into something that rang metallically off the van wall. The gun. Alex flung herself backward in an awkward, lurching scuttle and found metal at her back.

Jesus, Jesus, Jesus—

Marjorie found the gun.

Alex's numbed fingers reached the handle. Yanked down hard enough to rip a fingernail away. If it was locked she had no chance, none at all.

It was fucking locked. It didn't budge.

Marjorie lifted the gun.

Alex, screaming, threw herself backward with all her strength.

Not locked, after all. Just stuck.

She went out backward toward the pavement, twisted instinctively around and saw the ground coming. Too late. She hit with a slap and rolled, rolled, kept rolling with all the force she could muster, didn't care if it was a driveway into traffic, an onramp to the freeway, just get away, get away—

She was in the shade. Over her head an oil-spattered undercarriage loomed close enough to brush her nose. She rolled one more time, put herself as far up toward the middle as she could reach.

Marjorie Cassetti's feet came down from the rear

of the van. They were wearing white canvas shoes, spotted with pink that Alex identified as her own vomit.

Well, she'd done everything she could. There wasn't any more fighting left. Alex held to that, grimly, the consolation prize in the survival game.

Second best got buried.

The white shoes stopped, then backed away. A car was approaching fast, tires humming. A siren screamed. The shoes were running, now, to the side of the van, leaping into the opened door. The van's tires whirred on the pavement, backed up, and the van slammed into the car where Alex hid.

It shuddered, but held. Marjorie Cassetti's van sped away, back doors flopping open, plastic tarp sliding out the opening to waft gently out onto the parking lot.

The car braked to a stop, and a pair of women's shoes, sensible flat ones in black, got out to walk around. Alex wormed her way to the side and out into the sunlight, blinked back dizzy spots.

Shonberg stared down at her, stunned. Alex managed a smile.

"C-c-can you give m-me a ride back to the c-clinic?" she said, and started to cry in earnest.

Chapter Thirty-eight

With the blood rinsed off, the damage didn't look so bad.

"Hmm," the doctor said, and pulled at her nose. Alex made a strangled sound of pain, and he grinned. *Sadist,* she thought. "If you're not careful you'll end up looking like a prizefighter."

"Broken?" Alex croaked. He nodded cheerfully and taped it in place.

"Nothing much else wrong, though, a couple of loose teeth, scrapes, bruises. I've seen worse from schoolyard wrestling matches."

"So she's okay?" Detective Shonberg asked doubtfully. She looked the doctor over, evidently not finding much to trust in his big brown eyes and middle-eastern good looks. "You're sure?"

"Well, she's certainly walking wounded, but if you're asking me if she'll live, yes, certainly." He finished taping Alex's nose and gave her a brilliant, perfect-toothed smile. "Try not to be in again today."

Alex grunted and slid off of the examining table in a crinkle of paper. The doctor wrote her out a couple of scrawled prescriptions and handed them to her to give to the nurse. Shonberg watched him balefully as he headed down the hall for another patient.

"So? You saw the van and followed me?" Alex asked, as she paid the cashier again. Among the items left on the pavement when the van sped away had been the vomit-smeared plastic, and her purse, gun still intact.

"Don't know why," Shonberg confessed grimly. "We all figured if she was going to hit somebody—if she even existed—she'd go for Lipasky, not you. Not your lucky day."

"Lucky enough." Alex sighed and draped her purse over her shoulder. "Where to now?"

"Back to the station, I guess. Wait while I make a call."

Shonberg's conference with Markovsky was one-sided and, on her side, humbled. It mostly consisted of "But I—" and "Yes, but how—." Alex knew it was winding down when Shonberg actually managed something like a complete sentence.

"No, sir, I wasn't close enough to—yes, I think—she hasn't said—okay. Okay, I'll wait here. Yeah, I think she'll be able to walk." Shonberg raised her eyebrows at Alex for confirmation.

"Try to stop me," Alex muttered. "Any word on Detective Lipasky?"

Shonberg repeated the question, listened, covered the mouthpiece.

"Out of surgery, doing real well. Doctors say he can have visitors tomorrow."

"Make sure they're all brunette."

Shonberg smiled a little, didn't relay the joke. She

302

listened some more, gave him a terse one-word farewell and stood there, looking at the phone after hanging it up.

"Well?" Alex asked. Shonberg shrugged.

"We wait here for backup. Markovsky's not taking the chance of letting her get a second hit at you—or me, for that matter. Shouldn't take long."

Alex sat back in the uncomfortable waiting-room chair. Across from her, a stone-faced young man cradled a roughly bandaged hand, and a mother with two weary children coughed and sneezed. Nobody looked directly at her, though she must have been quite the topic of conversation, when absent. She picked up a three-month-old *People* magazine and flipped through it, tossed it back on the pile. Shonberg stayed where she was, in the corner next to the phone. Nervous, Alex thought. Just now figuring out what it felt like, to have a killer on your ass.

Shonberg, from the corner, had a pretty good field of fire if it came to that. Alex closed her burning, aching eyes for a second and tried not to think about the rainbow colors she'd be wearing instead of makeup in the morning. Her leg would be stiff, too. And her arms, probably.

She'd come awfully close to being stiff all over.

"Hey," Shonberg said. Alex opened her eyes. Shonberg was still in the corner, scanning what she could see of the parking lot through the clear glass door. She didn't look directly at Alex, any more than the other people in the room did. "That must have been quite a fight you put up, Hobbs. I'm impressed."

"That makes it all worthwhile," Alex sighed, and closed her eyes again.

"How come you got a safety pin on your shirt?" Shonberg asked. Alex's eyes flew open, wide, and she looked down. Just the safety pin, glittering clean in the overhead lights.

No picture.

"She p-pinned something to my shirt. We've got t-to find it." Alex stood up, winced at the creak in her leg. Shonberg took a last glance outside and abandoned her post to come up and put her hand under Alex's arm. "It m-must have blown out of the van with the plastic. Please. It was a picture or something, and she wrote a message on the back."

Shonberg looked indecisive, then stubborn. She shook her head.

"Please! It's important. I think she-she—" Alex couldn't put it into words, gave up trying. She pulled free of Shonberg and limped to the door.

"Hey, where do you think—"

"We have to *try!*" Alex shouted at her, and pushed through. The air on the other side was warm and windy, flavored with exhaust. "Where did you put the plastic?"

"It's in the trunk of my car. Look, Alex, it isn't safe out here. Come back inside. We'll go through everything at the station—"

"No!" Alex interrupted. Poor Shonberg. She couldn't even finish her sentences with a prisoner. "No, there's no time! It was important, and she thinks you've seen it. We have to find it or it may be too late."

"Too late for what?" Shonberg muttered, but made

a placating motion and pushed past Alex to unlock the trunk of her battered old Ford.

The smell of vomit rolled out, green and mildewy. Shonberg's face took on a stony expression of boredom that she probably reserved for things that might otherwise make her throw up.

The plastic was a mess, smeared with vomit and blood. Alex gingerly lifted a corner and looked underneath. No picture. She took a deep breath—through her mouth, which was all she was capable of at the moment anyway, and found a square corner. She looked at Shonberg.

"Grab the other corner."

"No. Hobbs, this is *evidence.*"

"Just shut up and grab the other corner. Look, it's my vomit and it's probably my blood, so just grab it, okay?"

Shonberg, alarmed by the way the wind already whipped at the corner Alex held, grabbed the other side.

Alex lifted it out. There, stuck to the edge by a thin film of vomit, was the picture. She whooped in triumph and grabbed it off. Shonberg grumbled and put the plastic back as carefully as she could.

Alex wiped the photo on her blouse and looked at it.

Just a house. Nothing she recognized. A wood-frame, middle-class house with some nice oak trees in front. There was a rusting old swingset just visible behind it, over the fence.

"Well?" Shonberg demanded over the cackle of plastic. The trunk lid slammed. Alex turned the picture over.

"I know this house," she read aloud.

"Anything else?"

"No. That's it." Alex sighed. "Damn, I figured she'd write something incriminating. A message or something."

"It is a message," Shonberg said, and took the photo by its edge, held it up to look at it critically. "It's just not to either of us. Come on. You've found your picture. Let's get back inside."

Alex hesitated a minute and scanned the street. No van in sight. Was she there, somewhere, watching?

Oh, yes. Somewhere.

Three old issues of *People* later, Markovsky arrived. He'd taken the whole situation a little more seriously, this time, and as he barreled into the waiting room Alex glimpsed two uniformed officers, both imposingly tall, standing beside the entrance outside. Markovsky gave her a quick, unnerving glance and went straight to Shonberg, who'd taken up her place in the corner again.

They had a quiet but intense discussion. Shonberg produced the photograph, safely bagged as evidence.

Markovsky stalked back over to Alex, dropped into a chair beside her. From the way his breath whistled, he'd been smoking a few too many of his thick cigars.

"Know this house?" he barked at her. She gave him a bland look. "Come on, Hobbs, you know we don't have time for this. Do you know this house?"

"Never saw it before," she said truthfully. He tapped it with a stubby finger as if he might tap something loose from her memory. "Honest, I haven't. I don't know why she pinned it on me. Maybe it's a message for Davies."

"I'm getting goddamn tired of maybes. All right, come on, we're taking you back to the station until we can organize some protective custody. You got any requests?"

"Can I call my editor?"

He gave her a tiny, meat-eating grin and shook his head.

"Can I see Lipasky in the hospital?"

"Later. We got other problems right now."

That was true enough. She stood up and found that her leg was stiffer than ever, treacherously determined to lock up on her if she put much weight on it.

It was a shock when Markovsky put his arm around her. She looked up into his face and found him smiling.

"You are the biggest damn fool I've ever met," he said, and Shonberg darted past to swing the door open. She smiled back through bruised lips.

"Yeah," she said softly. "I know."

The mutual admiration society limped outside, to the waiting unmarked car idling at the curb.

Chapter Thirty-nine
Davies

An excerpt from Gabriel Davies' diaries, found in his apartments.
Unpublished.

April 22, 1993

Barnes talked to me today. I have not seen him in some time, because I took all of the mirrors down in the apartment and stored them facedown in the closet. I thought he was locked safely in the dark.

He said that what was happening was my fault, my punishment for blaming him for everything. I had to learn, he said, that life sometimes was not tidy.

I had to admit to him that being untidy had its advantages.

I know where the infection has centered, now. I think it would be safe for me to look in the mirror, because he has drained out of my head, and now he is in my hands. If I look very hard I can see the blue eyes below the skin. I am tempted, sometimes, to try to cut them out, but I know that it would be a mistake.

I can't remember why it would be a mistake. Because I might miss him? And I might never have another chance to exorcise him?

I wish I could have peace. Is it so much to ask?

He tells me he has peace.

There is peace in death.

Even in the death of others.

Chapter Forty

"Hasn't said a word in hours," Markovsky rumbled. He was standing over Alex's shoulder; she sat in a chair in front of the one-way mirror, looking into the interrogation room. Gabriel Davies sat upright, perfectly calm, both hands folded in front of him. His eyes were closed.

He looked completely comfortable.

"He wouldn't," Alex said with certainty. "You're not asking him anything interesting. Have you told him about me?"

"No."

"Has he asked about Lipasky?"

"No." Markovsky evidently found that distasteful. Alex shifted in her chair and wished she could see Davies' eyes, know what he was thinking.

"He thinks he's dead. There doesn't seem to be much left for him to talk about, or anybody to talk to," she murmured. She felt Markovsky looking at her. Wondered if he found her distasteful, too. "He doesn't trust you. He doesn't trust anybody except Lipasky."

"And you."

"No way does he trust me. No way."

He didn't believe her. She hunched her shoulders and wished she'd hopped that plane to Bermuda, like she'd dreamed. No Gabriel Davies. No Marjorie Cassetti.

No Anthony Lipasky, either. She had to think about that one.

"You think he'll talk to you?"

"Not here. He's no dummy, he knows you're watching and recording everything. Look, you got some reason to hold him? Suspicion of something?" Alex tried not to think about the glasses, the barrette. Markovsky leaned against the wall and looked away from her, into the glass. She wondered what he saw when he looked at Davies. *I see somebody shattering into pieces,* she thought. *Lipasky sees a friend, dying from self-inflicted wounds. Davies sees a monster.*

Markovsky, she figured, *sees a problem.*

"He's a material witness," Markovsky rumbled.

"I've told you everything, Markovsky. There's nothing else he knows. You can talk to Lipasky and confirm it all. You don't *need* Davies."

"You're sure hot to get him off. Got an investment in him, Hobbs?"

She opened her mouth to lie, found she couldn't. For the first time in a long time, she couldn't. She met Markovsky's eyes squarely.

"Yeah," she said. "He's a mess. He needs help, not harassment. He won't help you because he *can't* help you, he can't trust you. He's not together enough to trust anybody. If you keep him here, keep picking at him, he's gonna come apart in your hands, like some

311

little rag doll with all the stitches cut. Give him a chance, Markovsky. Please. After everything he's done, don't you think he deserves that much?"

Markovsky stared at her. His eyes were bloodshot, stained yellow from too much smoking and bad food and long hours. His skin looked puffy and swollen, like a long-time alcoholic's.

"No," he finally said, and walked away. She sat looking after him as he dodged between desks, plodded down the hall. His shoulders were stooped and weak.

"Poor bastard," Alex whispered. She turned back to look in the mirror again.

Gabriel Davies wasn't there anymore. Not sitting at the table. Not walking around the room.

He just wasn't there. She blinked her swollen eyes and motioned quickly to Shonberg, who stood a few feet away, at the coffee machine. Shonberg walked over, stirring what looked like oil and black sludge in a coffee cup that read HAVE A NICE DAY.

"What's the problem?" she asked. Alex silently indicated the interrogation room.

Shonberg froze in the act of blowing on her sludge, blinked, blinked again. Her face paled under the freckles.

"That's not possible," she said. "He was just there. Couldn't have been a *minute.*"

Alex didn't have to point out the logical problem in Shonberg's thinking. He *was* gone, after all. Impossible or not.

Shonberg handed her coffee to Alex and lunged around the corner like Batgirl. Alex watched her open the door to the interrogation room, walk inside, look intensely around as if she'd somehow just overlooked her prisoner. *Oops, sorry, didn't see you sitting here in this empty room*—Alex took a stolen sip of coffee and was sorry she had. Crime didn't pay.

A hand touched her shoulder, just brushed it. Tentatively.

She saw his reflection on the glass in front of her. He was wearing a baseball cap and a thick-looking leather jacket, things he'd picked up from another prisoner or from the locker room. *If I don't turn,* she thought, *he won't be there. He'll fade away like a ghost.*

"Lipasky's alive," she said to his reflection, and saw his eyes close, then open again. "He'll be all right."

"And you?" Davies asked. She turned around, made him real. His eyes were blank and impossible to read.

"I'll be all right, too. She didn't get me."

The bastards really *hadn't* told him any of it, she realized as she watched him put things together. Her vomit-stained blouse. Her bruises. Her broken nose.

"I'm sorry," he said, and surprised her again. "I shouldn't have let you into this."

"This is a hell of a place to be discussing it," Alex said, and risked a glance over her shoulder. Shonberg had left the interrogation room, was probably dragging out everybody she could think of to help her search. "Let's get going."

"You should stay here."

"Should, my ass. Go. I'll follow you."

Getting up hurt just as much as she figured it would, but she accomplished it with only a little gasp and a lot of clenched teeth. As she shuffled past Shonberg's desk, she set the coffee down and casually picked up the evidence bag containing the photograph. Shonberg had noted the date and circumstances in neat, spidery writing.

Alex stuffed it inside her shirt and kept walking. Davies had disappeared around the corner, just another guy going off duty, or coming on. She followed him, knowing cops were watching her, checking her VISITOR badge, dismissing her.

If only she could get out before Shonberg got back—

"Hobbs!"

Jesus, Jesus, no time now for thinking, for doing the sensible thing. She had to choose. She could turn around and smile and go back to the desk, and leave Davies all alone out there, targeted, a wounded animal with no hiding places left.

He *had* to see the photograph. He *had* to.

She saw him ahead, pushing through a crowd of uniformed cops on their way in to go off-shift. The door was in sight.

Shonberg yelled her name again. It echoed loudly, but Alex kept walking. She pushed through the crowd and made it to the door, waiting for the sound of running feet, the command to stop. Actually, it would be *halt,* she supposed.

She looked back, that one glance that had turned Lot's wife into a pillar of salt.

Shonberg had her *back* to Alex, shouting out into the room. Nobody had even glanced toward the door.

Alex didn't know whether to be relieved or afraid, but it didn't stop her from pushing the door open and

314

limping out into the parking lot, past police who nodded to her, past rows of parked cars.

Gabriel Davies sat calmly on a bus-stop bench, waiting for her. She sank down next to him with a hiss of pain and stretched her leg out.

"Do you have any suggestions?" he asked her. She reached inside her shirt and pulled out the picture.

He stared at it. There was no change visible in his expression, but she'd learned how to see past that, to read the almost imperceptible flickers in his muscles. Distress, she identified. Pain.

He reached out and took it, turned it over. Read the message.

Without a word, he handed it back.

"Perhaps you should go back inside," he said. The words were mechanical, far from telling her what he really thought. She put the evidence bag in her purse, shoved it under the weight of the gun Shonberg had conveniently forgotten to confiscate.

The bus stop felt exposed. Alex darted nervous glances around, looking for a bus, a van, a running cop. Nothing, yet.

"So?" she asked Davies. He looked at her.

"It's Rachel's house. My ex-wife's."

My son's house, he meant, but was afraid to say. *Jeremy's house.*

Rusting swingset in the back yard. Marjorie Cassetti, pinning the picture to Alex's shirt, smiling.

"How long?" he asked. It sounded conversational.

"She gave it to me about two hours ago."

"Too long." The weight of his stare was enormous; she had trouble breathing under the burden. He continued to talk without expression, every word carefully calculated. "It takes five minutes for someone competent to dismember a child. Or less."

You're talking about your son, Alex wanted to say, and couldn't. *Your own child.*

He knew that very well. She saw it in the sudden trembling in his fingers, in the tension in his shoulders. He had probably visualized it many times, or dreamed of it.

He was so frightened, now. Fragile.

She was all he had left.

"We have to go," she said gently. Davies nodded, blank-eyed. "What if she's waiting for you?"

"Then," he said, "I will cut her up."

The bus wouldn't do, was too slow. Alex led the way down the block to a phone booth, called a cab. Davies mentioned casually that his wallet was still in the police property room.

Alex, laden down with money and weaponry, shrugged. They waited for the cab under a tree, like two picnickers in the park. Like two mugging victims.

She was glad to be in the air-conditioned cab, out of the heat, out of sight. As the cab drove by the police parking lot she saw Michelle Shonberg standing by her car, staring out into the distance.

"Sorry," Alex murmured to her, and rested her head against the cool leatherette upholstery.

The ride took thirty-six minutes. Alex opened her eyes to a tree-shaded street, quiet, genteel but sliding downward into shabbiness at the rate of about a thousand dollars a year off the price of the houses. The cab driver pulled up at the curb, and Alex looked up a hill at the house in the photograph.

Davies was already out of the cab. Alex leaned forward and gave the driver sixty dollars. He didn't want to wait. She clambered awkwardly out and watched his taillights disappear around the corner.

"You can stay here," Davies said tonelessly. She climbed the steps up to the sidewalk and looked uphill. It was a steep climb.

"No, I can't," Alex said. It occurred to her to wonder if she'd meant it as an answer to his question, or to the overwhelming strain of climbing up the walk. If it were the latter, she sounded whiny. She hated that.

She stiffened her aching shoulders and limped grimly up the walk. Davies cut around her and was gone, like the flash of a strobe light. She caught sight of him at the door, trying the knob. In a blink he was gone, and the door was swinging open.

Wait, she wanted to say if she'd had the breath. There was no time for waiting, not now. She managed a hopping run up the four cracked steps and pushed the door open with a cautious hand.

A dark living room, messy. The remains of at least a week's worth of papers lay piled untidily in the corner, the ones on the bottom curling up a little from age. Magazines scattered over every available inch of furniture, and where little gaps showed they were sugared with a fine thick coating of dust. Nothing fancy, Alex thought. Just a house, a busy mother, someone who liked to read.

There was a book lying on the floor, open. Its pages fluttered in the wind coming in the door. She took a sideways step toward it and saw that it was a romance.

The floor creaked in another room. Alex gasped for breath and clawed at her purse, found the .38, brought it out, and held it in a trembling hand. *Point and shoot,* she reminded herself. But not at Rachel or Jeremy Davies.

Or Gabriel, of course.

Unless—

Alex didn't want to move, to leave this familiar, cluttered living room where the TV stared with its dark eye, and nothing seemed strange or frightening. She knew that somewhere there would be a message from Marjorie Cassetti.

She didn't think she could stand to see it this time.

"Alex." The sound of her name startled her. Gabriel Davies came into view in the doorway to the kitchen. His face was impassive, but his eyes were wide and pupil-filled. "Check upstairs for Jeremy."

She wanted to tell him she couldn't, but her feet moved toward the staircase. It was covered with out-of-date powder-blue carpet, fraying at the sides, as if a dog had tried to dig holes. There were old stains here and there, memories of accidents with a glass of chocolate milk or a cup of morning coffee. Alex's leg burned as she climbed up.

She paused at the landing and huddled in the corner, shaking. Nothing came at her from the dark doorway at the top of the stairs. She heard movement below and saw Davies standing in the kitchen doorway again, staring at her.

He nodded slightly. *Go on,* he meant. She almost gagged on her own nervous swallowing, tightened her grip on the gun. Not the trigger, she reminded herself, almost too late.

Four more steps. Three. One.

A cool breeze on her face, as the air conditioner came on. She saw a light switch in the gloom and flicked it on. Hallway. It ran right and left, probably to two bedrooms. A small bathroom lay directly ahead. She stepped to that doorway and looked inside, found the light.

The tile was a dingy off-white, the shower curtain a bright cheery green. There was nothing to alarm her at all, not even when she, heart pounding, checked behind the curtain.

Nothing but an impressive bathtub ring.

She backed out of the bathroom, turned left. The hallway seemed unnaturally long. Light from the overhead fixture spilled a little way into the bedroom, reflecting dimly from an unmade bed and piles of clothes. She felt to her right on the wall and flicked the switch.

For a heart-stopping minute she thought there was a body in the bed, but it was only a tangle of sheets and blankets. Alex limped over and poked around, but there was nothing to find. The clothes on the floor were clean, mostly sheets and towels. They'd been lying there long enough to have creases, even in the towels.

There were pictures on the walls: Jeremy, age one. Jeremy, a chubby five or six. Jeremy in his mother's arms.

In one portrait, Jeremy, his dark-haired mother, and a smiling man that Alex's brain refused to match to the blank-eyed Gabriel Davies waiting on the first floor. This man looked peaceful, happy, proud. His eyes were smiling with his lips.

Same face, she thought. Different person.

"Alex?" His voice floated up from downstairs, faintly. She jerked in surprise.

"I'm okay. Still looking," she called back, and stepped over the piles of laundry to the closet. Nothing there—shoes piled haphazardly on the floor, heels worn down to metal nubs. Sneakers with the sides unraveling from the soles. The clothes of a woman who shopped rarely and sometimes unwisely.

Boxes piled in the corner. One of them was labelled GABE.

Clothes, Alex thought. Memories. Rachel Davies hadn't been able to throw him away.

Alex closed the closet door and moved left, to the private bathroom. The countertop was cluttered with cheap makeup, hairbrushes, curling irons left out to cool. A box of hot rollers with half of the rollers missing sat dustily on the corner, unplugged.

The shower curtain, a cheerful flower pattern, was drawn. Alex refused to let her imagination go anywhere with her, and batted it back. Plastic rings screeched on aluminum rod.

The bathtub was . . .

Alex opened her mouth. Nothing came out, not a scream, not a gasp, nothing. She couldn't even scream.

The bathtub was full.

She thought distantly that she should be vomiting again. She couldn't.

The bathtub was full of blood, and pieces of Rachel Davies. Her head bobbed gently, disconnected. The mouth was open.

No, Alex thought. *No, I am not seeing this.*

But she knew she was. There was no safety in fiction, not here. Alex backed away, toward the door. Turned.

Gabriel Davies was standing there. Alex instinctively reached out to him, to stop him from pushing past her. He moved her aside like a child and walked right up to the edge, stared into the horror.

Stared into the eyes of death.

"Check the other room," Davies said. She didn't move. He slowly turned his head to look at her, and to her shock, he smiled. There was madness there, hot in his eyes, twitching on his lips. She instinctively brought the gun up. He didn't blink. "Look for Jeremy."

She would have said, *I can't,* except that she knew she could. Her own strength appalled her.

She went back through the bedroom, through piles of laundry that would never be sorted, never be folded. Into the hallway, past the stairs that led downward out of the horror, into the clean afternoon light.

She kept walking, to the other bedroom.

Some people, she thought, *are cursed to be strong.*

There was nothing in the bedroom, no hiding little boy, no death. She sat down on the unmade twin bed, looked around. Jeremy was a sports fan. On the windowsill he had a collection of signed baseballs in their plastic shells, and on the walls he had pennants, bright with his favorite teams.

The photo album lying next to the bed had pictures of Jeremy, his mother, his father. In the later pictures,

Gabriel Davies looked curiously faded, as if he were being erased from their lives.

Rachel Davies was a smiling, beautiful woman. Alex put her fingertips on that smile and thought about the open mouth in the red bathroom, and felt something that wasn't quite horror well up inside. Rage. Yes. More like that.

There was a noise from the doorway. She didn't look up.

"He isn't here," she said quietly. "Did you know he kept pictures of you?"

When she looked up, finally, Davies was gone. She put the album away and went down the hall, down the stairs. Found him standing in the kitchen doorway again.

She looked over his shoulder and saw blood on the counters, blood on an assortment of kitchen knives, all laid out like surgical instruments.

"You knew when you sent me upstairs," Alex heard herself say. Davies didn't answer. He walked away, to the front door, to look out at the clean downsloping lawn.

"I knew before we came," he said tonelessly.

She walked over to the couch and picked up the phone. The weary voice of a 911 operator took her information and relayed the request for Detectives Shonberg and Markovsky. When she hung up, she saw that Davies had gone outside, to the porch.

She would have liked to have believed he was crying, but knew he was just waiting, staring, listening to the voice of Barnes Broward inside of him.

"Gabriel?" she called, and saw him turn. She'd been wrong.

There were tears on his face, drying even as she saw them.

"We can't wait for the police," he said. She opened the screen door and went outside to join him. He was so much taller than she was, but he seemed, in that single moment, to be so small, so lost. "Alex, did I do that? In there?"

She was too shocked to speak. How could he believe—

How could he not? Reality and fantasy were the same for him.

"No," she told him. "No, you didn't. Marjorie Cassetti did it. She wants other people to think you did it, but we know you didn't. I was with you, Gabriel. You didn't do anything. You have an ironclad alibi."

There was no visible reaction to her words, no sign of relief.

"This time," he murmured.

"You said we can't wait for the police. What else can we do? She didn't leave us a message this time," Alex said, and pushed away the thought that the next message would come chopped up in a small lawn-and-leaf bag. "The police can *help* you now. They know you're innocent."

He gave her a look that said he doubted that, but nodded. He looked down and saw that she still held the gun in her hand, forgotten.

"You might put that away before Detective Shonberg has to shoot you," he said, back to his old pleasant self. Alex fumbled open her purse and shoved the weapon in. "We have to go now. Come on."

He had taken four steps down the path, and she'd taken one, before she thought to ask where they were going. He threw a look back at her.

"Home," he said.

Chapter Forty-one

At a pay phone outside of a gas station three streets over, Alex called a cab. Davies waited impatiently, pacing in strange, jerky patterns while she sat wearily on the curb and watched for their ride.

Sirens, tearing this way. She thought of Markovsky and Shonberg, and wished she'd thought to tell the dispatcher where the body was. Cruel, to spring it on them unawares.

Davies was walking faster, winding up. She shaded her eyes against the setting sun to look up at him. He didn't seem to see her, just paced, staring straight ahead and muttering to himself. Should have scared her, she supposed. But he didn't.

She caught a word, here and there. He was having a conversation with Anthony Lipasky. Well, Lipasky had told her: it didn't much matter whether Davies talked to him or his answering machine. Or, apparently, the thin air. Davies had to work out his demons, and surely he had to be hag ridden now, torn between reality and nightmare.

She wished she had Lipasky's steadying hand, his

unshockable strength. She didn't think she had enough to go the distance.

Some people are cursed to be strong. Other people are just cursed.

Fuck it all. She picked up some road-chewed pebbles and let them dribble through her fingers. Gabriel's shadow paced over her, back and forth, growing longer and more frenetic. Lipasky would know what to do, where to go, who to call. She could only stand by and watch Davies disintegrate, one dream at a time.

The cab pulled up. The driver looked them over.

He hit the gas and split. Alex jumped stiffly to her feet and hobbled after him for a few painful steps, threw her handful of gravel. It was as ineffective as spitting at him. He hung a hard right at the next corner.

Davies had never stopped talking, never stopped moving, but now he slowed and looked at her.

Cold, wolflike eyes.

"I'll call someone else," she said, and dug another quarter out of her purse. She dialed another cab company.

Davies had stopped pacing. He stood now like a statue, hands at his side, staring off into the sunset. Alex gave the dispatcher the address and looked Davies over. If she were a cab driver, no way would she have stopped for him, or for herself, as battered as she looked.

A car cruised by. A gray Toyota. Alex turned her head to watch it go by and had to have the dispatcher repeat himself. Yeah, they'd wait. Ten minutes.

The gray car turned a corner. It didn't reappear. Alex breathed a sigh of relief and hung up. She sat back down on the curb.

Davies still didn't move.

Someone came walking around the corner, hands shoved into jacket pockets. Her hair was in a pony-tail, her sensible skirt exchanged for a pair of blue jeans and walking shoes. She stopped several feet away from Alex.

"You didn't go to the house," Alex observed, and wearily gestured for Shonberg to come sit down. She did, gingerly, watching Davies out of the corner of her eye.

"Markovsky did. And he took a forensic team. I was already off duty when your call came through, and he told me to go on home."

"You live around here?" Alex asked. Shonberg shrugged. "So, you gonna haul us in?"

Shonberg didn't say anything, just looked over at Davies, who looked off at the sunset. Her eyes were slitted almost closed, as if she had a pain somewhere deep inside.

"Whose house is it?" she asked.

"His ex-wife's. Rachel. She's—upstairs in the bathroom." Alex picked up another handful of pebbles and shook them. They felt as cool and dry as bones. "The kid is missing."

Shonberg was quiet for a while, digesting that. She nodded.

"You still think Cassetti—"

"It's the house in the picture, Michelle. Cassetti was here. She took the kid with her."

"We hope," Davies said. Alex jumped a little, saw

Shonberg do a double-take. Davies was still staring off into the distance, but it wasn't as trancelike as before. "We hope she didn't already dump him."

Dump him. Shonberg exchanged a quick, telling glance with Alex.

"We've put out a description of her and the van, but so far, nothing. I checked with GTE. She quit working there four days ago. The address she gave them was a phony, a gas station. Oh, you'll like this. I got them to fax me her job application. Under hobbies, she listed 'teaching children.' "

Davies turned his back on them, walked a few steps, turned back. He didn't look so crazy now. He was centering again, back on target.

"She loves children," he said, and came to sit down on the curb next to Alex. He wasn't acknowledging Shonberg's existence. "She has always said so. There's a chance—" He stopped himself. His hands rubbed together, kneading facts. "There's a chance that she's stealing Jeremy to take the place of her son. Of Charlie."

"That's good," Shonberg said. "It gives us a chance to find her and get him back."

Davies kept kneading his hands together. He did not look much cheered.

"She'll keep him only as long as she can keep up the fantasy. When he disappoints her—as Charlie disappointed her, with Jason Gardner—she'll kill him. Just as she did Rachel."

Shonberg gave him a long, sideways look. Measuring him for a white coat, Alex thought.

"What are you going to do?" Shonberg asked. It wasn't specifically directed at Davies, and he ignored her. Alex cleared her throat and leaned over to pick up another dry handful of pebbles.

"Go home," she said. It sounded strange even to her ears. "Wait for Cassetti to call."

"You think she will?"

"I think she can't resist torturing him." Alex jerked her head toward Davies, and Shonberg slowly nodded. "Listen, I know you're off duty and everything, but the cabs won't pick us up, not this late, not the way we look. You wouldn't—"

"Drive you home? Yeah, why not?" Shonberg, full of energy again, shot to her feet and waited impatiently for them. Davies rose with machinelike precision. Alex just wobbled up, bracing herself with one hand on the telephone booth.

"It's around the corner," Shonberg said, and started out at a brisk walk. Alex cursed her under her breath and started hobbling.

The hand under her arm surprised her. She looked over and saw that Davies' face was averted. Since he didn't want to acknowledge the kindness, neither did she.

His hand felt hot through the thin fabric of her shirt. She was glad when they arrived at Shonberg's car, and he released her.

Shonberg drove like a cop, careless but competent. She checked the rearview mirror a lot and made turns that Alex thought were unnecessary, except to confuse any followers. The world eased by, a glory of sunset reds and waking streetlights, other cars going with them or against them. I have a stripper story due, Alex thought suddenly. Maybe next week.

Normal life would come back. She'd worry about what to buy at the grocery store and what to fix for dinner, and whether or not she had enough deodorant to last through the week. She'd watch television programs and care what happened in them.

She closed her eyes and indulged, just for a minute, in a vision of Tony lying next to her in her new bed, warm and safe. Not so impossible. She just had to hang on.

Some people are just cursed, she thought again, and felt a chill.

Shonberg knew the way to the Alysium Apartments without prompting. Alex's vision fell into a rambling daydream and before she knew it Shonberg was braking, turning. Alex opened her eyes to see the fierce spiked fence looming over them.

Shonberg reached out and pressed a code into the keypad. The gates began to open.

"How'd you do that?" Alex asked. Shonberg smiled.

"Most of these places have an access code for the fire department, police, utility people."

"What is it?"

"I can't tell you that." Shonberg looked self-satisfied and more like a teenager than ever. She pulled around to the far side of Alex's building and found a parking space. Cut the engine.

"Thanks," Alex said, and popped her door open. Shonberg clamped a hand on her shoulder and held her in place.

"No way, Hobbs. You're not going anywhere I don't check out first."

"You're off duty," Alex reminded her, and pulled

loose. Shonberg bolted out of her own door, saw Davies sliding out of the back seat and walking away.

"Hey!" she yelled. "Hold it!"

Unmistakably a cop's yell, teenager or not. Davies didn't even glance back. Shonberg reached in her jacket and came out with her gun.

"What're you going to do with that? Shoot him?" Alex asked wearily. "Thanks for the ride, Michelle. Just go home, okay?"

Shonberg hesitated.

Inside her car, her radio crackled for her attention. She slid back inside and answered it, eyes fixed on Alex in baleful command. Alex waited.

Shonberg forgot her after the first few words, and concentrated on the news. She signed off and slammed her door, leaned over to look at Alex.

"Change of plans. They've sighted the van. I'm going."

"I'm going with you," Alex said, and started to squeeze back into the passenger seat. Shonberg leaned over to put her hand in the seat. Her face no longer looked so young, and nothing like naive.

"The hell you are. Go upstairs and lock your door, Alex. I'll call you when I know what's happening."

Alex clung to the open passenger door stubbornly, like a tick. Shonberg's glare was a blowtorch.

"You're wasting my time," Shonberg warned. Alex glared back.

"Tell me where Lipasky is."

"Sisters of Mercy. Close the goddamn door or I'll run you over."

Alex slammed the door. Shonberg gunned the car out, tires squealing. She stuck a flashing blue light on top of the car and roared out of the parking lot.

"Be careful," Alex sighed, and turned around. Her apartment waited. "Shit, not more stairs."

Fourteen of them. Alex paused at the top to dig in her purse, under the .38, under the loose cash. Keys jingled. She opened her deadbolt and went home.

Gabriel Davies, whom she hadn't even noticed standing in the shadows behind her, followed her in. She tossed her purse onto a dimly seen chair and flipped the overhead light switch.

"Don't you have a home here, too?" she asked wearily. The house was as she'd left it, stuffy and airless. She turned the air conditioning on. Her Pepsi had gone stale on the counter. She dumped it into the sink and watched it bleed thinly down the drain. Behind her, the couch creaked as Davies settled into it.

"I need to use your telephone," he said. She sighed and reached for a rag, ran it under a stream of cool water. Wiped at the sticky Pepsi residue.

"Suit yourself."

As he dialed, she looked in the refrigerator. Nothing there except two cold Coke cans, still held together by their plastic rings. Four down, two to go. Alex took them both out and left the plastic rings on the refrigerator shelf. She checked the freezer. No ice. She poured two glasses and carried them into the living room. She set one down in front of Davies. His eyes flickered, briefly, and he picked up the drink and held it. Watching her.

She sipped hers. He sipped his.

Everything was back to normal.

"I'd like to talk to Anthony Lipasky, he's a patient," Davies said. Alex jerked enough to slop a drop or two over the side of her glass. Davies continued to stare at her.

There was a long pause. Davies closed his eyes.

"Anthony?" he said then, in a very small voice. A child's voice, lost in the distance. "How are you?"

Alex heard the rumble, indistinct. Davies' hands were trembling, the level line of Coke bobbing like a heavy sea.

"I—I am fine. Alex is here. She—she has some bruises and scrapes, nothing serious."

How would you know, Alex thought gloomily. She supposed that, compared to Rachel Davies, she was in pretty good shape.

Davies' eyes opened, blind, unfocused. Glittering.

"She has my son, Anthony. I don't know what to do anymore. Nothing seems to make any difference."

He listened again.

"Rachel is dead. I couldn't stop that. I don't think I can save Jeremy and even if I do, what do I save him *for?* I can't be his father. No, Anthony, I *can't.* You know why I left him in the first place."

"So you're going to let him die?" Alex said. Davies' eyes focused on her. Furious. "You selfish

333

asshole. You're afraid to be his father, so you'd rather let her have him? What's *wrong* with you?"

Davies didn't answer her. He just held the phone out to her. She took it and pressed it cautiously against her ear.

"Tony?"

She hadn't known how much she missed him until she heard the sound of his voice, sandpaper-soft, deep in his throat. It vibrated deep inside of her, like she'd swallowed a tuning fork tuned to his pitch.

"Alex, are you okay?"

"Yeah," she said, and heard the unsteadiness in her voice. She swallowed it. "Yeah, I'm fine. Had a few bad moments with Miss Marjorie, but I got through it. And no bullet holes, how's that?"

"Pretty goddamn good," he sighed. He sounded weaker than she remembered. "Gabriel needs you. Don't leave him. He's having—problems."

"Yeah, no kidding. I've noticed."

"I'll bet. Listen. He's afraid to be around Jeremy, because once he—he tried to hurt him. He loves the kid, Alex. Don't judge him too harshly."

Lipasky, always the defender. Alex gripped the phone harder, tried to draw him closer to her.

"So what do the doctors say?"

"I'll live. Be out of here in about two weeks, less if I'm good. Hey, Hobbs?"

"Yeah?"

"I love you."

She sat, frozen, listening to the high metallic singing of wires somewhere in the phone noise. The sound of angels, she thought.

"You're nuts," she said. It sounded feeble.

"Yeah, I know. Give the phone back to Gabriel."

She held it out to him. When Davies' hand took the receiver, she felt more alone than ever, more vulnerable than she had since Marjorie Cassetti's gun had stared at her.

Davies had set his drink on the coffee table, on top of a coaster. He now had one hand wrapped around his stomach, holding himself together with physical strength. She remembered the laughing, smiling man in Jeremy's photo album, and grieved for him, that dead man.

"Help me," he begged a man confined to a hospital bed. "Please help me."

Alex retreated to the bathroom. Her face, in the merciless glow, looked like it had been tie-dyed. Her eyes were ringed with blue, edging to black; there was a thick, meaty-looking bruise on her forehead. Her nose was shades of red, black, and blue, and the rainbow spread out onto her cheeks.

Guess I can go without blush, she thought.

Apart from that, she was filthy, sweaty and completely exhausted. When Davies got off the phone she would throw him out, climb in a hot shower and collapse there for an hour. Then she'd drag herself off to bed.

What a blissful dream.

She went over to the tub and defiantly pushed the shower curtain back. Nothing, not even a soap ring. She closed the door and sat down on the toilet to pee; that reminded her, as always, of her tampon situation.

She'd have to go to the store.

In the morning, she told herself stubbornly.

She needed food.

In the morning.

Tonight, pizza. Delivered.

As she zipped up her pants she heard Davies' voice, and heard one clear thing.

"Goodbye."

He was done with Lipasky, she thought. Good. The shower was on the way.

The apartment door thudded, opening or closing. She froze. The bathroom was the worst place to be caught, noplace to hide, no weapons. She found a half-empty can of hair spray and jerked the door open, prepared to attack.

Nothing.

Davies was gone. She limped back into the living room and found his drink still there, barely touched. The phone was back in its cradle.

Alex found her own glass and drained it off in one quick, hard hit. Pretending it was rum.

The phone rang. She reached over and picked it up.

"Hello?"

"Hobbs? Shonberg." Alex could barely hear her over the wail of sirens and traffic noise. "Look, I'm out here with the van. It's the one, all right. It's been abandoned. Forensics is going over it now."

"Cassetti wasn't with it?"

"No, but she must have had the kid in here. They found a baseball cap, small. Got any ideas?"

Alex sat down heavily on the couch. Her apartment was dark around her, filled with mysteries. With monsters.

She closed her eyes. Davies, using her phone instead of his own.

Saying goodbye to the only person he loved.

Alex sat bolt upright with a gasp, felt her heart hammering against her chest.

"Alex?" Shonberg asked tinnily. Alex fought for breath.

"M-M-Michelle, she's here. She's here at the Alysium."

"What?"

"Not in my apartment. In *his*. He knew it. That's w-w-why he stayed down here and used the phone. He's gone upstairs to—"

Die, she thought. To die with his son.

"Alex, stay put. Lock your door and stay there. We're on our way." Shonberg clicked off, too busy to reassure her. Alex hung the receiver up and sat back on her couch.

The police were coming. That was enough.

He was alone. All alone.

And Jeremy—Jeremy, who kept those pictures of a dad who'd gone away.

Alex lunged across the couch and grabbed her purse. Money. More money. She dumped it out on the couch. The gun was the last thing out, cold, gleaming, deadly.

She picked it up and stuffed her keys in her pocket. A sign of hope, that. She intended to come back.

She opened the door and faced the stairs, one more floor, top of the next landing.

It hardly hurt, this time, to climb. She was too scared to feel pain. She got to the blank door at the top and put her hand on the knob. It felt cold, freezing cold. The door to hell.

Exclusive, she reminded herself. *Money. Position. Power.*

None of that meant as much, now, as Lipasky's voice telling her that he loved her. She wanted to live for that.

But she couldn't live without trying, at least, to save the other person he loved.

She turned the knob, quietly. It cooperated. She pushed. The door whispered open.

There was nobody in sight. She eased in and shut the door behind her, looked wildly around for a place to hide. Davies had a chair, a couch, a desk. She sprinted over and crouched next to the desk, where she'd have a clear view of anybody coming around the corner.

Somewhere, a child was crying. Alex closed her eyes and felt sweat drip down her face, sting in cuts and scrapes. She wasn't the maternal kind, but the sound of that child hurt, twisted in her guts like a knife. *If he's crying, he alive,* she told herself. It didn't help.

She eased up to peer over the desk. A picture, framed, stood on the corner, and she glanced at it, gave another long look. Shalanna North, smiling wanly. On the other corner was a framed yellow piece of newspaper. She was too far away to read it.

Pushed to the back of the desk, under the overhanging shelf, were a pair of small horn-rimmed glasses, a pink barrette, and a little girl's white scuffed purse. Alex froze, looking at them. The child continued to cry.

Nothing seemed out of the ordinary. She took a

deep breath and crawled awkwardly around the desk, took shelter under the pass-through bar to the kitchen.

It was dark, back that way.

"We're the same, you know," she heard Gabriel Davies say. He sounded perfectly calm, centered, sure. "Both infected by Barnes Broward. You want to kill me because you think that will stop you. That's why I killed Barnes. But it didn't stop. It doesn't—ever—stop."

"You should have left me alone," a woman answered. "I did what I had to do to Charlie, to stop him. People like you took my son away from me and taught him filthy things. And then, after all this time, you *threaten* me. You make me *think* about him again. That's not fair. You had your chance. You should have left me alone."

Alex couldn't move. She tried to force herself to go around the corner. Her muscles stayed locked in place, trembling.

"My job was to stop Barnes Broward. I never even noticed you, Marjorie." Davies sounded so fucking suicidally *calm*. "But I can help you now. I can help you get help."

Marjorie Cassetti laughed. There was panic in it, terrible fear. Alex got up from her crouch and eased around the corner. The bedroom door lay at the end of the hall, closed. Light leaked under it and puddled on the carpet. She took three steps and stopped, frozen again. *Just turn the knob, Hobbs,* she told herself. Her fingers extended, trembled, wouldn't grab it.

Marjorie Cassetti's gun roared. Alex, caught by surprise, threw herself to the floor, but there was no hole in the door, no Marjorie grinning down at her.

The shot had been inside the bedroom. As the ringing faded from her ears, Alex heard Davies moaning.

A child continued to cry.

"Pick it up," Marjorie said through the door. Alex, with her cheek pressed to the carpet, saw her feet, still in those white canvas shoes. Only a few feet away, Gabriel Davies lay on his side, eyes fixed on Cassetti's, staring. He was bleeding from his side.

On the carpet between them was something wooden, no, something wooden-handled. A knife. Cassetti kicked it and sent it spinning toward Davies. His fingers twitched, but he made no move to grab it.

"Pick it up," she said again. "It's your only chance. Or don't you like having a knife in your hand around your precious little boy? Does it scare you? Does it make you think bad things? Isn't that why you left him in the first place?"

Davies panted. His eyes were all pupil. The wooden handle was close to his fingers, but he didn't reach for it. Stupid to reach for it, Alex thought. He'd never make it anyway.

"If you pick it up, I'll let you go and get him from the bathroom. I'll let you both go." Alex couldn't see her face, but she could hear the smile, that crazy, hard smile. "You'll only have to hurt him a little, and I'll let you both go."

Davies closed his eyes.

"Or you can lie there and wait while I kill him. What do you want?"

He didn't move. Alex got up to her knees, then to her feet, felt her leg tremble with the strain. She reached out for the knob again.

"Don't you want to kill him? Really? I wanted to

kill Charlie, deep down. And you're just as bad as I am," Marjorie Cassetti whispered. Alex had the unnerving feeling that Davies' hand was reaching, going for the knife.

Alex's fingers closed around the doorknob.

It was locked.

Oh, God, she thought, and then it was too late, she had to do something even if it was the wrong thing. She balanced on one leg and slammed her foot into the door with all her strength.

It popped open, just like magic. Davies, on the floor, had the knife clutched in his hand. His eyes were unspeakable, spilling over with hatred. Marjorie Cassetti was already turning, little clicks of motion, gun leading. Alex's gun focused first.

"Drop it," she yelled. It was a stupid thing to do, she should have just shot her and been done with it, she knew it even as she yelled. Marjorie Cassetti wasn't going to surrender.

Cassetti, surprisingly, hesitated. Her gun lowered slightly, about to the level of Alex's crotch. Alex had a panicked second of disorientation. Was she going to drop it. Was she? What if—

Gabriel Davies came up off of the floor in a lunge. He was tall, standing, taller than Cassetti, and she took her eyes off of Alex to stare up at him. He was smiling.

"No!" Alex screamed.

He raised the knife, and those eyes, those eyes were black and bottomless, the eyes of a man in orgasm.

Alex fired. The gun kicked in her hands, and Marjorie Cassetti's face dissolved in a spray of red.

341

Women doesn't disfigure, she thought crazily. Davies had said it.

Alex, numb, stood over Marjorie's fallen body and fired again. Point blank.

The smile was gone. Thank God.

Cassetti's gun slid out of her fingers to the floor. She heard herself making a sound, a tiny, tiny sound that was so insignificant next to what she'd done.

Davies went to his knees, white-faced. He still had the knife clenched in one trembling hand and he bowed his head to stare at it. No blood on it. Clean.

He looked up at Alex, who clung to the doorpost. She found her voice, forced it through an abraded, tight throat.

"Please put it down, Gabriel," she whispered. "Please."

He didn't put it down so much as drop it, but she kicked it out of the way and checked Cassetti's pulse. Nothing that she could feel, through her numbed, stinging fingers. In the distance she heard the singing of sirens, or of angels.

Gabriel Davies slowly collapsed back to his un-wounded side, panting. She put her hand on his forehead and sat down next to him. He felt feverish and cold at the same time.

"Alex?" he asked. He still sounded so calm.

"Yes?"

"Thank you."

She sat for a while, her hand on his forehead. It was a little like touching a wild animal, magical, not to be trusted.

"Get Jeremy," he finally said. She nodded and got up. The bathroom door was shut; she opened it and

342

found Jeremy sitting in the corner of the bathtub, shivering. His tears were gone. He stared at her with huge, golden-brown eyes, and clung to her when she picked him up. Alex sat down on the floor with him, next to Gabriel, and waited for Shonberg to arrive.

So quiet. They were all so *quiet*.

Epilogue

Alex blew a strand of hair off of her face and wished she'd thought to buy more cheese at the store. Next time. She grinned to herself at that; she wouldn't remember. She'd tell Tony instead.

"Hey!" she yelled. "Dinner's ready!"

Lipasky, sitting in the living room, groaned. He came in lugging Jeremy under one arm like a sack of potatoes, sat him down in a chair. Jeremy grinned and reached for his glass, drank greedily.

"Haven't you had enough milk?" Alex asked him, as she poured some amoebalike stroganoff onto his plate. Jeremy shook his head and showed her his best milk-moustache smile. "Okay. One more glass."

She poured it with the flair of a waiter in a high-class restaurant, and reduced him to giggles with fake French. Lipasky watched them with his chin propped on one hand, a bemused smile on his lips.

"Are you going to eat my cooking?" she demanded. He moved his elbow out of his plate.

"But of course, *chérie*. Whatever it is."

"Shut up." She ladled out some stroganoff. "Did you get the mail?"

"Yeah." Lipasky eyed the mess on his plate dubiously, poked at it. It did not move independently. "Hey, kid, run upstairs and get the letter on my bed, okay?"

Jeremy was out of his chair and halfway up the stairs before Lipasky finished the sentence. Alex sat down in her chair, served herself some stroganoff.

"It's a letter from Gabriel."

"I figured," she said. "How is he?"

"They're—releasing him. He's passed all the tests."

Alex put the pan down and looked at him, shocked. Lipasky's lips were compressed into a tight, hurting line, but he didn't say anything.

"Don't they know—" she began, and stopped as Jeremy galloped down the stairs, waving an envelope. Lipasky took it from him and kissed him on the cheek before he bolted back to his chair. He handed it to Alex.

She unfolded it and read.

Anthony, it said. Never *Anthony and Alex.* He never mentioned Jeremy.

> *Anthony, Dr. Silberstein wanted me to write you and let you know that I'll be leaving here soon. The psychologists are of the opinion that there's nothing more they can do for me, and as you know, bed space is so often at a premium.*
>
> *I'll be coming back to Chicago, I expect, if that is acceptable to you. I still have*

*money left from father's estate, and I think
I will use it to buy a house, somewhere out
in the country. Away from people.*

*I am still fighting, Anthony. I will con-
tinue to fight, until I die.*

*Tell Jeremy that I think of him. You may
tell him I love him, if you think that is best.
Tell Alexandra I still think she should have
fired one more time.*

I am well, for now. I will write soon.

                       Gabriel Davies.

Alex looked up into Lipasky's warm gray eyes and
handed the letter back. There was something else in
the envelope; Lipasky took it out and handed it to
her.

It was a picture of Gabriel Davies, standing beside
an institutional gray building. He was neatly dressed,
as always, and wore a faint trace of a smile. Even so,
he looked faded, antique.

The smile frightened her. She handed the picture
back.

Jeremy looked up from his food.

"Can I have the picture? For my album?" he
asked. Lipasky hesitated, then handed it over to him.
Jeremy ran his fingers over it. Nothing showed on his
face. "He looks sad."

"He says to tell you that he thinks of you. That he
loves you." Lipasky looked over at Alex again.
Under the table, she reached for his hand and
squeezed it, not sure whether it was in support or in
warning.

Gabriel Davies had signed over all legal guardianship of his son to Anthony Lipasky and Alexandra Hobbs Lipasky.

She wondered what she'd do if he showed up at the doorstep to change his mind.

"Eat your stroganoff," she told Jeremy. He made a face and airplaned a forkful into his mouth. Such a bright kid. Hyperactive. Shadowed, sometimes, by what had happened to him.

But not like his father. She prayed, not like his father.

Jeremy blinked at her.

His eyes were golden brown, blank.

She looked away.

An excerpt from the private diary of Gabriel Davies.

Unpublished.

May 26, 1994

I have been in Chicago for some time now, and I think sometimes that Alex knows I am here. I see her, sometimes, looking out the windows blindly, searching for me. She does not see me, of course.

She is looking at the street, at the sidewalk. Not in the house across the street.

My lease here is up this month. I haven't decided to stay. Or to go. My life is in a kind of limbo.

I am waiting for something.

I am looking out the window now, and I can see Alex walking Jeremy to school. She goes with him everywhere, guarding him against the ghost of Barnes

Broward and Marjorie Cassetti, and me. I have not dared to call to talk to Anthony.

It's best that I don't, considering.

I think I will take a walk. There is a playground four blocks away, shaded, secluded.

I will go, I think, and sit a while. And watch.

HAUTALA'S HORROR — HOLD ON TO YOUR HEAD!

MOONDEATH   (1844-4, $3.95/$4.95)
Cooper Falls is a small, quiet New Hampshire town, the kind you'd miss if you blinked an eye. But when darkness falls and the full moon rises, an uneasy feeling filters through the air; an unnerving foreboding that causes the skin to prickle and the body to tense.

NIGHT STONE   (3030-4, $4.50/$5.50)
Their new house was a place of darkness and shadows, but with her secret doll, Beth was no longer afraid. For as she stared into the eyes of the wooden doll, she heard it call to her and felt the force of its evil power. And she knew it would tell her what she had to do.

MOON WALKER   (2598-X, $4.50/$5.50)
No one in Dyer, Maine ever questioned the strange disappearances that plagued their town. And they never discussed the eerie figures seen harvesting the potato fields by day . . . the slow, lumbering hulks with expressionless features and a blood-chilling deadness behind their eyes.

LITTLE BROTHERS   (2276-X, $3.95/$4.95)
It has been five years since Kip saw his mother horribly murdered by a blur of "little brown things." But the "little brothers" are about to emerge once again from their underground lair. Only this time there will be no escape for the young boy who witnessed their last feast!

MAYBE YOU SHOULD CHECK
UNDER YOUR BED . . . JUST ONE MORE TIME!
THE HORROR NOVELS OF

STEPHEN R. GEORGE

WILL SCARE YOU SENSELESS!